Trick Shot

S.E. Martin

Apostrophe H

eBook Edition ISBN-13: 979-8-9988419-4-1

Paperback ISBN-13: 979-8-9988419-5-8

Cover design by: All Write Well

This book turned into a love letter to the Tuscarora Nation, where I have so many happy childhood memories. Nyà•węę for all the strawberry shortcake, corn soup, and community.

Prologue

Summer, 13 years old

Sawyer

"Too slow *again*, Lanes."

I slam my lacrosse stick into the boards at Coach Jamie Montour's words. I elbow the plexiglass for good measure, just because.

We're running drills and practicing for odd-man rush situations. I'd been paired with my buddy, Neil Jonathan, as we ran down the floor towards the goal with a single defender in our path. I passed the ball to Neil, feeling confident he had a better shot at beating the goaltender. I still think he had the best shot, but as the defender slid to cover him, Neil pitched a perfect behind-the-back pass in my direction.

I wasn't expecting it. I never am. Until last year, my lacrosse training barely included BTBs. Sure, I'd throw the occasional trick shot playing backyard ball with friends, but it wasn't emphasized by my Canadian coaches. We practiced ball-handling skills and memorized plays where it was best to stick to the game script.

Then my parents divorced, and my mom remarried a Haudenosaunee man. My newly re-organized family moved to Six Nations Reserve, an Indigenous community in southern Ontario, and the script completely flipped.

I reacted too slowly to Neil's pass and missed it by a mile. The ball went skittering into the corner as the defense celebrated breaking up our play.

I was too slow. Again.

A blown whistle summons us for a team huddle. Anger and frustration roll through my body in waves as I slowly walk towards the midfield line.

"Sorry, man," Neil says, brushing his long braid off his shoulder. "It was a bad pass."

"It was a perfect pass, and you know it." I feel even worse that my friend is trying to make himself smaller in order to cheer me up. "I don't know why I still struggle with seeing those coming."

He taps his stick against mine. "Let's hang out and play some pickup lax this weekend. I'll impart all my BTB ancestral wisdom." He flashes me a lopsided grin, and I can't help but smile back.

Neil was one of the first Six Nations kids to befriend me after I moved. I struggled to make friends in those early days, feeling like an outsider in a new culture. I was afraid to make mistakes, say the wrong thing, or accidentally do something disrespectful. Neil took pity on me during my first disastrous season of Six Nations Minor Lacrosse, and we started shooting around after school. I still worry about making mistakes, but one year into this adventure I have a few people in my corner to help guide me around the potholes.

"Keep your head up, Lanes," Coach Randy Bissell says as I walk by. "You're on the cusp of a breakthrough; I know it."

"Thanks, Coach." I lift my eyes to his face shining with encouragement. I turn back to the huddle to find Coach Montour scowling at me, and my smile fades.

"Sawyer!"

I'm halfway to the locker room at the conclusion of practice when Coach Montour barks my name.

"I know you're still new around here, but right now what you're giving us isn't good enough." He looks down at me, although at five-foot-nine he's not much taller than I am after my summer growth spurt.

"I know, Coach. I'm sorry." I look at the floor. "I'm working really hard to get better."

"Well, work harder. You're hurting the team."

Sharp pain needles me in the chest as he walks away. My heart races as I turn toward the locker room. *I need to take some deep breaths and get out of here.*

I love lacrosse, even more now that I'm deeply immersed in its Indigenous roots as a form of healing and gratitude for the Creator. But lately, the pressure to succeed has been wearing me down. If it's not snide comments from Coach, there are the endless breakdowns of my poor play with my father. At least I don't have to see him very often.

"Take it easy on him, Jammer," I hear Coach Bissell say from down the hall. "He's a fish out of water here. He just needs some time to find his rhythm."

"That kid is a shitty ambassador for the Creator's Game," my stepdad, Rich Doxtater, mutters in the car on the way home. "He needs to remember he plays for his ancestors, not for himself. He thinks he's some hotshot, just because he plays college ball at Maryland."

I stare out the window, willing my pulse to return to normal. Rich knows me well enough by now to recognize when I'm spiraling, and immediately clocked my mental state when I got in the passenger seat.

He looks over at me. "Do you want to shoot around when we get home? I could dust off the old woodie and get out there with you. I'm sure I still remember a thing or two."

I force a pained smile. "Maybe."

"And remember, the Bissells are coming for dinner."

And suddenly, the sun bursts through the grayness of my mood.

"Oh, yeah. I forgot." My leg bounces frenetically as I sit up in my seat.

He smothers a grin.

I'm practicing behind-the-back shots in the yard when she emerges from the sliding back door. My heart skips a beat watching her quickly descend the steps and float towards me in black Converse sneakers and a cloud of espresso hair.

Sienna Bissell is the niece of my coach and the daughter of Rich's best friend. She's also become *my* best friend.

She's from the Tuscarora Nation near Niagara Falls, New York, so we don't see each other very often. But when we're together, we're inseparable. We're an unlikely pairing: she's beautiful, smart, and a total computer nerd. I'm awkward, academically mediocre at best, and a sports nut. But our friendship works, and she's been one of the people in my corner helping me navigate life as a white kid in Six Nations.

I also might be a little bit in love with her.

Sienna throws herself into my arms, smelling like strawberries and sunshine. I hug her tightly and bury my face in her hair.

"I'm so glad you're here, Sen."

She squeezes me. "Rich said you had a tough practice."

"I did. But I'm feeling better now."

She lets me hold her while my heart rate slows to match hers. My shoulders relax and my breath evens. Her presence signals calm to my body.

"Do you want to play pass with me? Rich has an extra stick."

She groans. "I will, but only because you'll feel so much better about yourself in comparison. I'm terrible at lacrosse."

"You can't possibly be that bad," I say with a laugh. "You're good at everything." I grab my stepfather's wooden stick leaning against the back porch and hand it to her. "Let's see what you've got."

She eyes it with trepidation. "Can I use your plastic one? I would be even worse with that heavy thing."

"No way. You're Native, you should take the woodie."

"You don't have to be Native to play with one, silly. Creator shared the game with everyone." She pushes the stick gently towards me.

I shake my head. "It's not for me. Maybe one day, but I want to be worthy of playing with a stick like this."

She wraps her hand on top of mine. "You *are* worthy of it, just the way you are."

I lean close to her ear and smile when goosebumps appear on her shoulder. "Take the stick, Bissell."

She puffs out a shaky laugh. "All right. But I can't be held responsible for any bruises I leave if I accidentally hit you with this."

I grin and pick my stick off the ground, scooping up a ball as I do so. "Game on."

Chapter 1

Čuhyeθáʔkye

Long Fruit Time / June

Sienna

"When are we getting to the interesting stuff?" Noah groans. "This is boring."

I raise an eyebrow. "This is *important*. There's a difference."

"*Bo-ring*." He spins in a swivel chair.

"To be fair, we were promised computers we could take apart and put back together," Vinny says, leaning against the countertop.

I harrumph. "We'll get there, but if you're not nailing your customer service skills, then I'm not turning you loose on hardware replacements."

"Can we at least remove some viruses, or something?" Noah asks. "If I have to hear anymore about being polite to elderly customers, I'm going to fall asleep."

"You should already be a pro at respecting your elders," I remind him.

Vinny smirks and opens his mouth to say something smart.

"Zip it, young buck." I point my pencil in his direction. "I'm not even thirty yet. I suppose we could switch to some hands-on practice for a bit, if you two are getting squirrelly."

Noah rubs his hands together. "What do you got for us?"

I emerge from the back room with a laptop. "A spyware-infected computer. Pull up the training manual and work through the checklist to get started."

Noah high-fives Vinny as he rolls across the room to the worktable.

"Make sure you're documenting what you do and any observations you have." I set the device in front of them. "I'm here when you have questions."

"Thanks, Sienna." Vinny smiles and takes the pad of paper I offer him.

I opened Three Sisters Tech five years ago to meet a need I saw in my hometown, the Tuscarora Nation. Elders and other community members were being taken advantage of by scammers and had nowhere they could trust to get their computers fixed. The big electronics stores were expensive, and the small fix-it shops were far away and shady. I knew I could be a familiar and trustworthy face in a sea of confusing technology, so after graduating with a Computer Science degree, I got my Master's in Business Administration and took a leap of faith.

The Three Sisters of corn, beans, and squash are planted together so that each contributes to the development of the others. The corn provides a stalk to support the growth of the beans, whose roots enrich the soil, while the squash leaves protect the dirt from weeds and bugs. They symbolize the balance my people strive for in life, and I like to think of my business as providing that sturdy stalk for my community. Plus, I like a little girl power infused in my work.

I should really get some shop keychains made: Corn, Beans, and Squash the Patriarchy.

I settle into a high stool at the counter to enter receipts into my accounting software. Business was slow in my first two years, and I'm grateful to have so many customers now. In fact, a recent contract with the reservation's elementary school has allowed me to hire my very first employees. Noah and Vinny are currently training to assist me in the shop, as well as with the school's Chromebooks. They're Tuscarora kids who attend the nearby high school, so they work when they can around school and sports. Investing in our youth has long been a secondary goal of mine with Three Sisters Tech, and I'm thrilled to be bringing that to life.

"Hey, Boss Lady?"

I look up over my tortoiseshell glasses to find Noah looking at me hopefully.

"How're you making out?" I ask.

"Good. We disabled the worst of the malware, and we've got a bunch of scans running." He pushes his dark hair out of his eyes. "Any chance we could take a break to shoot around?"

"Sure. How about I see you back here in twenty?"

It sounds like a herd of rhinos running by as the two teens grab their lacrosse sticks and head outside with shouts of "Thanks, boss!" and "See you soon!"

I shake my head and chuckle as I walk into the back room to grab some more laptops to fix.

Lacrosse is an important part of Tuscarora culture. We believe the Creator gave the game to us and all the Haudenosaunee people, a collective of six Tribal Nations located primarily in New York and parts of Canada. It provides us with medicine in the form of teamwork, physical exercise, and mental toughness. Our babies are given mini wooden sticks for their cribs, and there's a lacrosse net in most backyards.

I mindlessly install some Windows Updates while looking out the open shop window. It's a beautiful early summer day with a warm breeze. Vinny and Noah pass a lacrosse ball back and forth in the grass, trying to one-up each other with increasingly ridiculous shots.

Noah sends a leaping and twisting bullet over to his friend, who barely manages to snag it from the air.

"OK, Zeke Jacobs. I'm making you chase after that ball next time if I miss," Vinny teases before popping a behind-the-back pass over his shoulder.

"Ooh, a little Wes Harrison flair with the BTB." Noah easily catches it. "I like your style." He swings his stick and sends the ball between his legs.

"What the hell, man?" Vinny misses the low pass and jogs after it. "What kind of weird ass throw was that?"

"It's a trick shot." Noah grabs the ball when it sails back to him. "I've been watching Sawyer Lane videos lately. He did all kinds of crazy stuff in the Outlaws' last playoff series."

The pencil I was twirling falls from my fingers and clatters onto the floor. I scramble to pick it up and bang my head on a laptop as I stand.

Sawyer always sneaks up on me when I least expect him. I've done my best to avoid him for over a decade, but he pops up more than I'd like. I last saw him nine months ago at an international lacrosse tournament where my Uncle Randy was coaching. He's one of the star players on Buffalo's professional lacrosse team, the Outlaws, and a general pain in my ass.

But he used to be one of my closest friends. I found serenity in his presence that I've never been able to replicate with anyone else.

That was a long time ago.

The shop bell jingles as Noah and Vinny re-enter, looking sweaty and happy.

I rub the back of my head and hope I don't look as pained as I feel. "Welcome back. I think your scans just wrapped up."

"Perfect timing." Vinny gives me a warm smile. "Thanks for letting us get outside for a bit."

"No problem. It looked like you had fun out there."

"Yeah, until this jerk had me chasing down balls left and right." Vinny elbows his friend.

Noah elbows him back. "Hey, I need to practice showing off for the Junior Outlaws. Tryouts start next week."

There's that damn team again. I click through to start another round of updates on the computer I'm working on. "Junior Outlaws? What's that?"

Noah's face lights up. "The Outlaws have youth teams in the summer. You get a bunch of really cool team gear, and some of the Outlaws players are coaches."

"That sounds like a great opportunity. And you're going to try out?"

His smile falters. "Well, I want to. I just have to figure out a few things first."

"Like what?"

He scratches the back of his head. "Like a ride to the facility. My mom works nights, so she can't take me."

"We really need cars, bro," Vinny sighs. "Or at least friends with cars."

"What about your grandparents?" I ask.

Noah shakes his head. "They don't drive at night anymore."

"Aunts and uncles? Cousins? Friends?"

He fidgets with a loose thread on his shorts. "Tryouts go until 10pm, so no one wants to be down in Buffalo that late. It's at least a half-hour drive back here."

I pull up my digital calendar. "Which day is it?"

He blinks. "Monday. Why?"

"I can take you." I click to make a new event on my schedule.

"For real?" His face has lost some color. "You don't need to do that."

"It's not a problem. I can pick up some supplies for the shop while I'm downtown."

He smiles weakly. "I don't know what to say. That's really nice of you."

"Don't mention it. I'm happy to help." I close my laptop lid. "Now, tell me what your spyware scans came back with."

Two hours later we've managed to clean up the infected computer, plus I snuck in a lesson on communicating bad news to customers.

"Thanks for all your help today," I say as they gather their sticks and backpacks. "Training's going really well so far."

Vinny smiles. "It's been fun. Mostly."

I narrow my eyes at him, and he laughs.

"Do you want us to help you lock up?" Noah asks.

I shake my head. "I'll lock the door once you leave, but I'm staying late to do some more work."

Vinny frowns. "Well, don't stay too late. It's Friday night, you should be doing...auntie stuff. Whatever that is."

I hold back my chuckle. "I won't. Just want to finish up a couple more of these computers before the weekend."

Noah hangs back once his friend leaves. "Hey, so...I just wanted to thank you again for offering to drive me on Monday. If I find someone else before then, I'll let you know."

I wave him away. "Like I said, I stay up late. I don't mind."

"Well, I really appreciate it. It's been hard to get places since my mom's work schedule switched to nights at the casino." He shifts awkwardly on his feet. "I know this is a lot to ask, but I have one more hurdle for tryouts."

I set my glasses on the counter. "What do you need?"

He looks at the floor. "There's a $40 fee. I haven't gotten my first paycheck yet, and I don't want to bother my mom for the money. She works so hard just to cover our regular bills."

Noah's mom works two jobs to make ends meet. She's raised him alone with minimal help, and I know it's a struggle now that he's older and has more expensive needs.

"Well, that's simple." I grab my phone. "I'll give you an advance on your paycheck. I can send it electronically tonight."

"Thank you," he whispers.

I smile at him. "This is easy stuff. Always ask me when you need something. I might not always be able to help, but I can point you in the right direction, at least. *Ękwehę·we* take care of each other."

The corner of his mouth lifts. "My mom always says that, too. Native people look out for one another."

"She's a smart one, your mom. Now, get out of here so I can enjoy my lame Friday night in peace."

Noah grins. "Good night, Boss Lady. I'll see you on Monday."

Chapter 2

Sawyer

Friday

"Oh. Wow. OK." Addison repeatedly tucks a strand of blonde hair behind her ear, looking like she may vomit. "You're a professional athlete, so I'm sure you're good at every sport."

I smother a chuckle. "I'm not sure I'd classify mini golf as a sport, exactly."

She's on the verge of hyperventilating on a miniature golf course with clowns, windmills, and cartoon gophers.

I place a comforting hand on her elbow, and her eyes immediately shoot down. "Let's do something different. We could take a walk around the park, or grab a bite to eat nearby?"

"No, it's OK." She plasters on a fake smile. "Let's do this. Maybe you can help me? If you want, that is. If it's not too much trouble." Her face falls. "Oh God. This is too much. I'm so sorry."

Her anxiety is making my eye twitch. "I'd be happy to help you. Let's try a couple of holes and see how it goes."

I've been back on the dating apps for the past month, and so far it's been as fun as blocking 90mph shots in front of the net. Addison had seemed sweet when we traded messages last week, but she quickly clammed up when I revealed I play for the Outlaws.

"I don't know anything about lacrosse," she says as she clutches a club.

I smile warmly. "You don't need to. There's a lot more to my life than lacrosse."

That's not exactly true. My world has revolved around the game since I started playing in the peewee leagues growing up in Ontario. First, I played to keep up with my dad's unrealistic expectations, then I played to fit in with a new culture and community. Nowadays I play for myself, always seeing how far I can push my body to get stronger, faster, and more resilient. When I'm not playing, I'm thinking about playing, training for playing, and occasionally spending time with friends and family.

I might be a little obsessed.

And my date might truly be terrible at mini golf.

Addison lines up her shot, winds up, and sends the ball into a water feature two holes away.

"I don't think I'm cut out for this," she says with a sigh.

"You're doing great. Next time, try angling your body towards—"

She shakes her head. "No, I mean, I don't think I'm cut out for *this*." She gestures between the two of us. "It's not working."

I smile tightly. "It was really nice meeting you, Addison."

Saturday

Jacie plops down in the seat across from mine in a bustling coffee shop downtown. Her copper hair bounces around her shoulders as she takes a long sip of some kind of caramel frappa-something.

She slowly licks a dollop of whipped cream off her finger as she watches me drink my latte.

"So, Jacie, what do you do for a—"

"Do you want to go back to my place or yours after this?"

My last sip goes down the wrong pipe and I begin to cough violently.

She wrinkles her nose. "Are you OK?"

I pound my chest with my fist. "I'm good," I croak. "Sorry about that."

She leans on her elbows. "I know I'm being forward, but I kind of assumed we were on the same page with this...date."

I clear my throat one more time for good measure. "I'm sorry if I gave you the wrong impression. I'm looking for something more serious than a casual hookup."

Her foot brushes against my calf under the table, and I fight to hold back a cringe.

"Are you sure? That's not what I've heard."

I furrow my eyebrows. "What do you mean?"

Jacie shrugs and takes another sip of her sugary drink. "You're a professional athlete. You're hot. You're single. Your type isn't usually in the market for a long-term relationship."

Younger Sawyer would have jumped at the chance to fool around with a pretty redhead at the drop of a hat but, much to my chagrin, the proposition isn't landing for me anymore.

"Well, what can I say? My priorities have changed." I shoot her an apologetic grin. "It sounds like we're looking for different things."

She pouts around her straw. "That's too bad. I took an Everything Shower for this."

I chuckle and drain my beverage. "It was nice to meet you, Jacie."

Sunday

Danica sits on the barstool next to me with a sigh. "Well, shit."

I raise an eyebrow. "That's never a good start to a date."

She chews on her lip. "I was hoping it wasn't you."

I bark out a laugh. "That's even better."

"No offense, but your reputation precedes you." She keeps one foot on her stool, looking ready to bolt at a moment's notice.

"And what might that be?"

"You're a man whore, basically."

"OK, so I had a couple of busy years, but—" I pause. "You're the second person this week to say that. Is there some kind of spreadsheet of ex-girlfriends going around or something?"

She cringes. "There's a Facebook group."

"I was kidding. Holy shit."

Danica chuckles and sets her purse on the bar. *Maybe I have a chance with the feisty brunette after all?* And I have a real weak spot for feisty brunettes.

"It's a group for women who've dated or are dating Buffalo sports players." She flashes me a sheepish smile. "They share war stories about who's a cheater, who's just interested in a hookup, stuff like that."

My mouth inches upward. "And you're in that group?"

"Listen, I've dated a couple of football players. Maybe a hockey player." She coughs delicately into her fist. "I figure it's my duty to warn others."

"What's the group called?"

"The admins will never let you in."

"I know, but what's it called?"

She hesitates. "Buffalo Sports Hunks Anonymous."

I throw my head back in laughter. "This is gold."

A laugh bubbles up from her chest. "You're taking this well."

"Well, if I don't laugh, I'll cry, so there's that." I smile at her. "Will you stay for a drink with me?"

"It's tempting, but I'm just not interested in what you have to offer. I'm looking for a relationship."

"You may not believe it, but so am I."

She fiddles with one of her rings. "You're right. I don't believe it."

"I probably deserve that." I exhale. "I like you."

Her eyes scan me warily. "I like you, too. But I'm not willing to take a risk right now."

"I get it." I hold my hand out to her. "I'm really glad I got to meet you, Danica. Thanks for the intel."

She grins. "Best of luck to you."

I slink back to the apartment I share with my teammate, Outlaws defender Wes Harrison. It's been a full weekend of romantic strikeouts, and morale is low.

I had zero game with women until the latter half of my college years. Once I got drafted to the pros, I started attracting more interest, and I threw myself into the dating pool with gusto. I didn't have much time to feel lonely, that's for sure. I was a cocky and charismatic goal scorer, and I enjoyed the hell out of that lifestyle for a while.

Until it stopped being fun. And I've been left alone with my thoughts ever since.

"You're back early," Wes says when I walk into the kitchen. "Chels and I were just about to head out, in case you needed us gone."

I toss my keys onto the counter. "Nope. No need."

Wes' girlfriend, Chelsea, regards me cautiously. "How'd it go?"

I sink into the couch across from the two of them. "Swimmingly. I found out women are warning each other about me on the internet."

Wes and Chelsea exchange a look.

"Let me get you a glass. Come have a whiskey with us," he says.

"I appreciate you, man."

I regale them with the very brief tale of this weekend's failed dates. It's not my finest moment. It's pretty darn embarrassing, honestly.

"What is it you're looking for, Sawyer?" Chelsea asks. "Why are you back on the market after not seeing anyone for the past year?"

I tip a swig of whiskey into my mouth. "I want what you guys have."

Her eyes soften. "That's really sweet."

"It's true. My brother got engaged last summer, and that really woke me up. He's two years younger than me, and he's already found his person." I set my glass down on the coffee table. "Then I watched the two of you fall for each other, and I realized how lonely I've felt for a long time. I've always wanted to settle down with one person, but I got distracted."

Wes tucks Chelsea under his arm. "Is there anyone you've really sparked with in the past? Someone who's worth another try?"

I sigh. "I liked the girl tonight, but she knows better than to get involved with me. And I liked your friend I met in Utica last year, Chels."

"Lauren?" she snorts. "She'd eat you alive, Lanes."

"Don't threaten me with a good time." I run a palm over my face. "I love a sassy Native woman."

"That makes two of us." Wes grins at his girlfriend, and she blows him a kiss.

"But no, there hasn't been anybody else who's really lit me up. Not for a long time."

Not since—

I shake my head to silence the thought. There's no use going down that rabbit hole tonight.

"You'll find her," Chelsea says quietly. "You're a good guy, Sawyer, no matter what you think about yourself."

I smile softly. "Thanks, Chels. I sure hope so."

Chapter 3

Akęnha'kyeháh

Early Summer / July

Sawyer

I've been to a lot of Native celebrations, but the Tuscarora Picnic and Field Day is my favorite.

There's traditional music, games, and food vendors, including the best corn soup I've found on the American side of the border. I have to specify, because corn soup quality is a very sensitive topic in Haudenosaunee communities.

It's been too long since I've been on the Tuscarora reservation, and as I'm driving I mentally note changes since the last time I visited: someone's selling strawberries and green beans out of their house on the corner, the church has a new sign, and the outdoor lacrosse arena is in need of mowing.

I stroll into the picnic area as drummers are setting up near the stage. The Smoke Dance competition should be starting soon.

"Lanes! Good to see you, man."

Randy Bissell is one of the most legendary Buffalo Outlaws players of all time, and my former coach in minors. I wouldn't be where I am today if it weren't for his patience and encouragement.

"Hey Randy." We exchange handshakes and a bro hug.

"I love that you come out to this every year." He hands me a plastic cup of vibrant red liquid. "Strawberry juice, on the house."

"Thanks. I wouldn't miss this for the world." I take a sip and practically hum with nostalgia at the sweet taste.

My stepfather brought us to the Tuscarora picnic each July, braving the U.S.–Canadian border traffic in order to see his good friend (and Randy's brother) Scotty Bissell and his family. It's a casual, joyful event, and a highlight of my summers.

"What are you up to this off-season?" Randy asks.

"I'm playing summer ball in Niagara Falls and coaching for the Junior Outlaws."

"You're coaching now? That's great. Do you like it?"

"Love it. I'm coaching the U17 boys and it's so rewarding. They're right on the cusp of being men. They've got big dreams but still need guidance to reach them. A few potential superstars, too."

Randy nods and takes a drink. "That's one of my favorite ages to coach. Any Tuscarora kids?"

A light breeze carries the mouthwatering scent of corn soup, and now I know where I'm heading next.

"Yeah, Noah Printup. He's got an incredible amount of raw talent, but needs some help to stay focused on refining his skills. If he can do that, I think he has a real future as a player."

"Printup? He works for my niece, doesn't he?"

"Does he?" Movement catches my eye as a few dancers trickle into the performance area.

"I think so. I'll have to ask her." He finishes his juice and tosses the cup into a nearby trash can. "Her repair shop is doing really well. She's been able to hire a few local teens."

My insides warm. "That's awesome. I never doubted she'd be a success."

He claps me on the shoulder with a grin. "I need to get another strawberry juice before my wife realizes I gave hers away. We'll talk soon, I'm sure."

Women decked out in their finest regalia file into the dancing circle. Color explodes onto the grass with tunics, skirts, and leggings in all shades of the rainbow. Their hair is styled into intricate braids and ponytails tied with beaded wraps.

I'm sipping my strawberry juice and watching them settle into their starting positions when I see her. My hand freezes.

Sienna's lashes flutter down as she waits for the music to start. Her dark hair is plaited into two long braids that hang over her raspberry-colored tunic. Her lips are painted to match, and the vibrant shade flashes against her tawny skin. She's taller than the other women, with her five-foot-eleven frame regal and poised above them.

She's breathtaking.

The singing begins, and she unfurls her body in a circle. Drums quickly kick in, and her feet tap a million miles a minute. She moves as though on air, her knee-high moccasins barely touching the ground between steps. Her arms glide through the air while the trunk of her body remains still. By virtue of her height and skill, she takes up an impressive amount of space on the dance floor, and it's mesmerizing to watch.

The song is short, only about thirty seconds of soaring beats and movement. The singer concludes with a yell, and the dancers step into their final poses. Sienna spins, pauses, and looks up. Directly at me.

Her focused smile immediately tumbles as our eyes lock.

I smile weakly, raising my glass in acknowledgment.

She scowls and turns away, leaving the stage with the other dancers.

I chug the remainder of my juice, my forehead beading with sweat.

I'm a good-looking guy, and I know it. I spend hours in the gym each week getting strong and explosive for lacrosse, but the aesthetic side effects are a nice bonus. I enjoy looking and feeling my best, which tends to come with attention from women. In the past, I've used my looks and charm to get dates, but the most elusive prize has never given me the time of day: Sienna Bissell.

I've had heart eyes for her since we met in sixth grade upon my mom's remarriage. I was an awkward lax rat desperate to fit into my new home on the rez; she was an Indigenous siren with the mind of an engineer. Her father and my stepdad are longtime friends, so our families spent quite a bit of time together even though we lived seventy-five miles and an international border apart.

She was Ada Lovelace to my Bart Simpson. Her brain was a marvel to me, always seeking to take things apart to understand them, while taking no bullshit in the interim. She encouraged me when life in Six Nations got hard, or when I failed at lacrosse for the millionth time. She was my long-distance friend and impossible crush.

Until everything changed, and she was lost to me forever. She has barely tolerated my presence since high school, and I've had no luck changing her mind. Instead, I watch her kick ass at life from the sidelines and try my best to stay out of her way.

I take my time wandering around the various vendor booths, sampling food and admiring crafts. There's a break between dance competitions, so the area is swarming with happy chatter and the exchange of goods.

I'm taking a huge bite of frybread when I come upon a table with merch for Three Sisters Tech. *This is new.*

"Hey, Prints!" I dust off my hands and hit Noah with the handshake we came up with in our first Junior Outlaws practice. "It's good to see you, man. I heard you worked at the repair shop."

His eyes light up. "Hey, Sawy—I mean, Coach. What are you doing here?"

"I grew up coming to the annual picnic, so I never miss it. I spent a lot of time here when I was about your age." I flinch. "That makes me sound old, doesn't it?"

He laughs. "Yeah, but we'll just forget you said that."

I gesture at the paintings spread on the table. "What do you have here?"

He shakes his hair out of his eyes. "These are mine. My boss is letting me sell them here to raise money for my lacrosse fees." A flush creeps up his cheeks. "I'm sorry I haven't gotten that paid off yet, by the way. I'm getting close."

"No worries. I'll make sure the team office doesn't bug you about it."

A grateful smile. "Thanks."

"I missed you at practice this week." I pick up one of his watercolors to admire. *The kid's talented.*

Noah looks down. "Yeah, sorry about that. Something came up."

"I'll see you at the next one, right? We need your soft hands on the floor." My grin falters as Sienna approaches the table. She's changed from her regalia into a creamy pink ribbon skirt and white tank, her long hair still braided.

"Uh, yeah. I'm going to try really hard to be there." He counts a wad of dollar bills for the third time.

"Where's that?" Sienna asks him, ignoring me.

I wait for Noah, but he remains quiet while he fiddles with the cash box. "Noah's on the Junior Outlaws with me. He's one of my best players, although I don't think he believes that yet."

She frowns and looks down at him. "Do you need a ride to practice next week?"

He mumbles incoherently.
She looks up at me. "He'll be there."
Curious.
"Glad to hear it." I clear my throat. "Ring me up for the strawberry painting, would you?"

Me: Are you lazy bums coming out, or what?

Jammer: Cool your jets. I'm sitting in bridge traffic

Wes: Sorry, we got a late start leaving Buffalo. I've got Zeke and the girls with me

Me: All the corn soup will be gone at this rate

Jammer: You know they make a huge drum of that stuff, drama queen

Jammer: Gotta go. Heading into customs

"Sawyer! Just the man I need."
Scotty Bissell claps me on the shoulder as we embrace.

"Hey, Scotty. Long time no see." I smile warmly. "What can I do for you?"

"I've got a situation that could use your expertise." He leans in conspiratorially.

"Hit me with it."

His familiar laugh rolls over me. "The IDLA volunteers need some relief at their strawberry shortcake booth. Would you mind staffing it for an hour, for old times' sake?"

I would routinely get suckered into running the Indian Defense League of America's strawberry shack as a teen. The organization advocates for the treaty rights of Indigenous peoples, especially the right to free border crossing between the United States and Canada. And they make a damn good strawberry shortcake.

"Sure, I'd be happy to. Payment in strawberries, as usual?"

"You know the drill. Thanks so much, Sawyer." Scotty smiles. "Sienna will be helping you out. She's over there now."

Record scratch.

The last time his daughter and I worked the booth together was the summer before I started college, and I managed to piss her off so badly she refused to speak to me for most of the next four years. And that was *after* she dropped out of my life a few years prior.

Time to put on my mental armor and saddle up for another joust with her.

I glance down at the small strawberry tattoo on my arm before turning my baseball hat backward and plastering on a smile. "Great. We'll handle it."

Chapter 4

Sienna

U^{gh.}

Every year the Tuscarora picnic is a carefully balanced mix of things I love—dancing, eating, community—and things I dread. Namely, seeing Sawyer.

We usually manage to stay out of each other's paths, so I was pissed to see him at the end of my Smoke Dance performance. It's my favorite social dance, full of quick movements meant to evoke chasing smoke tendrils from our traditional longhouse dwellings. It's one of the few occasions I'm comfortable with people watching me, as I can blend into the frenetic drums and allow the music to flow through me. There's no reason to feel self-conscious when we're all moving to honor our culture and ancestors.

But now Sawyer's here, spoiling my brief moments of freedom and lightness in my body. With any luck, I won't see him anymore today.

My entire life, I've struggled with comments about my looks. Boys started looking at me far younger than I wanted, and I quickly realized they didn't care to get to know me past my appearance. I've learned to cut off romantic overtures at the knees, figuring anyone interested in me as a person would put in the time to work past my sharp tongue and frosty exterior.

Sadly, few have.

"Hi honey. I'm home."

You have got to be kidding me.

I spin slowly, clutching a paring knife in one hand and a strawberry in the other. It feels appropriate because I'm about to enter into battle.

Sawyer leans against the counter, his milk chocolate curls spilling from beneath a backward ball cap. Tattoos trickle from under the sleeves of his crisp white t-shirt as he rests on his forearms.

"No." I point the weapon in his general direction.

He throws up his hands. "Not exactly the warm welcome I was hoping for, but I get it."

"I'm not interested."

"In what? My delightful company?" He flashes me a grin that only serves to piss me off. "Well, I'm sorry to report you're stuck with me, Princess. Your dad told me to cover the booth with you."

A litany of curse words shoots off like fireworks in my mind. "You know I hate that nickname."

"I know." He inches inside the wooden structure like a zookeeper approaching a rampaging animal. "But it's fun to make you mad."

If my blood pressure gets much higher, I fear I can't be held responsible for my actions. "I hate you. Please go away."

"It kind of feels like you're flirting with me right now." That damn grin makes another appearance. I used to love it, back when he was the sweet, funny boy who looked at me like I controlled the tides. Now, it represents everything I can't stand about him: arrogance, cockiness, rakishness.

I want to scream into a pillow. Instead, I stomp my foot like a child and throw myself back into hulling berries. "Make yourself useful, please. We should see a rush of people once the men's dance qualifiers are over."

Many picnics ago, my parents begged me to enter the Miss Tuscarora pageant to help pay for college, since winners were awarded a small scholarship. It was my worst nightmare: getting dolled up for people to stare at me and ask questions. Much to my shock, I won, and the Princess moniker was born. That was the last time Sawyer and I were stuck in this small space together.

Shockingly, he does as I ask, sliding beside me to start slicing biscuits. We work efficiently together, if uncomfortably.

"You know I call you that in jest, right?" Sawyer nudges my shoulder, and I huff.

"And you know I don't have a sense of humor."

"That's not true. You're hilarious when you're trying to one-up me."

I roll my eyes.

Silence falls between us as we work, and it gives me entirely too much time to be alone with my thoughts. Sawyer and I have been needling and misunderstanding each other for well over a decade, with no sign of stopping. Sometimes I wish I were ready to move on from the hurt he caused me in high school, but I'm just not.

"Has Noah missed many practices with the Junior Outlaws?" I ask to change the topic.

"Just one," he replies. "But he misses a lot each time, so I want him to make it to the rest, if he can."

"He can," I say softly. "I'll make sure he gets there."

"Is everything OK with him?"

I work quickly with the paring knife, cutting out stems and slicing strawberries in barely a wink. My mom taught me knife skills at a young age, and I'm almost as quick as she is now. "He's a really good kid. A hard worker. Sometimes he just needs a little extra support."

"Noted."

"I can't picture you as a youth coach," I say after another long silence.

"Why not? Too evil?"

I bite my lip to hide an unexpected smile. "You've always seemed focused on your own game."

Sawyer preloads paper bowls with sliced biscuits. "I'm always focused on bettering myself as a player, but growing the game is important to me, too. So is giving back to the community."

"That makes it sound like you care about people other than yourself."

His jaw ticks. "Believe it or not, I actually do."

"Humph." I add some sugar to the vat of fruit.

He glances up. "Ah, the nephews have realized you're here."

I look to see a horde of teenagers making their way towards our stand.

"Don't be creepy." I ladle berries on top of biscuits.

"Just pointing out that teenage boys have found you attractive since the dawn of time."

"I'm sure it has nothing to do with the professional lax bro working the booth."

"Is that a compliment? I think it was almost a compliment."

"*Čwé:'n*, Sienna," the leader of the pack greets me in Tuscarora while smoothing a wayward curl in his hair.

"Told you," he whispers in my ear as he pushes me towards the front.

I crush his toes with the heel of my moccasin before painting on a cheerful smile. "*Čwé:'n*. What can I get you?"

We have a steady stream of customers for close to an hour as everyone grabs food between the men's and women's dance finals. Sawyer and I have accidentally (OK, maybe *occasionally* on purpose) stepped on each other at least two dozen times. We keep getting tangled in each other as we reach for shortcake ingredients and paper products.

I'm ready for a break from him.

I lick some wayward whipped cream from my thumb as the last people in line walk away with their desserts. "Whew. That was intense." I look over to find Sawyer watching me intently.

He swallows and looks away. "It was. But we managed to feed everyone and not kill each other."

"A miracle." I hand him a bowl. "Ready for our payment?"

His chestnut eyes sparkle. "You rebel. Our shift isn't over."

I start building my shortcake stack: biscuit, vanilla ice cream, berries, whipped cream. "I need to keep morale high to put up with you."

"That's fair."

My eyes close as I take my first delectable bite. The ice cream in this equation really puts it over the top. I hum happily as I go back for more.

"Save some for the rest of us, you two."

A smile pulls at my lips as Jamie Montour walks up to the booth.

"Sure took you long enough to get here." Sawyer sets his bowl down and leans across the counter to give his teammate and friend a hug.

"Yeah, yeah." Jamie grins. "You should be grateful I left the house on a Saturday." He turns to face me. "Hey Sienna. How's it going?"

We bump fists. "I'm good."

"Sorry you're stuck hanging out with this guy." He gestures at Sawyer with his chin.

My smile grows. "Your condolences are appreciated."

A warm set of green eyes emerges from behind Jamie. "Hi Sienna. We met briefly in Utica at the World Championships. I'm Wes." He holds out his hand. "And, unfortunately, I'm Sawyer's roommate."

"Hey!" Sawyer exclaims.

I smile and cautiously return his handshake. "It's nice to see you again. I'm sorry about your living situation."

New people make me nervous, but Wes' affability sets me at ease more than most.

"I like her," a dark-haired woman loudly whispers to Jamie.

He chuckles. "I told you that you would."

I swallow and fidget with one of my braids.

She smiles kindly at me. "I'm Chelsea. I kick Sawyer's ass at lacrosse practice every week."

A laugh bubbles up in my chest.

"I'm sensing a theme to these introductions." Sawyer fixes his friends with a withering stare.

"How are we doing over here?" A great, booming voice asks.

A grin splits my face. "Hi, Daddy."

"Hi sweetheart," my dad says. "You've got quite a crew of lacrosse players over here."

Sawyer chuckles. "Are you checking up on me, Scotty? You should keep a better eye on your daughter. She threatened me with a knife earlier."

I open my mouth to snap back a retort before realizing I have no leg to stand on. "I—"

Sawyer raises an eyebrow.

"It was just a paring knife," I mutter.

Jamie barks out a laugh.

"Can we be best friends?" Chelsea asks. "Seriously. I'll give you my number."

I glance at her with a hint of a smile pulling at my lips.

My dad shakes his head with a twinkle in his eye. "Why don't you take off early with your friends, Sawyer? I can cover the last fifteen minutes with Sienna. It may save your life."

"Can we get strawberry shortcake first, or...?" Wes asks, his eyes full of hope.

"Sure can, if you use some of that Outlaws salary to pay for it," my dad teases.

I jump when a warm hand grazes my lower back.

"It was good to see you again," Sawyer leans over to my ear.

"The feeling is not mutual."
He chuckles. "I'll see you around, Sienna."

Chapter 5

Sawyer

"Did you ever think we'd be coaching together someday, after I coached you in minors?"

I smile at Jamie as we dump buckets of balls before Junior Outlaws practice begins. "Hell no. That coach was an asshole."

"He really was."

"But I'm a forgiving man, what can I say?"

He taps my shin with his stick. "I don't tell you enough how appreciative I am that you gave me a chance to make things right. I was such a dick to you when we first met."

I wave him away. "You were going through a rough time back then."

"I was a fucking train wreck, but that's a nice way to put it." He scoops up a ball and fires it at the net. "I didn't deserve a second chance from anyone, and I'm grateful for our friendship now."

"You're getting soft in your old age, Jammer."

He smiles. "Maybe I am."

Movement in the bleachers catches my eye as high schoolers start filing onto the concrete playing surface. The metallic glint of a laptop opening, the white flash of wired headphones, and a cloud of long, espresso hair.

Jamie follows my gaze. "Is that Sienna?"

"Yeah." I watch as she types quickly on her keyboard, the glare from her screen reflected in her glasses. *Since when has she worn glasses?* I'm digging the look, and it's frustratingly distracting. "She must be waiting for Noah."

"Is she family?"

"He works for her. She gives him rides sometimes." I drag my eyes from her to find Jamie smirking. "What?"

He chuckles. "Nothing."

"What?" I repeat as kids start shooting around. "*Ow.*" A wayward pass hits me in the thigh.

"Sorry, Coach!" a mortified player squeaks.

Jamie claps me on the shoulder. "Keep your eyes on the ball, Lanes."

"Nice job on the power play drills, boys," I call out as the team regroups.

"Don't be a ball hog, Connor." Jamie elbows him as he walks past.

Connor Montour rolls his eyes.

I smother a grin. Jamie has so far avoided directly coaching his son, since his advice goes over like a lead balloon.

"Monty." I crook my finger at the surly teen. "You look good out there, kid. Just remember that when we have the man advantage, we want to pass the ball and apply pressure on the defense. You've got the skill to muscle in on goal, but you're going to get hurt and burnt out doing that every time."

Connor nods his head. "Thanks, Sawyer."

"Why does he listen to you and not me?" Jamie says as we gather the group for our final breakdown.

"He's *not* listening. He's uncoachable, just like his dad at this age." I grin. "He barely tolerates me, Jammer."

He shakes his head. "I don't know what I'm going to do with him. He's being recruited to play at Syracuse, and it's gone to his head."

"Sounds like someone I used to know," I tease.

He runs a hand through his short hair. "I don't want him to make the same mistakes I did. I ruined my life with my ego and bad decisions."

"Then you're the best person to help guide him. Now hit these kids up with a final pep talk, Coach, and let's wrap this up."

Jamie summarizes our objectives for the next practice as I walk along the edges of the group, making sure any squirrelly players stay on task.

"Who's the hot auntie up in the stands?" Connor whispers to Noah. "Anyone you know?"

Noah drops his eyes to the floor. "Dunno."

"She looks Native, and there aren't many of us on the team." Connor cranes his neck to get a better look.

"You're too young to be tangling with aunties, man." I step in front of his line of sight. "And that one, in particular, will disembowel you in front of your friends for love of the game, so I suggest you stay clear."

Noah tries to hold back a smile.

Connor grins. "Bet I could get her number."

"You know, I might enjoy seeing you try. Now zip it and listen to your coach." I gesture towards Jamie, who is finishing his final point.

The bleachers clang under my feet as I mount the steps after practice, the aluminum shaking with each step. I should've headed home, but, like always, I can't stay away from her.

After all, maybe this is the time I get her to crack a smile or chuckle at a joke. I haven't given up hope, even if I feel resigned to having lost her years ago.

Sienna briefly lifts her eyes before shifting them right back to her laptop screen.

"Two times in one month?" I drop onto the bench next to her. "Sure seems like you're stalking me."

"Your delusion is charming, as usual." Her keyboard clicks beneath her fingers. "What do you want?"

"Since when do you wear glasses?" I scan the arena, trying to ignore the sexy nerd look she's got going on.

"They're blue-light glasses. I wear them when I work."

I nod. "Very practical. How's the family?"

"You just saw us."

"I saw your dad. How's your sister? Your mom?"

"Hazel's good. Working crazy hours at the hospital, so I don't see her a ton." *Clickety clickety clack.* "Mom's looking forward to your brother's wedding in the fall."

I smile. "We all are. A week off to enjoy the Jamaican weather and celebrate Alex and Ellie? I can't wait." A beat passes. "You're not coming, right?"

"I'm not." She pushes her glasses up. "I can't leave the shop for that long."

"Got it." I quite literally twiddle my thumbs as I quickly flip through possible conversation topics. "You attracted a lot of attention up here."

She pauses. "What do you mean?"

The corner of my mouth lifts. "Some of those young guns were betting they could get your number after practice."

She puffs out a noise and resumes typing. "I'm almost old enough to be their mother."

"A young, hot mom, maybe." I jostle her with my shoulder, but she doesn't react. "You're definitely in deadly auntie territory."

"Do you think it embarrasses Noah to have me here?"

I look over in surprise. "Why on earth would you think that?"

Her keyboard clacking slows and becomes more erratic. "I don't want the other guys to give him a hard time if I wait for him. I tried to run errands, but everything closes early on weeknights."

I can feel the anxiety rolling off her. Every fiber in my body wants to reach out and tuck her hair behind her ear like I used to when we were kids and she'd get nervous. But nowadays she's more likely to sock me across the jaw rather than melt into my hand,

"It's not your fault you're—" *Devastatingly gorgeous. The most beautiful woman in the world. A motherflipping smoke show.*

She narrows her eyes. "Watch it."

"—dorky."

She kicks me, and laughter rumbles through my chest.

"Speaking of which, what are you working on over there, Lady Einstein?" I peer over her shoulder.

She huffs quietly. "I'm just doing some work."

"Well, yeah, I got that part." I squint at her screen. "Are you programming?"

"Yes."

"What is—"

"Do you actually care?" Her tone is short, and I draw back.

I take a couple of breaths to manage my irritation with her. I've never minded Sienna's sharp edges, but sometimes she cuts unfairly.

"I'm sorry." She looks down at her keyboard. "I shouldn't have—" She roughly pushes her hair away from her face. "I'm updating the ticketing system we use at the shop. Now that I have employees, we need to adjust how we're keeping track of progress on machines."

I lean back towards her, but keep more of a distance this time. "How so?"

She adjusts her glasses and I bite back a groan. She types in a keyboard shortcut and brings up a different window on her laptop. "This is what a ticket looks like currently. See how there's a section for case notes?"

I nod and watch as she switches back to her coding environment.

"Now that multiple people may be working on a single computer, it can get confusing having all those notes in one spot. Things get accidentally erased, and it's not clear how long it's been since a troubleshooting step was tried."

She highlights a section for my benefit.

"So instead, I'm adding a database where each person can keep track of a day's actions, so we can see at a glance what was done by who, and when." She tabs through the different headings and, honestly, it's unbelievably hot to see her intelligence so effortlessly on display.

"You designed this entire system yourself?"

Sienna shrugs. "It's not hard. It also saves me from purchasing a piece of software and allows me to customize it how I want."

"You're amazing. So incredibly smart."

The barest flush creeps into her cheeks, and damn it feels good to coax a positive emotion out of her for once.

"Oh, I'm—" She tucks her hair behind her ear.

I notice Noah emerging from the locker room on the other side of the arena.

I put her out of her misery. "Hey, I wanted to ask you something."

Her eyes slide over to mine. "What?"

"Who does Noah live with?"

She closes the lid of her computer and begins packing up. "His mom. She's wonderful, but she works multiple jobs to keep them afloat. So she's not often available to drive him places."

I fidget with my watchband. "So that's why he missed practice last week?"

She digs in her purse for her keys. "I didn't realize he needed a ride. It's my fault for not following up after his tryouts."

I open my mouth to reply, but we're interrupted by self-assured steps coming up the bleachers.

"Connor Montour." He smoothly extends his hand towards Sienna, which she looks at but does not take. "I saw you from the floor and had to come say hi. Which Nation are you from?

"Go easy on him, Sen," I murmur as she opens her mouth. "He has a family."

Her brown eyes flash to mine, and my stomach drops. I haven't called her that name since the Before Times, when our friendship was still thriving.

She turns back to Connor. "I'm from your imagi-Nation, because you should be hitting on someone your own age."

"Jesus Christ, Sienna." I choke on my laughter.

Connor's grin falters, and I feel a little bad for him. Then again, this kid needs to be taken down a peg for his own benefit. "Point taken."

Noah appears once Connor slinks away with his ego in tatters. "I'm sorry about that." He cringes. "I tried to talk him out of it."

The corner of Sienna's lips trembles with a repressed smirk. "No worries. Ready to head back to the rez?"

"Yeah. Just one second." He glances at me. "Do you mind if I talk to Coach Lane real quick?"

"Take your time." She heaves her substantial bag onto her shoulder. "I'll wait for you in the car."

I lean my hip against a nearby railing. "What's up, Prints?"

Noah shuffles his feet as he digs in his pocket. "I have some of my program deposit." He counts out cash with trembling fingers. "It's not the full amount, but I'm getting close."

"Hey, uh, let me check something real quick." I pull out my phone and navigate to a random website.

He runs a hand through his hair. "I'm really sorry it's taking me so long."

I scroll past the scores from tonight's baseball games. "There we go. I thought I saw this earlier." I look up. "You're good to go. All paid up."

He freezes. "What?"

"You're paid through the rest of the summer. I just verified." I tuck my phone into my back pocket.

"I don't understand." His voice cracks. "Are you sure?"

"Yep. I'm positive. Your mom must've taken care of it."

Noah blinks and slowly puts the cash away. "Oh. Wow, OK. That's...great. *Nya꞉we̜.*"

"Is that 'thank you' in Tuscarora?" I ask as we walk towards the parking lot. "It sounds a lot like Cayuga, which my stepdad speaks."

He nods. "Yeah. Tuscarora is pretty different because we lived in the Carolinas until joining the Five Nations in 1722. But a few words are the same."

"Would you be willing to teach me?" I ask. "I've always wanted to learn."

He grins. "Yeah? I'd be happy to give you the basics. We lost our last fluent speaker not too long ago, and we're a small tribe, so most language instruction happens in the rez school or in families."

"I'd love that." We approach Sienna's modest blue sedan. "Good practice tonight, Prints. Glad to see you back at it."

His smile reaches from his toes to his eyes. "*Nya·we̜*, Coach. I'll see you next week."

"See ya, man." I slap the hood and Sienna jumps, looking up from her phone in alarm. I grin widely. "Good night, Princess."

She glares at me and I laugh.

Chapter 6

Akęnha'kyehé·θu'

Late Summer / August

Sienna

I haven't had a day off in months, and I'm not quite sure what to do with myself.

Three Sisters Tech is overrun with customers, and I'm loving it. Settling into troubleshooting a computer is downright meditative for me. I love the feeling of figuring things out and bringing order to a machine. Computers are lifelines for people in my community, especially the elderly. They use them to communicate with family who live far away, look back on cherished photos and videos, and request help in emergencies. It's upsetting to be without such a critical piece of your daily routine, which is why I work overtime to get things fixed and back to their owners as quickly as possible.

I run system scans while folding laundry, install anti-virus software while processing payroll, and answer emails while visiting my parents. That last one often gets me into trouble. Something about needing to have a better work/life balance, or whatever. Let's just say I don't have much of a personal life.

But today, on a calm and sunny Saturday, I don't have anything to do. I'm caught up on work, thanks to Noah and Vinny, and my apartment is clean. I'm...*bored*.

I'm seriously considering going into the shop for a deep clean when my sister calls.

"You're alive!" I put my phone on speaker so I can make iced coffee while we talk.

Hazel chuckles, her voice low and tired. "Barely. I've been working overnights for the past month, and I'm stretched thin. Why did I want to be an ER nurse again?"

"Beats me. You couldn't pay me enough to work with people. Computers are much more predictable, and they rarely talk back."

She sighs. "I need to ask you a favor, but I also want to check in with you before I head to bed. How've you been?"

"I'm good. What's the favor?" I stir a splash of milk into my drink.

She ignores me. "I heard you worked the strawberry booth at the picnic last month."

"Yeah." My spoon clinks on the mug as I tap off the excess liquid. "It was fine. We made a lot of money for the Indian Defense League."

"I'm sure the dreamy lacrosse star you were working with had something to do with that."

I narrow my eyes even though she can't see me. "That man does not need any additional contributions to his ego. Let's say it was my friendly smile and winning personality that did the trick."

Hazel bursts into laughter. "Darling sister, I love you, but charisma with strangers is not a strength of yours."

I smile at her good-natured ribbing. "Maybe not." A pause. "And Sawyer is *not* dreamy."

She clucks her tongue. "I know you're biased when it comes to him, but you're not blind. Sawyer's hot."

I scoff. "Whatever."

"Still sticking to your guns about not forgiving him after all this time?"

I stab a metal straw into the milky ice. "Don't you need a favor?"

"Oh, right. Mom's having car trouble, and Dad's in Canada for the day." She talks through a yawn. "I could probably figure it out, but I'm honestly about to fall asleep driving home and really need sleep."

"I can head over there and take a look." I take a sip of liquid energy. "No promises, though. I know my way around hard drives and modems, not automobiles."

"Thank you so much. Call me in a few hours if you get stuck." Another heavy yawn fills the line. "I just need a power nap."

"Get some rest, Haze. I'll figure it out."

It's taking forever, but I'm making progress.

I'm sitting in the driver's seat of my mom's old Chevy Silverado, treating the vehicle like a computer that just came into my shop. First step: diagnose the problem.

Symptoms: Car turns on, but runs rough. Check Engine light is on. Shudders while driving.

Initial Research: Google suggests this could be due to a wide variety of problems. Needs further diagnostics.

My mom enters the garage and hands me a contraption. "Your father said to use this to scan for codes."

I furrow my brow. "To do what now?"

She shrugs. "No idea. That's what I have you for." She flashes me a winning smile. "My brilliant and accomplished daughter."

I chuckle as I consult the internet once more. This appears to be some sort of diagnostic device, which is right up my alley, but I have no idea how to use it. I stare at the end of it, which looks like it should be plugged in somewhere. But where?

"*Čwé:'n!*"

I jump so high that my head nearly hits the roof. Unfortunately, I would know that voice anywhere.

What in the ever-loving crap is he *doing here? And since when does he know Tuscarora greetings?*

Sawyer's face appears at my elbow. He's tan, bright-eyed, and fresh as a daisy. "Hey Princess. I heard you needed rescuing."

Oh, hell no.

"I've never needed a knight in shining armor, and I'm not about to start now." I go back to my Googling.

He leans his forearm on the open window. "How can I help?"

"You can go back home."

"Not a chance. Your dad sent me."

Dammit. My father and Sawyer's stepdad are spending the day together watching lacrosse and clearly have been comparing notes.

"I've got this under control."

"Clearly." He gestures to the jumble of plastic and cables in my hand. "Did you pull the codes from that?"

I blink at him, trying to interpret the alien language. "I was...just about to."

"Great. Well, plug 'er in and let's take a look."

One, two, three seconds tick by as I weigh my options. Send him into the house on a made-up errand so I can frantically look up the procedure? Admit I have no idea what I'm doing?

I'd rather jump over Niagara Falls than ask for help, especially from him.

"I—" I delicately clear my throat.

A smile tugs at his lips. "Can I show you where to plug it in?"

I huff and open the car door. "Fine."

"You used to be a lot nicer." He holds his hand out, and I slap the code scanner into it.

"And you used to be less of an ass."

He cocks his head. "You can fault me for a lot of things, but being an asshole isn't one of them. A *pain* in the ass, sure." His cocky smile is a little quieter than usual.

Sometimes I wonder if he truly doesn't remember what happened when we were teenagers, but that would be impossible. It was such a painful betrayal, so flagrant; how could he forget? I've *tried* to forget, but my pride and my self-esteem won't let me.

I cross my arms over my chest. "OK, pain in my ass. Let's get this show on the road."

Sawyer shows me a port tucked beneath the driver's seat, plugs in the scanner, and turns the car on. "Looks like a couple of the cylinders are misfiring. Let me do a quick search for the specifics."

I pace while he types on his phone, unsure of what to do with myself. I tidy some random tools on my dad's workbench and try to look busy.

The door to the house creaks as my mom enters the garage carrying two cans of Pepsi. She hands one to Sawyer and ruffles his hair affectionately. "How are things going? Thanks for coming up this way to help us out."

He smiles warmly. "No problem, Mrs. B. I'm happy to help, if I can."

"I was doing just fine on my own," I call over to them.

"I know you were." She brings me the second can. "But an extra pair of hands never hurts."

I grunt and take a sip.

Thirty minutes later, armed with a bag of spark plugs and other vehicular miscellany, I pull into my parents' driveway. We've attracted an audience.

Hazel and my cousin Gabby are sitting in folding chairs watching Sawyer. He has the hood of the truck propped open while he surveys the guts of the vehicle, sleeves pushed up to his elbows and his denim button-down hanging open.

"What's going on?" I ask.

Gabby takes a sip from her water bottle. "Oh, nothing. Hazel told me to come over."

I narrow my eyes at my sister. "I thought you were sleeping?"

Hazel smiles broadly. "Mom said you two were here fixing the truck, so I decided to come by. I'm feeling refreshed after a nap."

I look over at Sawyer and back at them. "So you're...supervising."

"Exactly," Gabby says.

I raise my eyebrow. "Are you two—?"

"Yes," Hazel replies.

"One hundred percent checking him out," Gabby adds with an emphatic nod.

"Oh my God," I mutter.

"What?" Hazel asks innocently. "Just enjoying what Creator has given us today."

I roll my eyes. "You're awful."

"Hey Princess," Sawyer calls. "You got those spark plugs?"

"Enjoy." My sister toasts me with a glass of lemonade before giving me a kick in the shins. "And loosen up. Everything doesn't have to be a battle with him."

I grumble and walk into the garage.

"All right, let's see 'em." Sawyer takes the box from my hands.

"I can do it," I say, pulling out my phone.

"Have you ever changed the spark plugs on this truck before?" he asks.

"No, but I'll watch a video." I type some search terms into YouTube.

"Wouldn't it be easier to let me do it?"

"And how do *you* know how to change the spark plugs on this vehicle?"

He smiles. "I watched a video while you were gone."

I grumble. "It's fine. I want to figure it out in case I need to do it again."

"Want me to show you? We could do it together."

I know it would save me time to let him. Time I could be spending catching up on work or chatting with my family. But it would kill me to accept help from him.

I hesitate. "It's no problem. You probably have other plans today."

"I've got nowhere to be that's as interesting or important as this." He sets the spark plugs on a nearby table. "Let me show you around the engine."

"Yeah, go help him, Sienna," Hazel yells across the driveway.

I glare at her.

"You take apart computers, right?" Sawyer says when I finally approach the truck.

"Yes." I peer under the hood.

"Well, this is the same thing. The parts are just bigger and do slightly different things."

Seems sensible. "So, what do spark plugs do?"

He leans against the bumper, hands shoved in his pockets. "They provide the spark that the engine needs for combustion. They keep everything running smoothly, like a heartbeat."

I nod, trying to ignore how my own heartbeat skips at his closeness. He's the essence of easy, breezy cool with his sunglasses perched on top of his head and a white tee fitting closely under his open shirt.

I realize I should have responded by now, and jolt myself back to life. "So, they're sort of like a motherboard."

"If you say so." He smiles and reaches for a socket wrench off the bench. "You would know better than I would."

I watch him remove the plastic engine cover and feel around inside the hood. "There they are. Come look."

I inch closer to him and tilt my head at an awkward angle to look deep inside the engine components. "How the heck are you supposed to get at those?"

He grins. "With a very long socket. You'll need to remove the plugs from here, here, and here." He points as he talks. "How about I take the first one out and you can do the rest?"

"I'm not a toddler," I huff. "I know how to use a wrench."

"I know you do." His tone is calm and reassuring, which irritates me. I wish he'd fight back when I get snippy with him. I wish I made him mad enough to avoid me.

That was the whole point of being a jerk to him, after all.

He leans close in order to get at the engine, and I take in a sharp breath of his cologne.

"Can you see?" He looks back at me.

"Um...yeah." I definitely cannot see past his broad shoulders.

He works the socket back and forth for a minute before reaching inside. He pulls out a corroded cylinder, his hand now streaked with black. "Here's one culprit."

I grasp for the wrench. "You'll get dirty. Let me do the rest."

"I don't mind. It feels good to work on an engine again." He tosses the old part into a nearby trash can. "I like using my hands for more than just lacrosse."

"I bet you do!" Hazel calls out.

He chuckles, and I sigh.

"I'm sorry about the sexual harassment." I raise my voice at the end of the sentence so my feral sister can hear me.

He hands me the socket and I contort myself to begin working. "Don't worry about it. I could use the self-esteem boost."

"In what universe do you not get enough attention from…" My voice trails as he strips off his denim shirt and tosses it at Hazel before wiping his hands with a rag.

She and Gabby whoop with laughter, and a smile brightens his face.

His biceps flex beneath his t-shirt, and I lose my grip on the wrench. I swear and re-center my tool. "Are you helping or showing off?"

He grins. "Both."

"You're doing great!" Gabby yells from her chair.

A tattooed forearm appears at my elbow. My attention is caught by a little strawberry folded in the midst of his lacrosse ink. "Good job. Let me grab that." He flicks the metal shell loose and pulls out the second spark plug.

I close my eyes and breathe. I've been single for too long if I'm having a hot flash over Sawyer.

We remove the remaining plugs, and Sawyer demonstrates how to put the new ones in. His patience and thoroughness make him a good teacher, much to my chagrin.

"Thanks for your help," I say as we clean up. "You explained things really well."

"See? I'm not so bad." He slams the hood closed. "Now, fire her up and let's see if that code has gone away."

"Thank you, Sawyer," my mom says, squeezing him around the waist as the engine roars to life beneath me. "We appreciate all your help."

"Anytime. Sienna did most of the work." He winks at me and my stomach does a full flip, like a traitor.

"Looks like the Check Engine light is gone," I say from the driver's seat. "You don't need to stick around."

He leans into the window, an impressive task given his height. "Trying to get rid of me, Princess?"

"Always." I look away from his gaze. "Thanks again."

"No problem." He hesitates before standing back up. "Let me know if you need anything else."

"Unlikely. I lost your number years ago."

He runs a hand through his hair with a chuckle. "Trust me, I noticed."

Chapter 7

Sawyer

*T*ick. Tock.

I watch as the minutes count down to the official opening of free agency at noon. That's when teams are allowed to contact players about signing new contracts. This is typically an easy day on the calendar for me, since I've never been interested in playing for anyone other than the Outlaws, so a quick call with our front office is all it takes to extend me for a year or two. But this time there's a gnawing unease in my belly, and it's become impossible to ignore.

I love Buffalo. It's a second home to me and is close enough to Canada that I can pop back and forth to visit family and friends. My mom and Rich are less than two hours away in Six Nations. My brother, Alex, lives in nearby Hamilton, Ontario, not far from our father. Not that I ever stop in to see him when spending time with Alex and his fiancée. That's a door I leave firmly shut as much as possible.

The Outlaws are like family. After a rocky start, Jamie and I have become the best of friends. Wes is my roommate, and often feels like my big brother when he dishes out wisdom beyond his years. Zeke is solid and steady while pushing me to become a better player. I love working with the entire team and staff, and every day of the past six years has been a joy, even the hard ones.

But what if there's something more out there? What if I could take my game and my lifestyle to the next level somewhere else? A change of scenery would certainly improve the dating scene.

National Lacrosse League players are paid peanuts compared to other professional sports. We're weekend warriors, working regular jobs Monday through Friday and traveling to play on days off. A few select cities can afford to compensate their players more than others, and I'd be lying if I said I hadn't considered those now that my contract with the Outlaws is up.

"You're making me nervous, man." Wes looks at me over his Kindle. "You've been staring at your phone for the past ten minutes."

The clock flips over to twelve. *Here we go.*

I prop my elbows on the kitchen island and rest my chin in my hands. "Yeah, well, you'll get to enjoy the delight of free agency next year, once your rookie contract expires."

One of his eyebrows ticks upward. "Are you not expecting to re-sign with the Outlaws?"

12:01.

"I think they'd like me to. But you never know." I fidget with the orange Every Child Matters bracelet I was given by a Native kid while visiting the local cancer hospital last year. "And maybe I should keep an open mind to other offers, if I get any."

Both eyebrows raise. "Don't tell me you're considering leaving."

"I wouldn't say I'm *considering* it." *12:02.* "I've only ever played here, and I wonder if I've gotten complacent. Maybe I need the challenge of a new city and a new team to get my game to the next level."

"I'm afraid to see you at the next level. You're a demon on the floor, Lanes. You're one of our top scorers."

I chuckle. "Thanks, but I know I can be better. Maybe somewhere else I could be the best version of myself."

My phone rings and it startles me so much I nearly fall off the barstool.

Wes sets his Kindle on the couch. "Who is it?"

"I don't know." I stare at the device as though it's a bomb. "I don't recognize the area code."

"Do you want me to answer it and pretend to be your agent?"

I need the laugh that gives me. "No need, but I appreciate the offer."

He slid onto the stool across from me. "Put it on speaker."

I swallow and tap the screen. "Sawyer Lane."

"Sawyer," says a smooth, deep voice. "This is Dominic Ocean, General Manager for the Miami Storm. How are you doing?"

My breath hitches. Miami's ownership pours money into its team, and it's known as the best location for player salaries.

"I'm doing well, sir. What can I do for you?"

"Sir?" Wes whispers with a smirk. "Could you sound any whiter?"

I wave him away.

"I'm hoping you'll do us the honor of playing for our team this year. We believe you're the best forward in the league, and we're prepared to offer you a salary befitting that role."

He gives me a number that makes my jaw drop. Wes scrambles to his feet for a piece of paper and jots down figures.

"We'd also pay for you to relocate to Miami, if you'd like," Dominic continues. "The city has incredible nightlife, much more so than Buffalo, I'd assume." A note of smugness creeps into his voice.

Wes starts adding numbers together and pushes the paper towards me with the total compensation.

"Oh my God," I mouth silently to him.

He nods, eyes wide.

"This is a very generous offer, Mr. Ocean." My leg bounces quickly up and down. "Could I have some time to review this with my agent?" I wink at Wes, who grins in response.

"Call me Dom, and take all the time you need," Dominic responds. "We want you to make the decision that's right for you." He pauses. "We're making a strong push for the championship this year, and we want you to be our Number One guy. You have what we need to put us over the top."

My insides warm at the praise. I've never had the chance to be a superstar in Buffalo. Jamie held that mantle when I was drafted, and then Zeke joined us two years ago. It's been hard to figure out where I fit in and what makes me unique compared to the rest of the team. In Miami, I would be their best player and lead goal scorer on Day One. I could step into the spotlight in a way I've only dreamed of up to this point.

"Thanks, Dom. I'm strongly considering Miami. I'll be in touch shortly."

Wes blows out a weighty exhale after I end the call. "Damn, Lanes. You're a wanted man."

My heart feels like it's about to beat out of my chest. I've gotten offers from other teams in the past, but nothing like this.

Sweat beads on my forehead. "I wasn't expecting that. This will be hard to turn down."

"You should make a pros and cons list." He flips his paper over and draws two lines. "List everything you can think of and see how that feels." He scribbles a couple of items and passes the paper to me.

Pros: Lack of snow

Cons: New roommate who isn't Wes

I smile as my stomach twists reading his words. Leaving behind my teammates would be the biggest drawback, by far. I take my relationships seriously, and losing these close friendships would be a blow.

But signing with a new team would give me a fresh start professionally and personally, and given my dating reputation in Buffalo, that may not be such a bad thing.

My phone screen lights up again.

"It's the Outlaws' GM," I say.

"You can probably be your own agent on this one." Wes raps his knuckles on the counter. "I'll give you some privacy. Let me know if you want to talk afterwards."

The pen feels awkward in my hand as I sign my name, as if my grip has been wrong my entire life and I'm just now noticing.

"Could you look at me for a picture?" the team photographer asks. "We're going to post on social media."

I raise my head and flash a megawatt smile, the same one I've been practicing since I was sixteen. That was the year I realized I needed to overhaul my image if I wanted to have a shot at professional lacrosse. Shy, anxious Sawyer wasn't going to entice college recruiters, especially with my grades that barely skirted academic eligibility. But confident, cocky Lanes? He might be able to make something of himself.

Fake it 'til you make it. Sienna had taught me that while encouraging me to look past my crippling perfectionism and relax into the game of her people. It had been her motto anytime she needed to put herself into spaces she felt she didn't belong, such as her coding classes. Her courage has always inspired me, especially knowing how deeply uncomfortable she felt around people she didn't yet trust.

"Great smile, Sawyer." The photographer snaps a dozen shots. "Can I get one with you and Coach?"

"Of course." I set the pen down and get to my feet.

Coach Travis pulls me into a hug, slapping me on the back. "We're glad to have you back for another year, Lanes. I know we weren't your only offer, and it means a lot that you wanted to continue your career here."

I smile tightly and clap him on the shoulder. "Thanks, Coach. I'm glad to be back."

"Can we get Dusty in the shot?" the photog asks.

The Outlaws' mascot, an opossum wearing a team jersey, bandana, and cowboy hat, peeks out at us from behind his pink paws.

I swing my arm in his direction. "Get over here, Dusty."

Coach and Dusty duck under my arms and pose for photos. The camera flashes as I paint on my smile and hope it reaches my eyes.

Turning down Miami's offer didn't feel good, but leaving the Outlaws felt worse. Maybe it's inertia, or maybe it's my imposter syndrome coming out. Being the top player for the Storm meant needing to live up to high expectations, especially during a championship push, and that sent my brain into a tizzy of insecurity. In any case, I'm back for another year in Buffalo and will re-assess after this season.

"I'll see you at training camp in two months?" Coach Travis says as I pack up.

"Sure will. Can't wait." I bite the inside of my cheek. "See you then, Coach."

Sienna

Noah catches a long pass from his goalie and charges up the floor. The Junior Outlaws are shorthanded with Connor Montour in the penalty box, but the goaltender made an incredible save and immediately threw the ball down to where Noah was coming off the bench.

His mom, Amber, flings her hand out to grab my leg.

"Go Noah!" I yell at the top of my vocal range, cupping my hands around my mouth to amplify the sound.

He has one defender to beat, who sticks to him like honey. Noah dodges to the right, sending the defender in that direction before quickly pivoting to the left and running behind the net.

The goaltender slides to cover his flank, but Noah dives into the crease and flings his stick towards the tiny space between the goalie's pads and the side of the net. The ball squirts past the goal line, and we erupt in cheers.

Junior teams across the NLL have gathered for their annual tournament in Ontario, and the Outlaws' squad has advanced to the finals. I've seen Noah's confidence grow with each game as he settles into the pace of play. He's not the fastest player on the floor, and he's not a pure goal scorer, but his creativity and enthusiasm are unmatched. He finds opportunities to move the ball that no one else sees, and those chances are starting to pay off in the form of goals and assists.

"I can't believe how much he's grown as a player this summer," Amber says while wiping her eyes. "This experience has been so good for him."

"It really has been." I squeeze her knee. "I'm so glad this worked out. I know the fee must've been really tough to manage."

She tilts her head slightly. "It was pretty reasonable, wasn't it? Noah said he covered it with money from his paycheck."

A funny little feeling tickles the edges of my nerves. Like I'm missing some critical information, but I'm not sure what.

"Oh, that's right." I adjust my ponytail. "Now I remember."

With less than a minute left in the game, the Junior Outlaws are locked in a tie. They've pulled their goaltender for an extra forward, and the players are huddled around Sawyer and Jamie during a timeout.

Sawyer draws figures on a handheld whiteboard, demonstrating positioning for their next play. The teenagers are hanging on his every word, nodding their heads in understanding as he talks them through the strategy. The whistle around his neck bounces as he gesticulates, lending him the unmistakable air of a coach.

He looks happy and at ease in a way I've never seen. I used to hope for the day Sawyer would feel comfortable in his skin and embrace his distinct upbringing straddling two cultures, Canadian and Native. And now here he is, but he may as well be an ocean away with how distant we've become.

"Are his coaches kind?" Amber asks, watching the bench. "Noah acts tough, but he has a sensitive soul."

I used to know a kid like that. "They are," I reply softly. "They're both good men."

She sighs. "That's a relief. I wish I could have been more involved with practices and getting to know the team. My work schedule takes me away from him so much."

"He's a great kid, so you're doing something right," I say with a smile. "I'm so glad you were able to come today."

"Me too. Oh!" Her braid whips around as play resumes with Noah in control of the ball.

The Junior Outlaws pass around the offensive zone as the game clock ticks toward zero. With seconds left, Noah sends a quick pass to a streaking Connor, who immediately shoots over the goalie's right shoulder before he can react.

The goal horn sounds, and we scream with jubilation. The team flings their equipment off: gloves, sticks, and helmets pile onto the floor as players jump onto Connor to celebrate his championship-winning goal. There are plenty of congratulatory fist bumps for Noah as well, since he fed Connor the perfect pass.

"This is so awesome." Amber beams. "I'm so proud of him."

"Me too."

Noah's face lights up like a starry sky when he sees us on the floor. "You came!"

"Of course I did. I couldn't miss this." Amber pulls him into a tight hug, and I step back to give them time to connect.

On my third footfall, I collide with a concrete wall.

"Behind you!" Sawyer grabs my shoulders to steady me against him. "Sorry, I didn't realize you'd be traveling backward."

I shrug off his touch. "I could've used that warning before you ran into me."

"You backed into me, and *I'm* the problem?"

I harrumph and look around for anyone else I may know that I could talk to instead. No dice.

"Congratulations on the big win, by the way," I finally say.

"*Nyà:wę*. The boys played with so much heart, and it paid off."

My eyes slide up to his. "Why are you using Tuscarora all of a sudden?"

He shrugs. "Noah's been teaching me. I figured I could speak with your parents if I got good enough."

I bark out a sharp laugh. "It's a very difficult language. I don't even know a lot."

"Maybe we could learn together."

"You're delusional."

"I'm a dreamer. There's a difference."

I look away from him, still not finding a good enough excuse to walk away. Noah is chatting animatedly with his mom, rehashing plays from the game.

"Oh, by the way," I say, "is Noah all paid up for the program?"

Sawyer fiddles with his wristband, and that's all the confirmation I need. That was always his nervous tell, and apparently some things never change.

"Yeah, he's all set."

"You paid for him, didn't you?"

He scans my face, no doubt trying to gauge my reaction before responding. "I did, yeah. But please don't tell him or his mom. They never asked for financial help, but it was clear they needed it. And I was happy to provide it."

A peculiar warming sensation begins pulsing in my chest. "I wish you'd let me know. I would've given you the money, or at least split it with you."

"Don't worry about it. You helped him out big time with driving to and from practice." He pushes a wayward curl out of his eyes. "He reminds me a lot of myself as a teenager. I want him to feel at ease so he can focus on the people and activities that are important to him."

I fear the warmth in my chest is the feeling of my grinch heart growing three sizes larger. This was the Sawyer I knew, the boy who had been my best friend. He's still there inside this grown man who aggravates and confounds me, and it's a confusing mix of emotions I'm not prepared to handle.

"Sawyer, I—"

"Lanes! Get over here for the team photo." Jamie calls out to him.

Sawyer motions towards the gathering group of players and staff. "I've got to split. I'll see you around, Sienna." He pauses. "Or maybe not. I don't think our paths will cross for a while."

"Probably not." I swallow. "Good luck with your upcoming season."

"Thanks. *Nyà:wę.*"

I watch him walk away, and the heat in my chest flares into an ache.

Chapter 9

Rahθeʔkyehé·θuʔ
Late Fall / October

Sienna

Soft oranges and pinks blossom on the horizon as the mid-October sunrise emerges. Red and yellow leaves are sprinkled throughout the trees outside my window, and I settle into the couch to watch the world wake up. I'll head into the shop soon, but my morning cup of coffee with the sun is my favorite part of the day.

I've stared at a lot of sunrises just like this one. They've brought me comfort during times of anxiety and grief. They're a daily opportunity for gratitude and thanksgiving for what the Creator has given us.

Thirteen years ago, I started the daily practice of waking early to watch the dawn, and I rarely miss a day. I began at a time when my confidence, and my heart, were in tatters, and for the first time in years I allow the memory to creep up on me like a rising tide.

It was Sawyer's sixteenth birthday, and he'd invited a few friends over to watch a movie at his dad's house. Things felt off about that night from the start. Sawyer and Alex almost never spent time at their father's place, since he lost interest in being an active parent the instant he walked out on their mom.

I entered the unfamiliar house with a knot in my stomach. I'd gotten to know Sawyer's friends from Six Nations, but none of them were here. Instead, his Canadian friends from primary school were represented, likely because his dad didn't know anything about Sawyer's current life. These friends were loud, brash, and not especially welcoming to me.

Sawyer was happy to see me, as he always was, but his friends demanded his undivided attention. It had been several years since they'd last seen each other, so I understood. Tori, in particular, was draped over him for much of the night, and she did her best to ignore me at every opportunity.

We gathered in the living room to watch *Guardians of the Galaxy*. I carried a steaming bowl of buttery popcorn, looking around for a place to sit. Panic rose in my throat as I realized the only openings were next to people I didn't know.

Tori and Sawyer were on the loveseat, talking animatedly. She glanced at me and I swear she smirked at my obvious discomfort.

I considered sitting in the back by myself when Sawyer saw me. His face lit up in a smile, and my lips began to curve upward.

Tori put her hand to his face and turned it back to hers as she continued talking. *And, you know what? I've had enough of this.*

She may have known him longer, but Sawyer was *my* person. We were special to each other, and we didn't get much time together. He'd been looking at me all night, and it felt like an opportunity to take a risk. To put myself out there, once and for all, and find out if he felt the same way I did.

"Excuse me." My voice was saccharine as I plopped between the two of them on a couch that definitely was not designed for three people. "I'm just going to squeeze in."

Tori scowled. "Do you mind? We were talking."

Sawyer's eyes flashed with surprise and delight. "It's OK. There's plenty of room." He moved his arm behind me to make space.

There wasn't plenty of room, but I did it. I pulled off a move that would ordinarily feel far too bold for me. I placed the popcorn bowl in his lap and scooted closer until I was pressed against his side.

He beamed at me, and I felt Tori's eyes boring into the back of my head.

"Everyone ready to start?" he asked, pointing a remote at the TV but continuing to look at me.

I snuggled into him as the movie went on. Our hands occasionally brushed as we reached for popcorn, and it felt electric to be so close to him for an extended period. We were in a roomful of people, but it felt like just the two of us.

The movie was wrapping up when I finally felt the tips of his fingers on my shoulder. I rested my head on his chest in encouragement, and he slowly brought the rest of his arm down to curl around me.

"Is this OK?" he asked quietly.

As though I wasn't doing mental cartwheels, I replied, "Yeah."

The popcorn bowl long since abandoned on an end table, I wrapped an arm across his midsection. His heart beat loudly beneath my ear, and I took in a shaky breath. I'd never been held like this. Never wanted to be, except by him. My body relaxed into his with an overwhelming sense of peace.

Sawyer placed his cheek against my hair, and my heart skipped a beat. "This is nice," he whispered.

I may have stopped breathing. His skin was warm against mine, and when I finally took a breath, the smell of his cologne made my stomach flip end over end.

He tilted my chin up with his fingers until we were eye to eye. "I'm really glad you're here tonight."

My gaze dropped to his lips. "Me too."

His tongue quickly darted out to lick them, and it did something to my insides.

"Sen, can I—"

The lights came on and it violently pulled me away from the safety of his arms and the promise of his kiss.

"Well, that was fun," Tori said, sitting back from the lamp. "Good movie."

My phone buzzes on the coffee table, wrenching me from the memory before it can continue. I set my coffee mug down and answer.

"Mom? It's early. Is everything OK?"

She sighs, and the tremor in her voice raises every alarm bell in my body. "Yes and no."

"Is it Dad?" He's had a cold for weeks, and his cough worried me when I stopped by the other day.

"Yes." People talk loudly near her. "He's all right, I don't want you to worry. But I brought him to the emergency room last night, and they are admitting him to the hospital."

I fly to my feet and rush to my closet. "What's going on? Which hospital? I can head right over."

"Don't come just yet," she says. "We're still waiting for a room, and who knows how long it'll take to get settled in."

I shove my legs into a pair of jeans. "I don't mind waiting with you. I can close the shop for the day."

"No, no. Don't do that." She yawns, and I realize she's likely been up all night. "He has an advanced case of pneumonia, and the doctor wants to keep him for treatment and monitoring. He's going to be OK, but we'll probably be here for a couple of days."

"I can come as soon as you give me the word. Promise you'll tell me once he can have visitors?"

"I promise." She clears her throat. "But, I, uh—We have a favor to ask you."

I sink onto the edge of my bed. "Anything. What do you need?"

"We were supposed to fly down to Jamaica for Alex Lane's wedding. We won't be able to travel, even after your dad is released." She pauses. "Would you consider going in our place?"

I exhale. "It would be tough to leave the shop right now. School is back in session, so I'm working on Chromebooks and don't have as many hours with Noah and Vinny."

"I know, sweetheart. It's a big ask. It would mean a lot to your dad if you considered it. Rich only invited a couple of friends, and he could use some companionship."

It's my turn to sigh. Rich Doxtator is from the Cayuga Nation, and one of the kindest, most genuine people I've ever met. I know he'll feel out of his element at a wedding without any other Natives.

"What date is the wedding?" I ask.

"A week from today. But we'd planned to fly out tomorrow."

"*Tomorrow?*" I practically screech. "Why so early?"

"The family is hosting a bunch of pre-wedding events, so we wanted to be there the whole time. But if you can't manage that much time away, that's completely understandable."

I flop backwards onto the comforter. "Let me make some phone calls and see what I can do."

Chapter 10

Sawyer

Eric Clapton blares in my headphones as I contemplate today's Wordle. My starter word is doing me no favors this morning.

It's a good morning for some blues and rock. I prop my feet on my carry-on and survey Gate 20 at the Buffalo Airport. My journey to Jamaica is beginning before the sun is up, and bleary-eyed passengers are chugging coffee and moving slowly around the waiting area.

The rest of my family is flying out of Toronto, so we'll meet up later today at the hotel in Montego Bay. We're booked at a resort for the week leading up to Alex's wedding, and I couldn't be more excited to take some time away and relax with my favorite people. *Sun, sand, and umbrella drinks—here I come.*

I close my eyes and let the sound of a soaring electric guitar wash over me. Clapton sings about Layla, the woman he loves but can't have. He begs and pleads for her to give their love a chance, even though he knows it's impossible.

My eyelids slowly drift open before blinking. Once, twice, three times.

As though my sleepy thoughts conjured her, my own personal Layla is walking down the aisle towards me. And she looks stressed as hell.

Sienna nearly runs me over before she notices and stops dead in her tracks.

"You've got to be kidding me."

I wiggle my fingers in a sheepish wave. "Morning, Princess."

She turns on her heel and heads in the opposite direction, rolling her suitcase behind her.

The angel and devil on my shoulders duke it out for a full minute before I gather my belongings and go after her. Eric Clapton would approve.

She huffs when I lower myself into the seat next to hers. "It should be illegal to deal with you this early in the morning."

I lean back and cross my ankle over my knee. "Do you want coffee? I can grab you one."

"I had some already. I'm used to being up early."

"Of course you are." I sip my own beverage. "To what do I owe the pleasure of your company before the birds are awake?"

She tilts forward and rests her elbows on her knees. "My parents asked me to attend the wedding since they can't. My dad's in the hospital."

I sit up with a start. "What happened? Is he OK?"

Her gaze is on the floor, and I wish I could throw an arm around her or squeeze her hand like I would any other friend.

"He's all right. He has pneumonia and needs some extra monitoring." She fiddles with her watch. "He should be discharged in the next day or two, but he can't fly in his condition."

"I'm sorry. This must be really stressful for you and your family. I can't believe you're packed and ready to travel on such short notice."

She chuckles. "I hope I'm packed. I had to outsource that to Hazel so I could prep the shop and make all my reservations. Who knows what she picked out for me."

I grin. "I truly cannot wait to see what you wind up wearing this week." I glance at the counter, where gate agents are setting up. "Hey, real quick. I know I'm not your favorite person, but would you rather sit with me on the plane or someone you don't know?"

Her head snaps up to look at me. "Ugh."

"I know, but I want you to be comfortable. Both flights are over two hours long."

Her shoulders droop. "I suppose you're the lesser of two evils."

"Stop buttering me up, or my helmet won't fit anymore." I hold out my hand. "Now gimme your boarding pass and I'll take care of you."

Forty-five minutes later we're seated together on the plane, courtesy of the outrageous flirting I did with a gate agent. It's my one useful superpower: the ability to charm my way into desirable situations.

Sienna takes the window seat so I can have the aisle to stretch my legs, though I know she'll be uncomfortable folding in her long frame.

"We can switch on the second flight," I offer.

"We'll see." She pulls her phone and a pair of headphones out of her bag, and I notice a slight tremor in her hands.

"Are you a nervous traveler?"

She pauses before plugging in her earbuds. "I haven't flown much. So, probably."

"It's the lack of control, I would guess."

She flicks her eyes over to mine. "I'm not some control freak."

"No, but you're used to being in charge. You get to set the rules in your everyday life." I slide my phone into the seatback pocket. "I'll let you boss me around today, if it helps."

She scoffs. "I've bossed you around for half your life."

A wide grin spreads across my face. "I know. And I like it."

She mutters under her breath, and I chuckle.

For all her sharpness, I've always found it easy to be with Sienna. I like that she challenges me, and that she isn't impressed by my nonsense. She's smarter, more accomplished, and better looking than I am. She's so far out of my league it's criminal to hold out hope for a chance with her.

All while I worry that one day I'll have to smile and shoot the shit with some undeserving future husband while her adorable children run around nearby. I need to be prepared for it, since we're both twenty-nine, but I'm nowhere close.

The plane's engines roar to life as we prepare for takeoff. Sienna grips both armrests, her knuckles turning pale.

"Do you want to hold my hand?"

"Shut up," she says through gritted teeth.

"I was kind of serious."

She closes her eyes. "Please don't judge me for being ridiculous."

"I promise. But you're not being ridiculous."

The fuselage lifts into the air, and she starts to tremble.

She'll probably claw my eyes out, but I can't sit here and watch her panic. I cover her hand with mine and lean close to her ear.

"Breathe, Sen. Take some deep breaths with me. Can you do that?"

She nods, and her eyes look a bit less wild. We breathe together until her inhales match mine and her body is still. I rub my thumb across the back of her hand until she pulls it away.

"Sorry about all that." Her hair spills into her eyes as she lowers her face.

"Don't worry about it." I rub my fingers together, missing the warmth of her skin. "You've helped me through plenty of those."

Her deep, shuddering exhale alerts me that she has a lot on her mind, and I don't push it.

"Do you still like to play cards?" I ask.

She looks up through her curtain of hair. "I do."

It was one of our favorite things to do together. She'd teach me a new game, and we'd play it for hours while talking. Then I'd force Alex to play with me so I could practice until I saw her again. We played Gin Rummy, Crazy Eights, Speed, Poker, Canasta; the list goes on. Other than Wes, who's been trying unsuccessfully to teach me Cribbage, I haven't had anyone willing to play with me in years.

"Excuse me." I flag down a flight attendant as she passes by.

She looks at me with a polished smile, flashes her gaze up and down, and relaxes into a cheeky grin. "Hi! How can I help you?"

"Does the airline have any decks of cards available?"

She tucks a stray piece of hair behind her ear. "We do. Let me go get you one." She leans in with a wink. "It's on the house."

"You're disgusting," Sienna says once the flight attendant leaves

I swing around. "What did I do this time?"

"You hit on anything that moves."

I guffaw with shock. "I do not."

She rolls her eyes. "You just flirted with the flight attendant."

"No way, I was just asking for cards. Trust me, you would know if I was flirting."

"What's that supposed to mean?"

I drop my eyes to her crossed legs and slowly drag them up her body until they meet hers again. She looks so pretty in her powder blue and white sundress, and I've been trying not to notice. "Do you want me to flirt with you so you can find out?"

She's definitely going to kill me this time. The faintest blush colors her cheeks, and I grin at my success.

"See, this is why I can't stand—"

"Here you go." The flight attendant returns before Sienna can attempt murder. "Let me know if you need anything else."

Her fingers linger on my palm as she presses a package into my hand.

"Thanks so much." I unwrap the deck of cards from a napkin and pause.

"Do you ever get tired of women throwing themselves at you?" Sienna asks with a smirk, eyeing the phone number scrawled in blue ink. The name Tammy is written underneath with a tiny heart.

I crumple the napkin and stuff it into the seatback pocket. "Not really, no." I unlatch my tray table so I can shuffle the cards.

She watches me. "Are you going to call her?"

"No."

"Why not?"

"Because I'm not interested. Will you just let me take your mind off flying for one damn minute?"

The corner of her lips quivers upward. "What are we playing?"

We played Hearts for the rest of the flight and switched to Gin on our second flight after a layover in Atlanta. If I didn't know better, I'd think Sienna was not just tolerating my presence, but even enjoying it a little bit.

She relishes kicking my ass at cards. She listens when I talk about the upcoming week of wedding events and how I'll be starting Outlaws training camp as soon as I'm back in Buffalo.

She even smiles slightly when I crack an especially good joke or two at my own expense.

It's so close to what we used to be, and I'm afraid to screw it up.

I'm laying down a set of queens when there's a commotion in the back of the plane. Flight attendants hustle down the aisle, and several passengers are out of their seats.

"What's going on?" Sienna asks, craning her neck.

I peer around my seat but can't see anything past the mass of people. "I'm not sure. Hopefully nothing serious."

We try to continue playing, but the situation in the rear of the airplane is too distracting. After several minutes, a flight attendant strides to the front, a concerned look on his face.

"Ladies and gentlemen, may I have your attention, please?"

We set our cards down as a voice comes over the public address system.

"Do we have any medical professionals on board? If so, please identify yourself to the nearest flight attendant. Thank you."

"That can't be good," I say.

For the next fifteen minutes, there's a flurry of activity. Flight attendants come and go, talk on phones, and bring refreshments to an elderly woman seated near the back.

The public address system dings again.

"Ladies and gentlemen, this is your captain speaking. This aircraft is being diverted to the Kingston airport due to a medical emergency on board."

Sienna and I exchange glances.

"We understand this is unexpected and will disrupt your plans. Please see a gate agent once we deplane, and they will help you find a way to your original destination."

"Well, shit." Sienna gathers the playing cards back into their box. "What are we going to do now?"

"We'll figure it out," I assure her. "If all else fails, I'll just flirt with someone who'll get us there."

She drops an elbow towards my obliques, and I dodge her with a laugh.

Chapter 11

Sienna

My emotions are out of control. There's a five-alarm fire raging inside my body, and I need to extinguish it immediately.

Sawyer's running a masterclass in how to win me over. All morning he's been nothing but kind, patient, funny, and pleasant to be around. He's noticing when I'm stressed and remembering how to calm me down. He even flirted a little, and I didn't want to strangle him. In fact, his deep voice talking me through a panic attack during takeoff immediately knitted my nervous system back together because it was unfortunately very sweet and *very* hot.

This is an unmitigated disaster. *This* is why I've gone out of my way to avoid him all these years. Deep down I knew I couldn't hang onto my hurt and rage if left alone with him for too long. I can't allow myself to get pulled back into his orbit.

I promised myself I would never let him hurt me again, and I have to see that through.

"What a mess," Sawyer says, surveying the chaos of passengers and luggage at our gate.

It turns out there are no direct flights between Kingston and Montego Bay. To fly across the island, we'd need to fly back to the U.S. and catch a different plane to Jamaica, and wouldn't arrive until the following day. The airline is attempting to organize a bus, but everything is still being figured out.

"Can we not just rent a car and drive?" he asks.

"I'm looking." I quickly connect to the airport wifi and start researching. "Looks like it's about three hours from here."

"Want to bail and do that, instead of waiting for hours on a bus that might not come?"

I pocket my phone. "Say less."

It seems we're not the first people to have this idea, as the rental car area is swarming with travelers.

"I'll take care of getting the car," he offers, gesturing towards a bank of seats. "Go take a load off."

"You sure?" I furrow my brow at the sight of the growing lines of surly travelers.

"Positive. I'll get us out of here before you've had a chance to get too comfortable." He winks and I scowl in response.

"Whatever. I'm going to see if I can make a reservation online and beat some of the crowds."

"Is this a competition for who can get a rental car first?" He smirks.

"No." *Maybe.*

"All right, Princess. You're on. I've always enjoyed our games."

I open my mouth to respond, but he spins and strides confidently towards the busy counter.

"This fucking guy," I mutter, pulling out my phone.

Me: We got rerouted to Kingston. Ugh. Need to fight a plane full of people for a rental car to get to the resort.

Hazel: This trip is cursed!

Hazel: Wait. Who's "we?"

Me: Sawyer and I were on the same flight, and I got stuck sitting with him

Hazel: What are the chances of that?!

Me: Well, I figured it was less terrible than squeezing next to a stranger

Hazel: ...You changed your seat so you two could sit together?

Me: You know how bad my social anxiety gets, especially when I'm already stressed about Dad and flying

Hazel: I do, and I'm glad he stepped up to support you. This may be a good time to tell you I packed your suitcase from MY closet because your wardrobe looks like it was donated by an elder.

Me: What's that supposed to mean?

Hazel: Enjoy your vacation, wear cute clothes, and snag a hot guy while you're down there. Sawyer absolutely counts.

Me: Haze. No.

I switch back and forth between the texts with my sister and the slowly loading rental car website. I glance up to find Sawyer somehow already leaning against a counter and grinning at an agent. She giggles and types on her computer terminal, tucking a spiral of dark curls behind her ear.

This. Fucking. Guy.

Sawyer leans back, and our eyes lock across the room. He winks, and it sends white-hot rage (that was rage, right?) zipping through my veins.

I refocus on navigating the achingly slow site. I've barely begun browsing the available car options when Sawyer strolls up to me.

"All set."

I stare at him. "There's no way."

"We're good. I'll grab the car and pull around out front for you."

I cross my arms. "You cut all these people waiting in line?"

"I did not." His lip quivers upward in a smile. "I found a very nice agent taking her break and asked if she could help me."

"So you flirted your way past lines of people. Got it."

"I can't help that I'm likeable."

I scoff. "You're insufferable."

"You're the only one who thinks so." He shoves his wallet into his pocket. "I'll pull around for you in a couple of minutes, OK?"

"Did you get *her* number, too?"

The snide question is out of my mouth before I can question its maturity.

Sawyer raises his eyebrows, and I regret everything. "Why, are you jealous?"

"Be for real."

"I am." He cocks his head to the side with a smirk. "You're acting jealous."

"I'm merely disgusted with your sense of entitlement."

"Entitle—? You know me better than that." His jaw ticks and I know I've landed a blow.

"I do. That's why I said it."

I'm being a huge bitch, but I'm too grouchy to care.

Sawyer inhales deeply, and not for the first time I hope he finally loses his temper with me. I've been picking fights with him for years, and he's never taken the bait. It would be easier to hate him if he'd snap at me. "Well, I'm going to get the car. If you can survive three hours with me, I'll buy you a margarita on the other side."

A few minutes later, I roll my suitcase towards the front entrance. The Kingston air is cooler than I expected, although still warmer than Buffalo. I'm lost in thought when a cacophony of noise startles me back to the present.

A white, open-top Jeep pulls around the corner, "Back in Black" by AC/DC blaring from its speakers.

Must be some jerk Americ—Oh, shit.

As the car gets closer, I notice Sawyer in the driver's seat, a broad smile stretching across his face. He's unbuttoned his Hawaiian shirt, and it flaps in the breeze around his torso.

And sweet strawberry jam, what a torso it is.

My mouth runs dry as he parks the car and strides over. I can't look away from the sinful amount of his chest and abdomen on display, each muscle chiseled from countless hours at the gym. My pulse races as he reaches for my bag, his fingertips brushing against mine as he grabs the handle from me.

I suck in a desperate inhale, unaware I'd been holding my breath. A shot of his woodsy cologne hits me square in the chest and floods my system.

I'm staring but unable to make myself stop. I stand rooted to the spot as he tosses my suitcase in the back before walking over to open the passenger door.

I finally wrench my eyes up to his when I realize he's standing there expectantly. "Sorry. Are you—?" I stammer.

"You should take a picture, Princess." He grins. "It'll last longer."

If my initial nervous system response to seeing Sawyer nearly shirtless was to freeze, it was now activated into fight mode.

"You should put some clothes on," I snap as I haul myself into the Jeep.

He closes the door behind me. "But then I wouldn't get to see you ogling me."

"I'm not *ogling*."

"You were just looking at me like I was Jessica Rabbit and we're in Toon Town."

"I was *not*!"

If a giant sinkhole would kindly come and swallow me up right now, I'd be most appreciative. I try to gain control of my heart rate as he walks to the driver's side and gets in.

"Objectify me out if you want." His eyes sparkle as he sets up the GPS on his phone. "I don't mind."

"Oh my God." I slink low in my seat and pull my sunglasses down. "You're so egotistical."

"I'm not bad, I'm just drawn that way."

I smack his arm so hard he drops his phone with a hearty laugh.

"Ready to punch it?" he asks, sliding his aviator Ray-Bans on.

"Let's just get this over with." I lean my head back against the seat with a sigh.

"You good with your hair down?"

"...what?"

"I wasn't sure if you wanted to pull your hair back, given the wind."

The reality of our situation hits me like a ton of bricks. "Why the heck did you rent an open-top Jeep?" I groan, digging around in my purse.

"First of all, options were very limited considering I flirted my way into a rental car." He wiggles his eyebrows. "Second, driving across the island in this is going to be freaking awesome."

"This is a nightmare." I pull my hair into a high ponytail.

"You're fun. I love traveling with you." He puts the car in gear.

We're less than a minute down the road when I realize I've made many errors in my attire.

Hair flies into my mouth as my ponytail whips around my head. I bat it away and squeak when my dress flies up towards my waist. I frantically push it down and tuck it under my thighs, spitting out hair along the way.

I hear Sawyer laughing and attempt an undignified glower in his direction.

"Don't worry, Marilyn Monroe. I'll keep my eyes on the road." He shifts into the next gear. "Do you want me to pull over so you can compose yourself?"

"Yes, please," I say through gritted teeth.

"What do you mean there are no rooms available?"

A soft-spoken front desk clerk smiles tightly with fear in his eyes. "I'm so sorry, Miss. I don't understand what happened."

"But my parents had this reservation booked for months." I blink back tears. It's been a long day, and I'm feeling about as stable as my last Windows upgrade. "I'm sure of it."

He fidgets with the collar of his immaculately pressed uniform. "I suspect the reservation was inadvertently canceled in the process of updating it to your name." He types quickly and scans his screen for at least the fiftieth time. "It shouldn't have happened, and I'm so sorry."

"It's not your fault." My voice comes out choked. "You're positive there are no other rooms available tonight?"

Sweat beads at his forehead. "I'm going to keep looking, but right now I'm not seeing anything available until next week."

I lean on the counter, my stomach clenching. "I appreciate you taking the extra time to look."

"Perhaps you could stay with another guest for a few days until a room becomes free?" he offers hopefully.

Like who? I don't know anyone at this wedding aside from Sawyer's family, and there are layers of awkwardness associated with asking any of them to bunk with me.

"I'll figure something out." I draw in a shaky breath.

My suitcase rolls loudly across the lobby floor, its wheels thumping into the tile grout every half second. I'm alone in a foreign country with no place to sleep and even fewer brain cells left to figure a way out of this mess. For the first time in years, I feel like crying in frustration.

I plop into a high-back chair at the bar, tucking my luggage and purse beneath the counter.

"Good evening, miss." The bartender smiles broadly at me. "What can I get you tonight?"

"Just a Coke, please."

I stare at the text conversation with my sister while I wait, but I don't have the heart to fill her in on the latest catastrophe. I'm exhausted from the long day of travel, the unexpected detours, and being forced to spend hours upon hours with Sawyer.

My mind is confused, so I focus on what I know is true: The man infuriates me with his very existence. He plays fast and loose with the rules, which is so personally abhorrent to me that it makes me want to scream. He's a womanizing playboy who doesn't care who he hurts along the way.

Heat rises in my cheeks as I'm reminded of my body's earlier response to him. I can't stand him, but Great Spirit, the man is easy on the eyes. I'd done my best to ignore him, but couldn't help but sneak a few glances as his shirt billowed back. He was singing classic rock at the top of his lungs, his chestnut waves blowing in the breeze, and his eyes sparkling beneath his sunglasses. His energy was so infectious I'd been tempted, just a bit, to throw my head back and enjoy the wind in my hair.

"Couldn't wait for me to buy you that drink, eh?" Sawyer sidles up to me at the bar, and I nearly scream at the unexpected intrusion.

"What the hell are you doing here?" I gasp, jumping straight out of my seat like a startled cat.

He's wearing a brown and white striped shirt, unbuttoned dangerously low for my liking. He's freshly showered, his hair damp and curling at the front. He smells like shampoo, cologne, and every one of my teenage daydreams.

Freaking hell.

"I'm meeting my family for dinner in a few minutes." He glances up at the bartender returning with my drink.

"Here you are, miss." The man gently slides the glass to me with a wink.

"Thank you." I smile gratefully at him.

Sawyer clears his throat, and I regretfully wrench my gaze back over to him.

"Could I get you something to drink, sir?" the bartender asks.

"I'll have what she's having," Sawyer says, nodding at my pop.

"Coming right up."

"Are you going home with the bartender tonight?" Sawyer asks, leaning against the bar. "Because it seems like he'd be interested in that."

I roll my eyes. "Oh, please. Who's jealous now?"

His eyes slide over to mine. "I guess we're even."

I blink and go back for another long drag of my beverage. "It's not a bad idea, however, since I have nowhere else to sleep."

His brow furrows. "What do you mean?"

"The hotel lost my dad's reservation, and they're booked solid the rest of the week."

"Oh, shit." He sets his glass down with a clatter. "Let me talk to the front desk for you. There has to be a way to fix this."

I shake my head. "The clerk is double-checking, but it's not looking promising."

"I'll talk to her."

"You're out of luck, Rico Suave. It's a guy."

"Maybe he's gay."

I barely hold back a sharp laugh, covering it with my drink.

"If we can't figure this out tonight, how about you stay with Alex and Ellie?"

I wrinkle my nose. "The almost-newlyweds? I'm not interrupting that vibe."

"My mom and Rich?"

I sigh. "Almost as awkward. I'm not a kid."

He swirls the dwindling ice in his glass. "I know this would be the worst of the worst for you, but what about my room?"

"No."

"I could probably get a rollaway cot from the front desk, and you could have the bed."

"Absolutely not."

"I'll be gone a lot with wedding prep, I'm sure. You'd barely see me."

"Hard pass."

"Sienna." He crosses his arms in front of his chest, and my eyes leap to the patch of exposed skin at his neck. "Don't be stubborn. I'm not a serial killer."

"You might be."

He drags a hand through his hair. "I'll sleep across the room with my back to you, how's that?"

My head falls into my hands. "I hate everything."

"Hey." A chair squeaks as he pulls closer to me. "This has been a tough day. We've been traveling since dawn, everything has gone wrong, and now you don't have a place to lay your head and decompress." A tentative hand touches my shoulder. "Let me help."

I harrumph, but don't look up.

"Here's my room key." He pushes a white paper pouch beneath my forearms and into view. "Go take a hot shower, change, sleep, whatever you need. I'll see what I can figure out with the front desk."

I stare at the electronic key. "Why are you being so nice to me? I treat you like shit."

"I like you."

That got my attention. I rotate my head to peer at him with one eye over my hands.

"I know the feeling's not mutual, but I've always respected the hell out of you." He pushes his empty drink away. "I care about your well-being and whether you have a safe place to stay."

I press the heels of my palms into my eye sockets and sigh. "Fine. We can try this for one night. But I'm calling to check availability at other hotels in the morning."

"Deal." He stands up and offers me his hand.

I stare as if he's sprouted tentacles. "What's this for?"

"A guy can't be chivalrous anymore?"

"I told you, I've never needed a knight in shining armor."

"But you need my hotel room." He smirks as he lowers his hand and grabs my suitcase instead.

"One night." I poke him in the chest with my extended index finger.

"We'll see."

Chapter 12

Sawyer

I sent Sienna to my room with strict instructions to eat and relax. I'm fairly certain she'll do neither, but at least I tried.

Alex grabs me in a bear hug when I walk into the restaurant. "It's so good to see you, man. It's been a minute."

I clap him on the back. "Not my fault you've been tied up with wedding planning for the past month."

"It's *my* fault." My brother's fiancée smiles as she pulls me away from Alex and into her arms. "But you could've come over to make reception favors, you jerk."

I give Ellie a squeeze. "Sorry about that. My days have been packed with tournaments, coaching, and getting in shape for training camp."

"Yeah, yeah." She ruffles my hair. "I might forgive you eventually."

"Come inside. Mom and Rich are holding a table for us," Alex says.

I follow them through the rows decked out with fine dishware and bouquets of fresh flowers. The restaurant glows with candles and dimmed lighting.

"Hey, so, uh…" I say to Alex, "do you know when Dad is arriving?"

He shakes his head. "No clue. I think we were lucky to get an RSVP card back from him, to be honest."

I chuckle sardonically. "Why am I not surprised?"

"I hope it wasn't a mistake to invite him." Alex bites his lip. "It didn't feel right to leave him out when we were writing invitations, but now I'm thinking it's just asking for trouble on a happy occasion."

Ellie squeezes his arm.

"Everything will be fine." I smile with as much gusto as I can manage. "No matter what happens, we have each other, and we'll deal with whatever chaos he may bring."

I haven't seen my father in a couple of years, although he calls regularly during the NLL season. He seems to forget I exist unless there's a reason to judge my play. I never lived up to his expectations, which he likes to remind me of at every opportunity. I thought making it to the pros would silence most of his commentary, as well as my internal criticism, but it hasn't.

"Hey kid." Rich pulls me in for a hug. "I'm glad you made it. Sounds like you had quite a journey to get here."

I laugh. "You can say that again. But I'm here."

"Did you run into Sienna?" my mom asks, squeezing between us to join our embrace. "Anne Bissell called yesterday to tell us they couldn't make it, and it sounded like Sienna might be on the same flight out of Buffalo."

"She was, yeah. We drove together from Kingston, too."

Alex's eyebrows shoot up. "And she didn't kill you? I'm shocked."

I hold up my hands. "I survived to tell the tale, somehow."

"Is this your friend Sienna from high school?" Ellie asks.

I nod as we get to our seats. "I'm not sure we exactly qualify as friends anymore, but yeah."

She brightens. "I've always wanted to meet her. You'll have to introduce us."

"I was so sad when the two of you stopped being close," my mom says. "You were so good for each other."

I smile tightly. "Me too."

"What did you do to piss her off?"

We all turn to look at Rich, who grins in response.

"If she dropped you like a hot pot, then you did something, even if you don't know it." He takes a sip of water.

"Richard," my mom hisses. "I'm sure they just grew apart."

My stepdad shakes his head. "You don't have to believe me, but I've ticked off my fair share of Native women." He kisses my mom's hand. "You always tell me when you're angry with me, *Kegehjih*."

She narrows her eyes at him.

"See? You're communicating it to me right now."

"So, what did you do, Sawyer?" Alex asks, his eyes sparkling with glee.

"Hell if I know," I reply. "If I knew, I would've begged her to forgive me years ago."

Ellie leans over while we're eating. "Do you want me to talk to Sienna for you? People always open up to me."

I chuckle as I take a drink from my glass. "You haven't met this woman yet. She's like Fort Knox."

She sits back with a smile. "I'll see what I can do."

I walk back to my room, my body humming with happiness. My family are the most important people in my life, and I'm thrilled to be here with them to celebrate the addition of Ellie to our crew.

I breathe deeply to steel myself before entering the room. My interactions with Sienna have been all over the map today, so I'm not sure what I'll be walking into.

Driving across the island with the wind whipping through my hair and the most beautiful woman I've ever seen in the passenger seat was definitely a Top Five life moment. She wanted to kill me the entire time, but no matter.

Actually, that wasn't true. Murder wasn't on her mind the entire trip, based on the way I caught her staring at me earlier. She was downright flustered by my bare chest and when I checked her out on the plane. I'd flirt with her more often if I wasn't worried she'd bite me.

I enter the room and find it empty. *Maybe she left to grab food?* I kick my shoes into the closet and stride towards the bed, only for the bathroom door to open in a cloud of steam.

Sienna screams and nearly drops her towel when she sees me.

I get an accidental eyeful of her toffee skin before I spin around and put myself in the corner like a misbehaving child. "I'm sorry! I didn't see anything, I swear."

"Don't move."

"I'm going nowhere." I rest my forehead against the wall and try not to let my mind flood with images of her: the curves of her breasts above the towel, the expanse of skin across her chest, the grooves of her shoulders. I can hear her towel fall to the floor and the rustling sounds of her pulling on clothes.

I'm not well. This is very, very bad for my mental and physical health.

"OK, I'm dressed."

I slowly turn with my eyes on the ground. "Sorry. I should've knocked." Hesitantly, I look up at her and almost collapse from cardiac arrest.

Sienna is shoving clothes back into her suitcase, a pink satin robe cinched tightly at her waist. It rides up her thighs as she bends over, and I am not a strong man at the moment.

She stands up straight and catches me drowning for her. "What's the matter?" she asks.

My mouth is bone dry, but I manage a shaky smile. "Nothing. Just picturing your sister picking out your clothes."

She glances down and scowls. "I wouldn't normally wear something like this to bed, but it'll have to do."

My brain conjures images of every possible sleepwear option she might wear. I tamp down a quiet groan at the thought of her in one of my t-shirts and nothing else.

She sits on the end of the bed and starts braiding her damp hair. "Did you ask the front desk about a rollaway cot?"

I wrench my eyes away and dig through my own suitcase for something to sleep in. "Yeah, so, about that…"

She stills. "No cots?"

I shake my head. "But I can sleep on the floor, no problem."

Her braiding recommences. "You shouldn't sleep on the floor. This is your room."

"I don't mind. Don't worry about it."

As soon as I get to the bathroom, I bend over the sink and take several deep breaths. *Pull yourself together, man. Don't be a creep.* I splash my face with water and head back out to battle.

She's reading on her phone when I emerge. "I don't want you to sleep on the floor."

I push down the flicker of hope that ignites at her words. "I really don't mind. You deserve some privacy."

She watches me set up a pillow and extra blankets on the ground. I plug my phone in nearby and lay on my side.

"See? Just fine." *These floors are uncomfortable as hell.*

I scroll through social media for a minute before looking up to find her still watching me.

"Come to bed." Her voice is a mixture of tired and commanding.

"Sienna—"

"Come. To. Bed. I'll put some pillows between us so you stay on your side."

"Are you sure? I'm really—"

"Yes, I'm sure." She pulls back the covers and starts rearranging pillows. "I won't sleep knowing you're suffering down there."

I climb into bed as she tosses her robe on the floor, leaving her in a tiny camisole and sleep shorts that will haunt my dreams.

"Let me know if you change your mind." I turn my back to her and scoot to the edge. "I can leave if you want."

She sighs, and the sound reverberates through my chest. "Stay. Please."

"Good night, Princess."

"*θaθręhnakwáhsnę·k.*"

"Are you talking dirty to me in Tuscarora?"

"Good night, Sawyer."

Chapter 13

Sienna

I wake up disoriented. My internal clock typically rouses me, helped by the sun, but it is pitch black where I am. And I never close my bedroom curtains.

I fling my arms wide and bang into something warm and solid. And it grumbles when I hit it.

My body freezes. *Where. Am. I?*

I force myself to breathe deeply while I unscramble my brain. Bits of memories come back to me until they complete the puzzle: airplane, Jeep, resort, Sawyer.

Sawyer. It's Sawyer.

My muscles relax with relief. Sawyer is next to me, and I must've forgotten to open the curtains before bed.

Shit. Sawyer's in bed next to me.

My eyes start to adjust to the dark, and I can make out his broad form sleeping near me. He stayed on his side of the bed, as requested, although I'm wrapped around the pillows between us.

I have no idea what time it is, and I'm too exhausted to care. My heavy eyes close, and I attempt to drift back to sleep.

Attempt being the keyword, as my tired mind immediately floods with uncomfortable images from the past.

Sawyer's dad's living room. Summoning every bit of strength and hope I possessed to sit with him on the couch. The safety I felt wrapped in his arms. How sure I was that he was about to kiss me.

And then the aftermath, when I realized I knew nothing at all, because the past several years had clearly been a lie.

It's painful, and I resist, but the memory comes to me unbidden.

Tori turning on the lights interrupted us, but Sawyer stayed near me as we began to clean up.

His pinky finger wound around mine as I grabbed our popcorn bowl from the end table.

"Can I see you before you leave?" he asked with the softest smile tugging at his lips.

Gosh, he's so gorgeous. I'd always found him attractive, but Sawyer had definitely grown into his body in the past year. He was wearing his dark hair a bit longer, and now the waves turned to curls at the ends. He was finally the same height as me, while his chest and legs filled out from lacrosse and the gym. I caught other girls looking at him, whereas before I'd been the only one.

And now this sweet and beautiful boy was looking at *me* like I was the only one in the room.

I looked down shyly. "Yeah, we can do that. My dad should be here soon."

"OK." He squeezed my hand. "Let me clean up the kitchen real quick, and then I'll come find you."

He left, and I clapped a hand over my mouth to quiet my squeal of excitement. *This is it. This is when he finally tells me he likes me, too, and we can be together.*

I gathered the bowls scattered throughout the room, humming happily as I worked. I stacked them inside each other as I approached the kitchen. The sound of voices stopped me short.

"I don't know. She's just kind of...weird." It was a female voice, so it must be Tori.

"She's a really nice person." That was Sawyer. "And a very good friend."

I smiled at his words.

"You already *have* friends here," Tori says. "I don't know how you're surviving living on the reservation. It must be awful."

I rolled my eyes, unfortunately used to casual racism.

"Tori."

"What? You know it's true. And we never get to see you anymore. You see her all the time."

He sighed. "I don't, actually. She lives in the States. And she's important to me."

My insides warmed as I continued my gratuitous eavesdropping.

"Well," she scoffed, "you two sure seemed cozy during the movie. She was all over you."

Thump. Thump. My heart thudded in my chest, hanging on his next words.

He cleared his throat. "We're just friends."

If it were possible for my heart to physically break, it would have. *Had I completely misread our relationship? Was Tori right? Did I throw myself at him tonight?* My hands shook as I clenched them around the bowls.

"Really?" Tori sounded surprised.

"Yeah." Sawyer's voice was flat. "Don't concern yourself with her."

Sharp pains hit me in the chest, and it hurt to breathe. I frantically looked around for a place to set down the bowls in my hands, desperate to be anywhere but here before I succumbed to the emotion gathering in my throat.

"Well, in that case..."

I peeked around the corner as I put my stack of dishware on the ground and found Tori wrapping her arms around Sawyer's neck.

"What are you—"

She cut him off with a kiss, and his hands rose to her waist.

Now I think I really will vomit.

The dishes rattled as I left them and ran to the bathroom, the clatter of plastic echoing in my ears.

I cried my eyes out for five minutes, desperately trying to stay quiet so no one heard me. Shame and embarrassment rolled through me like thunder. I put myself out there and made a fool of myself. Of course, we were just friends. How could I assume we were anything more? Boys were never interested in me once they got to know me. I was too cold, too serious, too inflexible.

Sawyer may have liked me early on, but over the years he figured out he didn't want to date someone like me. And I couldn't blame him.

I pulled myself together, because being found like this would be much worse. My eyes were still puffy, but I had to get out of this house. I opened the door and ran right into Sawyer.

"Hey!" He grabbed my shoulders to steady me. "I was just looking for you." His smile fell when he saw my face. "What's wrong?"

"I need to go home." I pushed him away and walked quickly down the hallway.

"Wait, Sen!" He jogged and immediately caught up with me. "Is everything OK? You look upset."

I blindly shoved my arms into my coat with a haze of tears creeping in. "I'm not feeling well. I should go."

"Oh, OK." He straightened the collar on my jacket, and his hands lingered there. "Do you want me to call your dad?"

I shook my head. "He'll be here any minute." I put my hands on his to remove them from my lapel, but he tightened his grip and pulled me an inch closer.

"I'm sorry you're not feeling good," he said softly. "Can we find another time soon to talk? I can call you."

My stomach flipped, and I wanted so badly to trust him. *Maybe I misheard him in the kitchen. Maybe he's not into Tori.*

What a stupid girl I was.

Headlights turned into the driveway, and I saw my dad's New York license plates.

"I have to go," I rasped, pulling away.

My coat slipped out of his hands as he let me leave. I wanted him to chase after me, to wrap me in his arms and finish the kiss we almost started. I wanted to sob and punch him in the chest and yell at him. And above all, I never wanted to see him again.

"Sienna?" Sawyer's insistent voice breaks through my dream, and I'm so confused.

I open my eyes to find him looking at me with deep concern. He swipes under my eye with his thumb, and I feel wetness on my lashes.

We're back in the hotel room. I must've dozed off.

"Are you OK?" he asks, his palm covering my cheek. "You've been crying."

I wrench myself away, feeling absolutely mortified. "I'm sorry. I don't know what happened." I rub the heels of my hands across my face. "What time is it?"

He glances around me to look at the digital clock. "Eight a.m."

"Oh, shit." I throw my legs off the bed and hurriedly pull on my robe. "I need to start working."

"Aren't you on vacation?" He watches me fling items from my suitcase as I pull an outfit together.

"Vacations don't exist when you're a business owner." I settle on an entirely too short pair of denim cutoffs and an open-knit tank before zipping into the bathroom to change.

Five minutes later I'm dressed, packed, and heading out. "I'll see you later at some point."

"Bye!" Sawyer calls from bed as I close the door behind me.

Chapter 14

Sienna

The breeze is warm, the sun is shining, and people start drinking *really* early here.

I'd wanted to work in a quiet corner of the lobby, but that felt too anti-social, even for me. I set up on the outskirts of the pool at a table in the shade, similar to how young children parallel play: you do your thing, I'll do my thing, and we'll be happy coexisting.

This week I had to reduce shop hours. Given the sudden change, I want to stay on top of emails and help facilitate computer drop-offs when Noah and Vinny are available. There's already a backlog of requests in my inbox, and I've been plugging away at them for a while.

Unfortunately, I keep getting interrupted.

"Is this seat taken?" An insanely gorgeous man with blond hair and bright blue eyes smiles at me.

I blink. "No."

Much to my chagrin, he pulls out the chair across from me and sits down. *Dammit*. I'd been hoping he just wanted to borrow the chair.

He leans forward. "What's your name?"

I'm immediately over it. "Actually, I'm working, so I'm not able to talk right now."

He grins as he flicks his gaze down my bare legs. "You're too pretty to be working."

"Does that line usually work for you? Because it's lame." I turn my attention back to my computer screen.

His smile falters. "You're feisty."

"Please go."

I dispatch with him, but more arrive in his place over the next few hours. I become more curt with each intrusion, offering up an "I'm not interested" the instant a guy opens his mouth.

I'm typing a checklist of priorities for Noah and Vinny when someone sits at my table.

"Not interested," I say without looking away from my screen.

"Sheesh, tough crowd."

I glance up to find Alex Lane grinning at me.

"Oh, thank God it's just you." I get to my feet and am swallowed up by my friend's arms.

"As usual, I'm not sure whether you're complimenting or insulting me." He squeezes me and spins me around. "It's great to see you, Sienna. It's been too long."

"It's been ages since we've had a big family get-together." His smile brings out mine. Everything is brighter on Alex's side of the Lane brothers coin: his honey brown hair and hazel eyes are lighter than Sawyer's, his laugh is louder, and his clothes more colorful. Big younger brother energy from this one.

"Well, yeah. No one wants to clean up the blood spill from you and Sawyer being stuck in the same room." He chuckles.

Oh, the irony.

"Speaking of rooms, is everything good with yours?" He sits back down and leans back in his chair.

I hesitate. The family does not need the stress of my lack of a room. "Yeah, everything's great."

"You should join us for dinner one night, as long as Sawyer won't annoy you too much."

I smile weakly. "Maybe. We'll see how the next few days pan out. I'm pretty swamped with work while I'm here."

A pretty blonde in a striped bikini and a nylon cover-up tied at her waist deposits herself in his lap.

Alex beams and kisses her. "Hey, babe."

"Hi honey." She turns to face me, and the exuberant energy shining from her smile catches me off guard. "You must be Sienna."

"And I'm hoping you're Ellie," I say with amusement.

Her laughter is like wind chimes in a gentle breeze. "If I'm not, then we definitely need to tell her to call off the wedding." She leans forward with sparkling eyes. "I knew it was you, because first of all, you're gorgeous, and secondly, your earrings are incredible."

My cheeks warm unexpectedly. "Oh, thank you." I run my fingers over the dangling beaded strawberries. "They're made by a local Tuscarora artist."

"I love them. Does she have an online shop?"

Alex taps his bride-to-be on the hip before scooting out from beneath her. "I think that's my cue to move along. I promised my mom I'd help her pull together the photos we're displaying at the reception."

"I can't tell you how excited I am to finally meet you." Ellie pulls her chair closer after he leaves. "I've heard so much about you."

I cringe. "Hopefully nothing too terrible."

She tilts her head. "No way. Only the best things. The boys have so many great memories of spending time with you and your family."

A smile tugs at my lips. "That's nice to hear. I feel the same."

"Will you have a drink with me? I'd love to stay and chat." She flags down a passing waiter.

"Oh, I shouldn't, I'm—" I glance at my laptop, and Ellie raises an eyebrow. "I'll have one drink." I smile and gently close the lid.

"So, tell me about your shop. I'm so impressed you're a badass business owner in a male-dominated field."

Ellie and I talk for over an hour, and I can't remember the last time I had this much fun.

Making friends with other women has never been a strength of mine. They either think I'll steal their boyfriends or that I have the personality of a dial-up modem. Usually both.

But Ellie seems genuinely interested in my life, even though we're so different. It's...nice.

"So, I have to know." She finishes the last of her margarita. "What were Alex and Sawyer like as teenagers?"

I open my mouth to respond, just as a man approaches our table.

Ellie turns to face him. "No."

"But I—OK." He thinks better of his opening line and heads in the opposite direction.

She spins back to me. "As you were saying?"

"I think I love you."

She giggles and sits back. "So, the boys?"

I take my last sip. "Alex was still Alex. You get what you see with him. He's just grown up now."

"And Sawyer?"

I run my finger along the salt rim of the margarita glass. "He was sweet and sensitive. Shy, although he started to open up in high school." A quiet smile emerges on my lips. "He was funny, kind, and open-minded. I always appreciated how willing he and Alex were to learn a new culture in Six Nations and embrace life there."

She rests her chin on her hand. "I've never known Sawyer to be anything *but* those things. Except shy." She grins. "The man is a shameless flirt."

I roll my eyes. "That's for sure."

She watches me. "You two used to be close, right? But you're not anymore?"

I shake my head, my throat tight. "I thought we were closer than we actually were."

Her face softens. "I know you mean a lot to Sawyer. Whenever he talks about you, he—"

"Hi ladies." A grinning greaseball in a speedo stands in front of us. "How are you doing today?"

Ellie sighs. "We're spending time together, just the two of us. So, no thanks."

He wags his eyebrows up and down. "Sounds hot."

"Could you please lea—"

"Hey baby." A blur of cream and cologne comes from behind and kisses me on the cheek.

I flinch in Sawyer's arms as he wraps them around my shoulders. "Just play along," he whispers in my ear.

A thousand goosebumps break across my arms as I turn to look at him in surprise.

"Hey." He smiles down at me, and my insides melt. "You ready to get some lunch?"

My ability to speak English has left the building, and my mouth feels like cotton.

Ellie clears her throat, and we both look over to where she's smothering a smile. "Our gentleman caller left. Thanks, Sawyer."

"Happy to be of service." He releases me, and I finally exhale. "But that was a rescue effort for the gentleman. You two are no damsels in distress."

"Damn right." She pushes back her chair. "I need to go track down some of my bridesmaids who just arrived. Sienna, thank you *so* much for hanging out."

She hugs me warmly, and I squeeze her in gratitude.

"This was really nice. Let's do it again," I say.

I reach for my laptop once Ellie heads towards the lobby.

"Nope." Sawyer pushes the lid closed. "Get up, loser. I'm taking you to lunch."

"Excuse me?"

"Put away your computer and grab a bite to eat with me." He nudges me with his foot. "I can't stand seeing you waste beautiful weather like this."

"But I need to—"

He fixes me with a stern look.

I huff and pack up. "Your family is really quite bossy."

"So why aren't you calling Tammy?"

"Who?"

"The flight attendant."

"Are you still on about this?"

I'm now two margaritas deep at lunch and feeling delightfully buzzed. I rarely drink, so I'm a lightweight. I'm also, unfortunately, finding Sawyer looking good enough to eat, and it's very distracting. His skin is tan against his cream polo, the sleeves snug on his biceps. I have to keep reminding myself not to stare.

"Is it because you're seeing someone?" I fidget with one of my earrings.

A smile lifts the corner of his mouth. "I'm not seeing anyone. Are you?"

I scoff. "No. Definitely not."

"You said that with a lot of venom for a strong, independent woman."

"I have terrible taste in men."

"All nerds like you?" He winks at me over his glass as he takes a drink. "Tuscarora guys?"

"The nerds never pan out. I intimidate them."

He coughs as his beverage goes down the wrong pipe. "I bet you do."

"And the rez is tiny. Not enough interesting men to go around."

"Have you tried Six Nations? Jamie's single."

I kick his shin, but he intercepts my foot. His hand is warm on my calf as he redirects me with a grin.

"Well, what are you looking for in a partner?" he asks before popping a french fry into his mouth.

I pull out my fingers and start counting. "Kind. Smart. Doesn't hate that I'm tall. Enjoyable in bed, but I don't think that exists."

His foot brushes against mine, and I'm not convinced it wasn't on purpose. "You're fun when you're tipsy."

"I am *not* tipsy."

"Mmm hmm." His eyes sparkle. "Tell me more about your sex life. *Ow!*"

This time I make contact with his shin.

"I've always been underwhelmed by that part of a relationship. There's too much to think about: Does he like this? Do I like that? I'd rather give up."

"Oh, please." Sawyer licks some sauce off his thumb. "You just need a decent man who'll take over and let you enjoy yourself. You make every decision every day. You don't need that bullshit in the bedroom."

I chew a bite of my sandwich. "I'll have to take your word for it. I don't believe these mythical, women-pleasing men exist."

"They do. I have eyewitness testimony to support my case."

I scoff. "Of course you do."

"What's that supposed to mean?"

"If I looked up 'slut' in the dictionary, I'd find a picture of your face."

He chokes on his food, pounding the table with his fist as he laughs. "Jesus, Sen. I'm not *that* bad."

"That's not the impression you give."

He sips his drink, and we sit in silence for a minute.

I sneak a peek to find him staring off into the distance, and his unexpected reaction leaves me feeling uncomfortable.

So I do something really freaking dumb to fill the space.

"Well, I think I'm a lost cause, so your evidence doesn't do me any good."

He looks over at me and cocks his head. "What do you mean?"

I dust the crumbs off my hands. "I've never enjoyed sex all that much. I must be broken."

His jaw ticks. "Doubtful. It's typically user error from the other team."

I smother a smile at his IT humor for my benefit. "Maybe, maybe not. I guess we'll never know."

His hand clenches around his water cup as he takes a long, slow inhale. "Sienna."

"Yes?"

"Are you telling me you've never...?"

"With someone else? Never."

Sawyer swears under his breath and sets his glass on the table with an icy rattle.

"What kind of losers have you been dating?"

"I told you, I don't have good luck with men." I shrug. "Never have." *And it started with you.*

He watches me. "You should have someone to take care of you. I can tell you run yourself ragged, and you carry around a lot of stress."

"Probably." I drum my fingers on the table. "No time for a boyfriend currently, however."

"You need to unwind," he says sternly, and it makes something flip low in my belly.

I'm playing with fire, but I don't care. I blame the margaritas.

"And how would you suggest I do that?" I ask, leaning forward on my elbows.

His jaw is so tight I could carve ice with it.

"You've got options."

"Such as?"

"A bottle of wine. A good workout. An orgasm."

I shrug again.

"It'll have to wait until I get home. Unexpected roommates are a bit of a buzzkill."

"You're baiting me," he states.

"Maybe I am."

I'm about to melt under the heat of his gaze.

"All right, Princess. I'll play your game." He leans back in his seat. "Do you need to get off?"

"It would probably help." I cross my legs, and it's impossible not to notice his eyes following them.

"Do you need time alone in the room?" He swallows. "Or do you want help with this problem?"

Walk away, Sienna.

"I don't think you'd be much help. I'm batting zero."

"All you need is a batting coach. And some new pitchers, because clearly you suck at signing free agents."

We stare at each other intently.

"You want to bet on it?"

A smile plays at the corner of his mouth. "What do you have in mind?"

I tap my chin in thought. Every rational brain cell is telling me to laugh it off and pretend this is all a joke. Unfortunately, my hormones are distinctly *irrational*, and they are leading the charge at the moment.

"If you can get me off, and that's a big if, what do you want?"

"I want you to be my date for my brother's wedding."

His lack of hesitation takes me aback. "You don't have a plus one?"

Sawyer shakes his head. "There wasn't anyone I wanted to bring."

"Would this be for your own enjoyment or my torture?"

A slow grin spreads across his face. "A little bit of both."

"Good thing you won't win this bet, then."

He leans his forearms on the table. "I'm so confident I'll win that I want you to make it harder. Give me a time limit."

I tilt my head.

"It'll be too easy just to get you off. Give me an amount of time to do it in."

Given that my prior record is nonexistent, I have no idea of a reasonable length of time.

"Um, twenty minutes? Is that achievable?"

His eyes flash. "That's fair. When are we doing this?"

My heart races. "Can we play it by ear and I'll let you know?"

"Absolutely."

"Shake on it?" I hold out my hand.

He grasps my hand in his. "It's a deal."

Chapter 15

Sawyer

I fucked up. I really, really fucked up.

I never should have engaged with Sienna. I should have shut the conversation down the instant she started getting spicy, but I was having so much fun I couldn't help myself.

And now all I can think about is touching her.

I increase the speed on the treadmill in an attempt to distract myself, but instead the images flash through my mind at a quicker pace.

I think of taking her to bed and feeling her writhe beneath me as I bring her to the edge again and again. Would she want me to kiss her while I touch her? I would sell my left kidney to dust my lips down her body while she begs for more.

My lungs burn as I attempt to outrun my thoughts. Part of me is ecstatic at the chance to live out my fantasies with her, while the other knows this is a one-way ticket to emotional hell.

There's no way I'll be able to touch her so intimately and then go back to our uneasy blend of antagonistic friendship.

My phone screen lights up with the Outlaws group chat.

Jammer: Daily check-in. What's everyone doing for training today? Remember, camp starts in eleven days

Wes: I'm hitting weights with Chels after she's done with work. Might run a bit before she gets to the gym

Jammer: Nice. Get that cardio up.

Jammer: I'm doing old man mobility stretches today from the training plan Paige gave me

Wes: How did you get a custom plan from the team trainer?! I want one!

Jammer: I asked nicely

Z: I'm shooting around with Genny later, then we have some kind of cake tasting?

Jammer: That's the only thing that sounds enjoyable to me about planning a wedding. Speaking of weddings, where the hell is Sawyer?

Me: He's trying not to die after a treadmill sprint. Weights next

Wes: *fist bump emoji*

A half hour of dumbbells and a hot shower has done little to calm me down. Sienna wasn't in the room when I came back from the gym, and I'm grateful because I am a mess.

I run some product through my hair and smile at her skincare bottles neatly arranged on the counter. God forbid the woman ever set something down out of place.

I can't wait to make her come undone.

Alex texts to find him near the pool once I'm done with my workout, so I throw a shirt over my swim trunks and head out.

I find my family, plus Sienna, congregating around a wrought-iron table. Photo albums are laid out across the surface, the pages covered in plastic with frayed edges.

"What do we have here?" I ask.

I'm struggling to keep my eyes from the sight of Sienna in those damn cutoffs, now paired with a red bikini top.

"Oh, Sawyer. I'm so glad you're here. Come sit." My mom gestures to the open chair on the other side of Sienna.

I walk behind her to my seat and have to bite the inside of my cheek to hold back a groan. Her top is held together by flimsy strings at her neck and back, and they spill onto her skin where delicate, inky writing in Tuscarora trickles down her spine.

Sienna freaking Bissell has a tattoo, and it sends me into a death spiral.

"What's up?" My smile is tight.

My mom pushes an album towards me. "Here are the childhood photos Alex picked to show at the reception. Do you have any objections?"

I furrow my brow. "Why would I obj—Oh, God."

"I love your mullet phase because you make me look so good in comparison," Alex jokes.

I made some ill-advised style decisions in my college years, but my hair was by far the worst. I grew it long in the back, kept it trimmed in front, and shaved a fade on the sides. I thought I looked super cool.

"Is that a...mohawk mullet?" Sienna gapes.

"Sure was." I cringe. "Not my finest choice."

"Have you never seen him with that hair?" my mom asks her.

Sienna shakes her head. "I didn't see him for a few years around that time," she says quietly.

Ah yes. The fallout from teasing her about the Miss Tuscarora win. Her avoidance of me reached new heights after that.

Rich turns the page with a smirk. "Here are some later variations of that style."

Next is a picture of me and Alex after my first Outlaws game, our arms around each other and my sweaty helmet hair curling in crazy directions.

"Oh my gosh." Sienna grins, and it lights a flame in my chest. "Look at your *curls*."

"He doesn't listen when I tell him to cut it shorter," Alex says with a smile. "It gets wild."

"Don't you dare." She flips to another photo. "I love your curls."

My heart stops at the same instant she realizes what she said.

Sienna clears her throat. "It looks more natural than when you kept it short."

She. Loves. My. Curls. Now I'm consumed by a need to get her hands in them immediately.

She sneaks a peek at me and I raise an eyebrow. She manages a decent glare before turning her flushed cheeks back to the photos.

My mom smiles and pushes a second album in my direction. "If you can live with those, here are some others to consider."

Chapter 16

Sienna

Halfway through my bedtime routine, I realized I'd forgotten to check with the front desk for updated room availability. I considered calling, but honestly, Sawyer hasn't been *that* bad as a roommate. He's not in the room much, he gets up later than me, and he's largely left me alone.

Except for accosting me at the pool and forcing me to have lunch with him. But that had wound up being...almost fun.

We're just going to pretend my harebrained idea for a competition didn't happen. It's easier that way, and I can't imagine he actually cares.

I may have taken an Everything Shower the next morning, but that was just a coincidence. I was due anyway. Now I'm freshly shaved, moisturized, and updating shop tickets while wedding guests enjoy the nearby pool.

"Sienna! We need you!"

I glance over my laptop screen to find Alex waving his arms above his head.

"What's up?"

"We're short one player for volleyball. Want to play?"

I suppress a groan. I'm enjoying my quiet time working in the shade, and have zero desire to be thrown into the water with rambunctious people.

"Um..."

"C'mon, Sienna. I need you on my team!" Ellie calls with a smile.

I scan the pool and count eight men and seven women. If I don't play, then someone will need to sit out.

I reluctantly zip the computer into my nearby bag. "I can play for a few minutes, I suppose."

"Yeah!" Sawyer pumps his fist. "Come on in, Princess. You're with me."

Oh, mothereffing...

I shoot a glare at Alex as I slip out of my black cotton cover-up. He flashes me the patented Lane Brothers grin, full of wickedness and charm.

"So, we just need to get the ball over the net?" I ask as Sawyer swims up to the steps.

He raises an eyebrow. "Have you never played volleyball before?"

"Only under duress, so this is on brand."

He chuckles. "Yes. Either hit the ball over the net, or pass it to someone else with a better shot."

I gnaw at my lower lip. "OK, I'll try. I'm terrible at sports."

"Good thing you're partnered with a professional, then." He walks backward in the water as I enter. "You should get on over here, where the water's a little deeper."

"Huh?"

"On my shoulders. It's safer for you to get up once we're out of the shallow end."

I blink at him. "On your—?" I look around to see Ellie squeal as Alex rises out of the water with her balanced precariously on his shoulders. "Oh. Hell no."

"You're allergic to fun." Sawyer sinks lower. "I won't drop you, if that's what you're worried about."

I watch as other women pop out of the water looking carefree and graceful. "We would be the tallest pair."

"Exactly. We're going to dominate."

"I don't know about this."

He spins around and crouches in front of me. "Let's just give it a try. If you hate it, we can adjust."

I swallow. The last thing in the world I want is to be towering over everyone, seconds away from tumbling into the water with one errant move.

He looks back. "You good?"

"I—I don't know how to do this."

He steps closer to me. "Climb onto my shoulders and I'll do the rest. I'll go underwater for a few seconds so you can get in place."

My pulse quickens. "OK."

Sawyer sinks beneath the water with a stream of bubbles. Summoning all my nerve, I place my hands on his shoulders. I grip and maneuver my legs to drape over him, feeling like an uncoordinated koala. He starts to stand up and I shriek, slipping down his back.

"I'm not ready!" I press down to send him back underwater before considering I'm about to drown him. I quickly scale his shoulders again and wrap myself around his neck.

He lifts up and gulps in air. "Are you trying to kill me?"

"If you can believe it, no. This could've been my chance." I whimper as he stands up taller.

"Let me adjust you, OK?" He splutters water. "My life is flashing before my eyes." He submerges again, and I attempt to reposition.

He reaches overhead and grabs my backside. I squeak in surprise as he pushes me forward and then tucks my legs along his sides.

"You two OK over there?" Alex asks with an amused grin.

"Not rea—"

Sawyer rises and I fold myself around his neck again.

"Please don't drop me," I whisper in his ear.

"I've got you." His warm and sturdy hands grip my knees. "Can you sit up, or am I going to need to wear you like a scarf all game?" He *oof*s when I dig my heel into his side.

"I should have mentioned I'm afraid of heights."

"How can an Amazonian warrior be afraid of heights?"

"I'm like a baby deer up here. All gangly limbs and poor abdominal control."

"You're perfect." His voice softens, and my stomach begins to unclench. "Sit up for me."

I slowly peel my spine up and away from his head. My abs and legs quiver with effort, but I manage to make myself somewhat straight. I dig my fingers into his wet hair, and his grip on my legs tightens.

"Sen," he croaks, "getting suffocated by your thighs would be a hell of a way to go, but I can't keep you upright if I lose much more oxygen."

A strange and unfamiliar sound bubbles up from my chest as I relax.

"Everyone ready?" Alex calls.

"Yeah, one sec." Sawyer's hands crawl up my sides until he can tilt me over. "Hey, look at me."

I bend over as much as I comfortably can until his eyes lock onto mine. "What's wrong?"

A grin pulls at the edges of his lips. "Did you just *giggle*?"

"What? No."

"Yes, you did. I heard you giggle."

"You must have water in your ears." I sit back up and shove his head forward. "I've never giggled in my life."

"That's going in my obituary: 'Sawyer Lane, dead by suffocation. Best known for winning the NLL Cup and making Sienna Bissell giggle once'."

I feel *another* giggle threatening to burst through. This is concerning.

Turns out I'm still terrible at volleyball. But this time it's less painful because I'm genuinely enjoying myself. Ellie cleans up most of my bad passes, and Sawyer gives me encouraging feedback from below. I eventually forget that I'm afraid to fall, until Sawyer slips on the pool bottom and we tilt dramatically to the side.

"Hold on." He struggles to right himself before I careen off his shoulders, handicapped by my vise grip around his neck. He wrenches himself upright with a wince, and I manage to stay airborne. "You OK?"

"Am *I* OK? You probably pulled a muscle trying to save me."

"I don't need that oblique, anyway."

I wrap my upper body around his head so I'm close to his ear. "Thank you," I whisper.

He squeezes my thighs, and my skin heats at his touch. "Anytime."

I want this man. It's a rather unfortunate turn of events, but I can't deny it any longer. He's cracked my frosty exterior and let the light in for the first time in over a decade. And I think I like the sunshine.

I promised myself I would never embarrass myself in front of him again, never go back to the way things were between us. But maybe I just need to get him out of my system, dismantle the *what if?* thoughts that still tug at me. He's an itch I could scratch and be done with years of drama.

"So, uh…" I wrap a towel around my waist after we exit the pool, tucking and re-tucking the ends. "Tonight would be good. After we get back to the room. If you're still up for it."

Sawyer looks up. "Tonight? For the—"

"Yeah. For the bet." I count the water droplets dripping from my hands onto the concrete.

"OK." He clears his throat. "Game on."

I don't know what to do with my body once we get back to the room. It's the story of my life with any vaguely sexual encounter.

"Do you have that deck of cards from the plane?" Sawyer asks.

"Yes, why?"

"Teach me a game." He sits at the small table in the corner.

"You want to play cards right now?" I rifle through my purse until I find the deck in question.

"You can read me the phone book for all I care." He pats his leg. "Play Solitaire, whatever. I just want you to relax."

Well, now I'm the exact opposite of relaxed. I start to lower myself into the chair next to him, but he grabs me by the waist.

"Get over here." He wrestles me onto his lap. "I want you to get used to my touch before we do anything."

I try to stand back up, but he wraps his arms around my torso and pins me in place. "I just had your hands all over my legs for an hour in the pool."

"Yeah, you did." His breath skates over my neck, and goosebumps rise in reaction. "Did that feel good?"

It felt amazing, but I wasn't about to tell him that. I felt safe and taken care of, and it allowed me to focus on the game instead of my fear. There's probably an uncomfortable truth to be found in that, but I'm ignoring it for now.

"It felt OK."

"Just OK?" He holds me still with one arm while dragging the pads of his fingers softly down my arm. He reaches my fingertips and continues, his nails gently circling my knee. "Sienna?"

"Hmm?" I'm transfixed by the sight of his large hand moving over my body. My wrist looks tiny next to his.

He rests his cheek against the back of my shoulder. "Was it just OK earlier when I was touching you? Or did it feel good?" His palm inches upward. "I liked having my hands on you."

"Sawyer!" My voice comes out with a scandalized squeak.

He chuckles. "You better deal before I distract you too much."

I grasp for the nearby deck of cards. "You can't distract me."

"We'll see."

I begin laying down columns of cards on the table in front of us. My hands tremble as Sawyer moves his grip further up my legs and onto my hips.

"We should set some ground rules for this," he says.

I nod and continue dealing. "Good idea."

He fidgets with the ties of my bikini bottoms, and my brain short-circuits.

"Sienna." He squeezes my outer thigh. "Answer the question."

I close my eyes and attempt to block out the intrusive thoughts. "Could you repeat it?"

He smiles against my shoulder. "Do you want me to touch you tonight?"

I blink. "Come again?"

His chuckle is low and diabolical. "Ladies first."

I roll my eyes. "Don't you have to touch me for this?"

"Not necessarily. We can get creative. But I want to make sure you're comfortable."

I harrumph and finish setting up my game.

He gathers my hair and gently sweeps it to one side. "Tell me what you want. I want you to feel safe."

I pause again. This is shaping up to be the longest ever game of Solitaire.

The room is silent as he waits for my reply. His hands are motionless on my thighs, and I very much wish he would start moving them again.

I breathe in deeply. "Yes, I want you to touch me."

His fingers press into my skin. "OK."

A minute passes as I move cards between columns, and he continues grazing my legs.

My skin is warm, and it's getting more difficult to sit still. I'm painfully aware of the single layer of fabric between me and his leg.

"You're good if I use my fingers?"

My heart rate skyrockets. "Jesus Christ, Sawyer."

He wraps an arm around my midsection. "Just checking."

My card game is all but forgotten at this point. It's become essential to focus on not rubbing against him like a cat in heat.

How on earth did I get myself into this situation? Things are getting too real and too dangerous. This incredibly dumb idea was supposed to be a bit of fun mixed in with squashing his ego. I know he won't be able to get me off because it's just not possible. My body doesn't work like that when someone else is around.

But I'm also more turned on just by sitting with his hands on me than I ever was fooling around with past boyfriends.

Sawyer jostles me with his leg. "I'm losing you again, Bissell."

I move a card randomly to another pile just to give myself something to do. "Yeah. Fingers are good."

He softly kisses the back of my shoulder, and I practically melt. "You call the shots, OK?"

His hands are easy and assured, tracing lazy patterns down my arms and legs. I twitch as his palm slips underneath my cotton cover-up and flexes wide across my bare stomach.

"Doing all right?" His voice is low in my ear, and it triggers an avalanche of hormones.

"Yeah." I squirm ever so slightly in his lap.

He pulls me an inch closer, and my traitorous body shudders. My skin blazes when he dusts his lips across the side of my neck.

I should tell him to stop. I should put an end to this ridiculous game.

Instead, I moan. Quietly, nearly imperceptively, but a moan nonetheless.

Everything about him tenses. His hand on my abdomen tightens, the other fists in my cover-up, and his mouth presses hard against me.

"Am I turning you on?" His voice is husky as he nips at my skin.

The cards slip from my hands. "Absolutely not." I try desperately to pull myself back from the precipice I'm in danger of tumbling over with him.

He chuckles against my neck. "I can't wait to make you eat your words."

"Not a chance. Oh, fuck." I exhale shakily as he kisses down the column of my throat.

He hums. "You like your neck kissed. Noted."

"No," I say in the most unconvincing tone imaginable, attempting to wiggle free.

"You're not going anywhere." His touch is firmer now. His arm pins me in place while his other hand grasps my inner thigh.

A full-body shudder rolls through me, and there's nothing I can do to stop it. I've never felt less in control, and I hate it.

His breath is warm against the shell of my ear. "You're ready."

Chapter 17

Sawyer

I hook my arms beneath her and stand.

She clutches my shoulders, her long legs dangling. "What are you doing?"

"Rocking your world, remember?"

I set her down on top of the desk while sweepin everything to the side with one hand.

"We're not doing this on the bed?" She watches me wedge pillows into the corner with the dresser.

"Next time." I lean her back against the soft pile and her eyes widen. "I've got better leverage at this angle, and I'm working with a time limit."

"Oh." Her chest is rising and falling quickly. "You've planned this out?"

You have no idea. "I've spent some time considering the most effective options."

She looks down at her cotton dress. "Do you want me to take this off?"

I bunch the cover-up around her waist. "I want you just like this."

She bites her lip and lifts her backside to help me.

"Do you need anything from me?" I ask.

"You're already doing everything."

"What would help? I want you to be into it." Insecurity coils in my stomach.

Sienna sits back up and brings a hesitant hand to my collar. "Take this off."

"You want my shirt off?" Without hesitation, I slowly start unbuttoning the linen fabric, and her eyes follow.

She nods and I smirk.

"I knew you'd been checking me out."

"Shut up." She watches intently as I reveal more of my chest and abdomen before reaching the last button. Her eyes blaze as I strip off the shirt and toss it to the floor.

"Better?"

"Better." She swallows as she drinks in every line and divot of my torso.

"Do you want to touch me?"

Her eyes flick up to mine. "I don't understand the question."

I smother a smile. "You can touch me if you'd like. You look like you want to."

"Oh, I don't—" She looks everywhere but at my eyes.

I take her hand and place it against my chest. "I got to touch you. It's only fair."

She swallows. "I don't—" Her fingers trace down the groove between my pecs. "—need to."

I lower my forehead to hers. "I think you do."

She reaches my abdomen and exhales with a shudder. Her thumb brushes across to my hip bone and ever so slowly drifts lower.

I hold my breath and stay as still as possible.

Her fingers reach the waistband of my swim trunks and pause. "We should probably get started." Her voice is quiet.

"Like I said, you're the one calling the shots here." I pull out my phone, set up an alarm, and place it on the nearby dresser. "One last thing."

"What's that?" She looks like she wants to devour me, and it goes straight to my ego.

With more nervousness than I'd anticipated, I lean forward to cradle her face in my hands. "I could do this without kissing you, but it doesn't feel right. I want you to feel cherished."

Sienna blinks. "What?"

I run a thumb across her cheek. "I'm going to kiss you now, OK?"

Her tongue darts across her lip. "Are you sure?"

"What kind of question is that?"

"Last time you didn't—" She presses her lips together, and the torment behind her eyes breaks my heart.

"I should've." I breathe in the scent of sunscreen and coconut emanating from her skin. "And I've been waiting thirteen years for another chance."

Her eyes fall to my lips, and the flashback hits me hard. This isn't the first time we've been in this position. But this time, I'm going to finish the job.

She takes in a breath to respond, but I kiss her before I lose my nerve. And it's absolute heaven.

I brush her lips softly at first, savoring their fullness and holding back the urge to claim them. She's still, and I draw away slowly to gauge her reaction.

Her eyes are closed but flutter open to lock onto mine. She stares into my soul for several seconds, and I can feel every thump of my heart as I wait. *One. Two. Three. Four.* Her exhale washes over me before she loops her arms around my neck and pulls me back in.

On my deathbed I'll remember that Sienna Bissell tasted like strawberry lip gloss and melted in my arms when I kissed her. Her lips are soft and pliable, parting easily for my tongue. She moans quietly into my mouth, and I'm ready to hand over my lifetime earnings and firstborn child to hear that again.

My hand slides to the back of her neck to deepen the kiss. Her breath is ragged as I barely hold myself back from devouring her whole. I didn't expect her to respond this way, and her enthusiasm is shooting liquid fire through my veins.

Her fingers tangle in my hair, pressing me closer against her. I want to scream, cry, and spontaneously combust because this is the best kiss of my whole damn life.

I groan and tear my mouth from hers before I do something stupid like make this mean something.

Her chest heaves as she gulps in air. Her eyes are heavy with desire and tinged with shock.

"That's how I should've kissed you on my birthday." I drink her in, feeling high at the sight of her clearly wanting more.

Her eyes flick back up to mine. "You—?"

I indulge myself in one last quick, hard kiss to cut her off from asking a question I shouldn't answer. "Are you ready?" I ask softly.

She blinks and slowly nods, not breaking eye contact. "Yes."

"Tell me if at any point you want to stop, no questions asked."

I take my eyes off her for two seconds to start the timer. I've got twenty minutes to memorize every curve and sound of the girl I've never been able to forget.

I grip her hip with one hand and dip the fingers of the other beneath her black bikini bottoms. My thumb flicks across her, and she bucks off the desk in response. I press her gently back down with my palm.

"Has no one found your clit before, Princess?" I ask with a smirk.

She huffs in annoyance. "It's just been a while."

"How long?" I trace lazy circles over her, and she squirms beneath my touch.

"A couple of years."

I mutter under my breath. "It's been two fucking years since this gorgeous body has been touched? That's criminal."

She keeps her eyes on me but doesn't respond.

"Has anyone tried to make you come before?" She's already swollen and sensitive, her breath catching as my thumb continues moving against her.

She closes her eyes for a few seconds. "Yes, but they gave up after a while."

The thought of some bozo not worshipping at the feet of this magnificent creature in his bed makes me see red. I'm determined to change how she thinks about her pleasure.

I lean in close. "You know what I've never, ever done when faced with a challenge?"

She turns to look at me, her pupils wide.

"Given up." I drop a kiss at the base of her jaw, and she releases an exhale.

She's turned on but trying to fight it. I see her holding back, and that is just not going to fly. I need to hear every sound I can rip from her throat tonight, because I might not get another chance.

"You may hate me, but your body doesn't." My fingers brush against her, and she silences the whimper that starts to break through. "You're soaked."

"I do hate you," she whispers.

"Liar." I slip one finger inside her and nearly lose my composure from how warm and wet she is.

Sienna gasps softly and looks at me with wild eyes that unravel me.

"Does that feel good?" I rasp. "Do you want more?"

She's not quiet anymore. She nods through a moan, and I add a second finger.

I slap my hand against the wall behind her so I don't collapse. "You feel *so fucking good*, Sienna."

She whimpers and I'm already cooked. There's no way I'm going to recover from this.

"Keep making those little noises for me." I pull my hand from the wall and cup her cheek. "I can't get enough of them."

Her gaze darts around. "I wish I didn't have to look at you," she says, but her words lack bite and her breathing is heavy.

I keep up the pace of my fingers. "I'll blindfold you next time, how's that?"

She moans loudly as her eyes flutter closed. "Fuck you."

"If you're offering, the answer's yes."

The sight of her splayed open on the desk and taking my fingers has me painfully hard. This is better than any dream I've ever had. I try to memorize how she looks and sounds writhing under my touch. The taste of her strawberry gloss lingers on my lips, and I need more. I need enough to last a lifetime.

She's clearly enjoying herself, but not getting closer to the edge. Her body is tense, but in the wrong way.

"Maybe I *should've* blindfolded you. You need to get out of your head." I pull my fingers back, and she whines. "Close your eyes for me, sweetheart. And don't open them until I tell you to."

She looks at me with disappointment and desperation. "Are you giving up on me already?"

"What did I tell you? I would never give up on you." I grip her thigh. "You're going to get there. Close your eyes."

She swallows, and her lids flutter closed. "I don't like being bossed around."

"I think you need to be every once in a while."

The ghost of a smile whispers across her lips, and I take the opportunity to catch that pillowy lower one between my teeth. She gasps and meets my gaze.

"Keep those beautiful eyes closed, or I'll stop."

She huffs and shuts them again. "So fucking bossy."

"You'll thank me later." I kiss up one side of her neck while tracing my fingers down the other.

She shivers and reaches for my shoulders.

"Focus on what you're feeling and tune everything else out. Chase the pleasure."

I continue kissing her neck, harder this time, while my fingers drift their way back down her body. "I want you to tell me when you need more or less of something, got it?"

"Why should I help you?"

I chuckle against her skin, tempted beyond belief to give her a hickey for her insolence. "Because I'm going to make you feel amazing."

Her soft gasps and moans are driving me crazy. It's so intimate, like I shouldn't be hearing her like this. I'm dialed into how her body shifts against me with each one, sometimes pressing closer and other times pulling back slightly.

"Are you telling me what you need?" I graze my teeth against her earlobe, and she shudders.

"More," she breathes.

"Harder? Faster? More of my fingers?"

"Harder."

I increase the pressure of my thumb and she moans. Her hips grind against my hand, and a groan slips past my lips knowing she's using my body for her pleasure.

"That's it, Sen. Take what you need from me."

She gulps. "Could you go slower with your fingers?"

I pull back on the pace, and she visibly relaxes. "Your body knows what it wants. Listen to it."

She whimpers and I smile. I'm going to make this woman climax if it takes me all night.

"Sawyer?"

"Yeah, baby?"

Her eyelids flutter open and I cluck in disapproval.

"You don't have to do this."

"I'm having the time of my life. And you're close." I press harder with my thumb and watch panic and pleasure bloom in her eyes. She turns to look at the timer on my phone, and a look of defeat flashes across her face.

"No, I'm not." She barely has enough breath to get the words out.

"That's a lot of denial for someone about to come on my fingers with time left on the clock." Her muscles clench around me, and I grin. This uptight princess likes a little disrespect in the bedroom, and I am here for it.

"Do you want me to beg you to let go?" I nip at her earlobe. "I'd get on my knees for you in a heartbeat."

"Fuck, Sawyer." Her voice is strained, and her eyes are desperate. "I'm going to—"

I give her a little more pressure and movement. "I want to see you lose control for once in your goddamn life and know it's because of me."

She falls over the edge with a choked sob, and I kiss her roughly.

"That's my girl." My teeth sink into her lower lip. "So damn beautiful."

Her climax goes on and on, her body shaking so much the desk rattles against the wall.

"Fuck, Sienna." I hold her close as she starts to come down. "You needed that so badly."

She's incapable of speech, her breath ragged and her eyes unfocused. It's the hottest thing I've ever seen.

I'm in trouble. I'm in big, big trouble. I don't think I can come back from seeing, not to mention *feeling*, this woman climax for me.

"Do you still hate me?"

I grin when she manages a weak nod in my direction.

"Well, you're about to hate me even more, because I'm not letting you go." My thumb takes back up its firm circles, and she jumps beneath my hand. "There's still time left."

"Wait, I'm—"

"You have years of pent-up stress to release. You need more."

"There's no way—" Her head falls back as I pick up the pace with my fingers.

"You can." I smile and kiss down her jawline. "Just trust me. The first one is the hardest. The rest are a piece of cake."

"You're so full of yourself," she rasps.

"You like it."

"I don't. I hate it."

"You have no leg to stand on right now, sweetheart." I curl my fingers inside her, and she moans loudly. "Because you're a needy mess for me."

She tries to snap back with a retort, but her breath is stolen by the second orgasm ripping through her body.

"So pretty when you're falling apart," I whisper in her ear as she shudders.

She wraps her arms around my neck and pulls me to her to ride out the tremors. Her fingers tangle in my hair and tug with each pulse.

The timer goes off with a triumphant flourish, and I smile against her. "I mopped the floor with you."

"I can't stand you."

I fumble blindly for the phone and manage to turn off the noise.

"You're not done yet, Princess. I'm going to need you to start counting."

She squirms against me, but I pin her into place with my body.

"We're done. You won. You can let me go now." Emotion tinges her voice.

"What if I don't want to?" I kiss away whatever firestorm is raging inside her. "What if I want to see how much you can take? What if I want to give you the attention you should've had all these years?"

Her legs fold around my waist, and I groan at the sensation before putting my fingers back to work.

"I'm going to get you back for this somehow," she gasps, unable to do much more than take everything I'm throwing at her.

"Is that a promise?"

She yells my name as she comes again, and the sound of it sends lightning zipping down my spine.

"How many was that?" I murmur against her ear.

"I hate you."

"That's not a number. Should we start over?"

"Three, you asshole."

"And how many did you think I'd get, hmm?"

"Go jump in the ocean."

"Not yet." I'm pushing my luck, but I slide my fingers into her once more. "I've got some attitude left to get out of you."

"Sawyer, I can't," she rasps. Her legs fall heavy to the sides of me and she's beginning to slide down the desk.

I grab a handful of her backside and prop her back up. "You can. Give me one more, baby, and then I'll tuck you into bed, OK?" I plunder her mouth with my tongue as I increase the pressure on her clit.

She's shaking and panting against me. I hold her close with one hand splayed on her back while the other brings her to the edge.

"Tell me I'm the only one who's ever made you feel this good." I lock eyes with her and curl my fingers inward. "Tell me, Sen."

Her brown eyes are oceans of emotion as she struggles to catch her breath.

I'm desperate for her. Desperate to leave a mark on her memories. Crawling out of my skin to dull the light of any man that may come after me. Because no one else will ever love her as well as I would.

"It's you." Her voice is thick. "Only you."

I kiss her roughly and rub the spot I know makes her come undone. "And don't you fucking forget it," I rumble against her lips.

She tightens around me with a shudder. Her wide eyes lock onto mine before rolling back.

I swallow her moan as she shatters beneath me. I kiss her through the climax, savoring the dying seconds of the best half hour of my life.

I would keep her here all night, but she's worn out. Her body melts onto the desk as she comes down from her high. Ever so gently, I tug her bikini bottoms back into place and clean us up with a nearby towel.

She mumbles nonsense as I pull her forward and scoop her into my arms. She rests her head against my shoulder until I carefully lay her down on the bed.

I tug the blanket over her before crouching next to her. "Do you want me to stay with you or get you some food?"

Her voice is faint, but she manages to say "food."

"I'll be back soon, then." I can't help myself, leaning in for one last kiss of her exhausted lips. "Don't go anywhere."

My world is upside down as I stumble to the bathroom. I manage to wash my hands and splash my face with water before an emotional tsunami overwhelms me. I hang over the sink, droplets dripping unabated from my chin as I gulp for air.

That was so much better than I ever dreamed, and so much worse than I feared.

How the hell do we go back to normal after this?

Chapter 18

Sienna

My eyes open at 5:44am and it all comes flooding back.

Me, spread out on a hotel room desk, hanging on for dear life as Sawyer gets me off with his fingers. Him carrying me to bed afterwards like I wasn't an unwieldy gazelle and kissing me like it meant something. The takeout tacos he brought me later, which I'd inhaled before passing out again.

Oh. My. God. I just let the pompous asshole who broke my heart in high school do *what*?!

And I didn't just let him. I wanted it. I asked for it. I ground myself against his hand and came so hard, and so often, I saw stars.

I couldn't even blame it on the margaritas this time. The only thing I'd been drunk on was *him*.

I roll over with a soft groan and come face to face with the pompous asshole in question.

The hotel room is dark, but a small sliver of daybreak illuminates his obnoxiously gorgeous face. His breathing is slow and even as he sleeps, his chest rising and falling beneath his gray Outlaws t-shirt. The soft fabric hugs his chest and biceps, and I could weep at how goddamn chiseled he is.

Honestly, any woman would have folded. I lasted longer than most.

I stare at his lips while I remember how delicious they felt on me, alternating between soft, sweet, hot, and desperate. How his warm breath tickled my neck while he whispered in my ear. How he kissed me through climaxes and never let me feel uncomfortable.

Dammit. I need a cold shower and a lobotomy. I carefully crawl out of bed and grab a handful of clothes from my suitcase. I stub my toe on a shoe and bite my cheek to prevent myself from swearing as I make my way to the bathroom.

I'm confused. Painfully turned on, but confused. I thought I was prepared to remain emotionally disconnected while fooling around with Sawyer, that one physical encounter would close out my curiosity about him and allow me to move on.

Never did I think he would touch me with such passionate reverence. Or kiss me like he'd been waiting for it since we were sixteen.

I can't ignore that last night unlocked something. I've never thought of myself as a sensual being, preferring to spend time with partners outside of the bedroom where I didn't feel bored or guilted into lackluster sex.

But with Sawyer, I felt ablaze. Alluring. *Alive.*

I try to scrub away the recollection in the shower, to minimal effect. I'm annoyed. I'm disgusted. I'm ready to climb the walls because I want him so badly. All of this is greatly unappreciated at 6am.

Coffee. Coffee will help.

Ten minutes later I'm gulping down my first heavenly sip while checking my email. Noah and Vinny are going to the school later today to update Chromebooks, and I need to send them a detailed checklist in advance.

The resort café is quiet, as most vacationers aren't psychopaths awake with the sun like me. The low hum of waitstaff and the occasional flip of newspaper pages is my only soundtrack. It's a relief to slip into uninterrupted work, my mind distracted from the drama of last night.

"You snuck out before morning after cuddles."

Sawyer's voice is husky with sleep, and I jump in my chair.

He chuckles and places a hand on my shoulder to steady me. "Easy, Princess. It's just me."

Ah, so we're back to Princess. I can handle our typical dynamic, although the warmth of his hand on my bare skin is...distracting.

"Don't you have other people to annoy this morning?" My fingers return to their steady typing.

He plops into the seat across from mine, his large frame dwarfing the wrought-iron chair. "Nope. Just you."

I ignore him as he drinks his coffee.

It's quiet. Too quiet. I glance up to find Sawyer watching me, his chestnut eyes soft. His curls tumble haphazardly as though he had simply run a hand through them before going out the door.

"What?" I ask.

"Nothing. I just—" He swallows. "Just waking up, still."

"You can wake up across the room from me, you know."

"Well, I *wanted* to wake up in bed *with* you, so this is my second choice."

My breath leaves me in a *whoosh*, as though he sucker-punched me in the gut. I look over my laptop to find him still gazing at me with an unreadable expression. I open my mouth to reply, but it's bone dry.

"Are you working?" he asks, gesturing to my computer.

I gulp down some more coffee. "Yes."

"Is Noah holding down the fort?"

"He is. He's doing a great job."

We sit in silence for another few minutes. The cafe is gradually filling up as more guests arrive for breakfast.

"I hope you packed your dancing shoes for Saturday. I'm dying to see your Electric Slide."

"There will be no dancing. That wasn't part of the deal." My keyboard clicks under my fingers.

"Baby, you're my date. There sure as hell will be dancing."

"Don't call me baby."

"You didn't seem to mind it while you were—"

I kick him hard in the shins and he spills his coffee. His laughter echoes across the half-empty room.

My cheeks warm. "Do *not* be insufferable about this."

His smirk is infuriating. "Are you feeling shy?"

I slam my laptop closed. "And that's my cue to leave."

Sawyer grabs my hand as I start to stand. "Sienna, wait." His thumb traces circles on my palm, and I freeze. "I'm sorry. I genuinely don't want you to feel uncomfortable."

I stare at his hand swallowing mine.

"I had fun last night." His thumb moves to my ring finger, rubbing at its base. "If you ever want to do that again, just say the word."

"I want to do that again."

No one is more surprised than I am to hear those words come out of my mouth, but Sawyer's shocked eyes come close.

"Seriously?"

"Don't question it, or I'll change my mind."

"When?"

"Tonight."

"Jesus, Sen." He blows out a shaky exhale. "I've got karaoke with Alex tonight, so after that?"

"OK." *What the hell am I doing?!* "But we're using the bed this time."

A slow grin spreads across his face. "You're the boss, applesauce."

"Good." I pull my hand away and immediately miss his comforting touch.

He sips the remainder of his coffee and watches me reopen my computer.

"If I win, you're doing three group dances with me: Electric Slide, Macarena, Cupid Shuffle."

I smother a smile. "We're going to have to lower the time limit."

"I agree. Ten minutes?"

"Ten minutes. No warm-up."

"No warm-up?" He scoffs. "That was for your benefit more than mine."

"It gave you an unfair advantage."

"I can't help that you got hot and bothered from my hands on you."

I guffaw, but my body shudders at the memory. And he notices.

I feel his eyes running over every inch of me. "It's a deal?"

"It's a deal."

He drops a kiss on top of my hand when he shakes it, before leaning close to my ear.

"I'll see you later, baby."

Chapter 19

Sawyer

*H*oly shit.

My legs were shaking when I walked out of the café earlier, after Sienna asked for me again tonight.

Again. Tonight. Me and Sienna.

I would have given anything to have another chance with her, and she just offered it up like it was no big deal.

I'm going to hold her again. I get to kiss those pouty, glossy lips again. I'm going to hear her moan my name while she falls to pieces around me again.

It's the best gift I've ever received.

"Sawyer?"

Alex nudges my foot, and I shake my head, wrenching myself back to the present.

We're at a karaoke bar celebrating my brother's bachelor party. Pretty low key, if you ask me, but it's what he wanted.

"What's up?" I fumble for the rum and Coke I've been nursing all night.

He narrows his eyes. "Are you going to tell me what's going on, or do I need to guess?"

Alex is tenacious when he's on the scent of gossip. I won't get out of here without throwing him something to chew on.

I sip my drink. "There's a girl."

He lights up and claps me on the shoulder. "A girl! Is this a girl you like, or a girl you're sleeping with?"

"Are those things mutually exclusive?"

"For you, yes, they usually are."

I roll my eyes. "See, this is why I can't hold down a relationship. I've got a toxic family."

He elbows me. "Well?"

"It's a girl I like."

Alex slaps the table. "Finally! Tell me about her. Did you meet her here?"

"Not exactly."

"Why are you so cagey?"

"It's a girl I can't have."

"Why the hell not?"

Why the hell not, indeed? I've asked myself that question countless times since Sienna abruptly removed herself from my life. I've turned my memories over every which way and can't figure out what happened between almost kissing her at my birthday party and running into her upset. We hadn't even been apart for more than ten minutes before then, but it felt like a nuclear bomb had detonated in the interim.

I roll the ice around in my glass. "I just can't."

He looks at me. "What's her name?"

A smile tugs at my lips. "Layla."

"You're such a classic rock junkie."

"Hey!" One of Alex's groomsmen comes crashing into view. "We're up next. Are you ready?"

I groan and check my watch. "You've got me for one song, Alex."

He scoffs. "Miss me with that bullshit. It's my bachelor party!"

"Don't be a diva."

He puts me in a headlock. "Three songs, or I riot."

I smack his forearm. "I've got important business back in the room."

"Jerking off? It can wait."

"Toxic family!" I yell when he finally releases me.

After rousing renditions of Sweet Caroline, Life is a Highway, and Call Me Maybe, I beg off any further musical debauchery.

"Come on, Sawyer!" Alex says too loudly. "You've got to stay out with us."

"Can't. I need my beauty sleep." I turn towards the only quiet and unassuming groomsman. "Mike, can you make sure he gets tucked into bed eventually? Call me if you need help with him."

He nods seriously, his eyes shifting nervously from side to side.

I sigh. "Maybe I'll just come back in an hour and check on things. Keep him out of trouble until then?"

I dump Alex's drink in a planter and slide a glass of water in front of him instead. "Have fun, brother. I'll be back soon, OK?"

"OK!" He chugs the water and heads back to request another song.

My heart hammers in my chest as I walk back to my room. Knowing that Sienna is waiting for me to come back and do unspeakable things to her is making me feral and anxious. What if I can't get her over the edge again? What if she's changed her mind?

What if I fall all the way back in love with her and say something stupid about it?

Who am I kidding? I'm already there.

My hands are sweaty as I scan my keycard and push the door open. *Starting things off real sexy, just like I planned.*

Sienna's still in her sundress from breakfast, propped up against the headboard with a computer in her lap. Fast asleep.

I swallow my disappointment. I'm certainly not going to wake her. I know she was up early, sneaking out of our bed before the sun was up.

I gently slide the laptop from her hands and close the lid, placing it on the bedside table. She stirs slightly.

"Sawyer?" Her voice is breathy, and it goes straight to my dick.

I cup her cheek as her eyes flutter open. *God bless, she looks beautiful.* "You should change. You won't be comfortable sleeping in this."

Her gaze is heated. "Could you bring me a t-shirt?"

I rub my thumb against her jaw. "Which one?"

"One of yours."

I exhale and bury my face in her neck. "Goddamn, Sienna."

She tugs me closer. "Come to bed."

I'm falling apart. I can't be with her like this and not fall head over heels.

My breath is ragged. "Let me get you that shirt. And I want to jump in the shower."

She makes a displeased noise, and I smile. "I'll be quick. I smell like old beer and karaoke bar."

"Super quick."

"Trust me, I'm highly motivated."

"That's how I like you."

My chuckle is wicked as I kiss her forehead. "Just you wait."

Chapter 20

Sienna

My body is humming and desperate for him to touch me. I was dreaming about Sawyer when he woke me, and I'm already climbing out of my skin for more.

The shower starts, and I hop out of bed to peel off my dress. I swipe makeup remover across my face before pulling on an old college lacrosse t-shirt Sawyer tossed me on his way to the bathroom. It smells woodsy and clean, like him. I glance in the mirror to find it hits me at mid-thigh, even at my height. I used to envy women in movies who wore their boyfriends' shirts and looked adorably swamped by fabric, because that was never me. I was lucky if those shirts were even large enough to fit me.

The past twenty-four hours have been my teenage dreams come true, and I'm losing control of my emotions. I was once a lovesick girl for him, but I thought those days were long gone. I prop my hip against the nightstand to gather my wits about me.

What am I doing? This is such a tremendously bad idea. It was emotionally reckless getting involved with Sawyer last night, and asking for a repeat is out of this world dumb. It took me years to get over him, and now I'm opening myself back up to getting attached. *I'm in his fucking t-shirt waiting for him like an Outlaws groupie.* I need to get a hold of myself before this spirals past the point of no return.

I'm digging through my suitcase for actual pajamas to change into when he emerges from the bathroom in a cloud of steam. He's wearing a pair of cotton drawstring shorts slung low on his hips, and nothing else.

"Well, shit," I mutter.

"You're telling me." His eyes drink me in, slowly tracing up my bare legs. "You're a damn bombshell."

The way he looks at me makes me weak. "No, I'm not," I whisper. "I'm not wearing any makeup. My hair is a mess. I'm nothing special."

He tosses his towel on the floor and slowly stalks towards me.

My breath catches as he backs me up against the desk, hooking his hands beneath my thighs to lift me onto it.

"You're the hottest woman I've ever met." He winds a hand in my hair while the other parts my legs. "And now you're wearing *my* shirt and waiting for me to have my way with you."

I give up. It's a lost cause. Someone alert the authorities, because I'm a goner.

"Tell me to stop if this is too much." He pulls back slightly to drink in the sight of me. "My God, look at you. I've never seen anything more beautiful."

"Don't you dare stop." I'm practically panting when he runs his knuckles up the front of my panties. "Sawyer, please. I need you."

"I'll give you anything you want if you keep begging for me like that."

I whimper as he slips his fingers under the cotton material. "Please. I need more of you."

"You're so wet. You didn't need that warm-up after all." He holds me in place while he kisses me breathless. "Were you thinking about me earlier?"

"Yes." I can barely get the word out between his mouth devouring mine.

He groans and tightens his grip. "Are you going to moan my name again?" His fingers slide inside me, and the stretch is so delicious. "Because I liked that a whole lot yesterday."

I press against him, desperate for more contact.

"Tell me what you need, baby."

"This. More of this." I grind on his hand.

His enthusiasm for me is intoxicating, thrilling, and confusing. I've caught his flirtatious comments over the years, wrapped up in our vitriol-laced dialogue, but never thought it meant anything. He had scores of women to hit on and hook up with. *Is he like this with all of them? There's no way this is just for me.*

He pulls out of me, and I whine at the loss.

He smirks. "So impatient." He wraps my legs around his waist and pulls me off the desk. "You said you wanted to be in the bed, right?"

I tightly grip his neck as he carries me there. He lays me down gently and tugs at my panties. "Take these off."

I've never shed an article of clothing faster, kicking them to the side.

"So, you *do* listen occasionally." He chuckles against my neck.

"Fuck—and I cannot emphasize this enough—you."

"I'd like to see you try." He flips me from my back to my stomach, and I squeal as he throws me around.

"Please come bac—" I gasp with pleasure as he reaches between my legs from behind, his hands assured as he sinks back into me. "Sawyer," I breathe.

His other arm pins me in place. "Does this position feel all right?" He drops a kiss between my shoulder blades.

I can't respond. I can only try to breathe through the heat flooding my veins.

"Your body remembers me," he rumbles. "I'm not even going to need that ten-minute timer."

I'm a mumbling mess with my face in a pillow. I try to thrust back onto his fingers, but he has me held so I can only lie there and take him. It heightens the sensations, and I already feel a climax building.

"How are you doing this?" I moan.

"Science." I can hear the smile in his voice. "And I'm learning what you like."

He increases the pressure, and I melt into a puddle. My body is starting to shake, and words are failing me.

"Fucking hell, Sawyer." I'm an absolute mess, completely overcome by everything he's doing.

His breath skates across my neck. "I love knowing I make you come unglued like this. Best ego trip of my life."

"Shut. Up." I'm so close and trying to catch the spark.

"Sienna Bissell takes my fingers like a fucking champ," he murmurs in my ear. "Do you know how many times I've dreamed about this? About you not giving me the time of day until you find out how good I can make you feel?"

The way he talks to me is filthy. Degrading. And it turns me all the way on.

"Sawy—"

I come with a yell I can't hold back, and Sawyer clamps a hand over my mouth.

"Easy, beautiful. You'll wake the hotel." He nips at my earlobe and rocks me back against him. "I need to get you somewhere you can be as loud as you want."

I moan into his hand and ride the wave of the most intense climax I've had since...well, yesterday. But it's a revelation after my utterly uninspiring love life up to this point.

He holds me in place while he nibbles a path down my neck. "If this is what you're like after you loosen up a bit, we're going to have a real problem."

"This is already a problem." I'm out of breath as my body goes slack against him.

He turns my chin to kiss me hungrily. "You're going to look so fucking cute on the dance floor, baby."

"I honestly can't stand you."

"Imagine how you'd act if you liked me."

I turn and bury my face in his chest to hide my giggles.

Sawyer wraps his arms around me and holds me there while tracing his fingers up and down my spine. Tonight has been unabashedly intimate, far beyond a casual hookup. And it feels *right*, which scares the living daylights out of me.

He kisses my forehead. "Do you want more? I'm not stopping you at one."

I'm getting too attached and losing control of my heart.

"Actually, can we talk?"

I look up to find something unreadable in his eyes.

His smile is tight. "Why do I feel like a poor performance review is coming?"

"Definitely not." I prop myself up on my forearm. "You've made all of this feel different from what I've experienced in the past. Easier. Better." The edges of my lips lift. "Hotter."

"So, you think I'm hot?"

I roll my eyes with a scoff.

He tucks a piece of hair behind my ear, and I already feel my resolve weakening. "I love that you're having a sexual awakening on my behalf."

I swallow. "I am, and for that I'm grateful."

His drawn eyes tell me he knows what's coming next.

I pull in a shaky breath. "But I think this should be the last time we do this. We risk a lot of complications if we continue."

He nods slowly. "You're probably right."

If I'm right, then why does everything about this feel wrong?

"Can we be friends?" The words feel like poison on my tongue, and I'm uncertain if that's because we haven't been friends in over a decade, or because I don't want to be *just* friends with him.

He smiles weakly. "Absolutely. I've enjoyed spending time with you again this week."

My stomach clenches painfully. "Thank you for everything. Truly. You've helped me achieve something I didn't think was possible."

He runs his thumb under my chin. "You already knew how. You just needed to feel safe enough to let it happen."

I'm starting to feel distinctly ill.

Sawyer doesn't look like he feels much better. "Thank you for trusting me." My chest aches as his palm slides over my cheek. "Can I give you one last kiss to close this out? A bookend."

What a horrifically bad idea this would be. I nod in agreement, and he pulls close.

His lips brush gently against mine, and everything is different.

Our first kiss had been full of anticipation, desire, and longing. The last kiss is overwhelming with its grief.

His tongue traces my lips before meeting mine, as though he's attempting to memorize the shape and taste of me. Tears prick my eyes at how freaking *sad* it feels. At how sad *I* feel.

We pull apart slowly, and I barely resist the urge to hold him in place.

"You're worth the world, Sen," he says quietly. "I hope you know that. Don't settle."

I really, truly may vomit. "Thanks," I whisper.

He sits up with finality. "Well, I should go rescue Alex from the grip of drunken karaoke. I'll try not to wake you when I get back."

"OK." I pull the covers around me like a vise. "Good luck."

I lay in bed for an hour after he leaves, trying to quiet my brain enough to sleep with no success.

Chapter 21

Sawyer

If someone were to take an ice pick to my temple, it might feel better than the blinding pain currently stabbing my head.

I groan and roll over, hoping to redistribute the pounding. The inside of my mouth tastes like tequila and regret.

Last night, I found Alex looking slightly more sober than I had left him, to my relief. I was back at the karaoke bar on a targeted mission: retrieve my brother, make him chug a glass of water, and deposit him safely back in his hotel room. Easy peasy.

He pulled me into a bear hug when I arrived. "You're back! All done with your top secret task?"

I chuckled without humor. "I'm here to take you back to Ellie."

"Have one more drink with me." He tugged me toward the bar. "And then we'll leave."

"Can I—?" Mike, the groomsman, asked, looking longingly towards the exit.

I waved him off, his security guard duties completed for the night.

"What are we drinking?" I asked.

"Depends." Alex lightly punched my upper arm. "How's your girl?"

"Who?"

"The one you clearly snuck off to see an hour ago."

I blew out a weighty exhale. "I don't have a girl. She was never mine to begin with."

His face fell slightly. "Does that mean Layla is living up to her nickname?"

I shrugged and attempted to look casual. "I guess I'm just not her type."

He squeezed my shoulder. "Then we're doing shots."

I was absolutely gutted that Sienna didn't want to continue our...whatever that was. I thought I knew the rules: help her push past her mental block, secure her as my date to Alex's wedding, and don't let any emotions get involved. It was an absurd proposition from the start, but I deluded myself into thinking it was possible to be intimate with her without actual intimacy. It wasn't. I failed, she noticed, and then called it off.

It was a small comfort that she was willing to consider us friends again, but the word was a dagger in my heart. Because I didn't want to be friends with her anymore. I needed her to be my everything, or nothing else would do.

After multiple rounds of tequila shots, we stumbled back to our rooms. I handed Alex off to a sleepy and annoyed Ellie, then made my way back to Sienna.

Not to Sienna. To our room. No, *my* room. The bed we shared with a gaping chasm between us.

I was supposed to do something before going to sleep, but I couldn't remember what it was. *Oh, right. Drink water.* I needed to find some water, but that felt difficult. I stripped off my clothes and crawled beneath the covers. *I'll just close my eyes for a minute, and then I'll get up for water.*

That was a bad choice with very painful consequences.

The mattress sags as Sienna gets out of bed, so it must be morning. I groan quietly from the movement and hear her pause.

"Are you OK?" Her voice is close, and it feels like she's shouting.

"I've been better."

Her warm hand lays across my forehead, and it feels so soothing I nearly weep. "You don't have a fever." A moment passes. "But you smell like a frat house."

"Karaoke bar."

Her warmth disappears. I hear loud rustling that sounds like gunshots before an even louder symphony begins near my head.

"Sit up."

If I wasn't on death's door, I would've enjoyed her bossing me around. "Why?"

Thump. She sets something on the nightstand. *Rattle.* She pours out what sounds like an army of marbles.

"I'm trying to help you, dumbass."

With great effort, I manage to come to a seated position, the covers pooling below my bare chest.

"Take these and drink this entire bottle." She shoves pills and water into my hands.

"Thank you," I croak before downing the life-giving liquid.

"I'll be back soon." She leaves with all the subtlety of a hurricane, shoving her feet into sandals, roughly grabbing her belongings, and loudly closing the door. I'm not sure if I've pissed her off, but I'll cross that bridge later. Right now I need to survive.

I crawl back into bed after brushing my teeth and nearly losing the contents of my stomach. I should check on Alex, but that's another thing that'll need to wait. Sleep washes over me until Tropical Cyclone Sienna re-enters the room.

She sets things down on the desk before marching towards the window and throwing open the curtains with gusto.

This must be what vampires feel like. I yank the covers over my face to block out the sunshine. "What the hell, Sienna?"

"I'll help you, but I'm not going to coddle you." She stalks across the room and deposits something on the table next to me. "Come eat and have coffee."

She wrenches the blankets from me before swearing like a sailor.

I've been sleeping in a t-shirt and shorts out of respect for her, but in last night's drunken haze I forgot and stripped to my boxer briefs.

"Can you—ugh!" She heads to my suitcase and starts digging around. "Put some clothes on."

A shirt hits me in the face as I take my first sip of coffee. "Can you give me a damn minute to ingest what you brought first?"

She huffs and plops down on the edge of the bed. "Do you need anything else?"

I spear a bite of breakfast potatoes and moan as the greasy food works its magic on my hangover. "Yeah, I need to know why you're so mad at me."

Sienna folds her arms. "I'm not mad at you."

I raise an eyebrow. "Am I supposed to believe this is your version of joyful charity?"

She watches me inhale my food. "I thought you were just bringing Alex back to his room last night?"

"Why, did you wait up for me?"

Her eye twitches, and I realize I've landed an unintentional blow. *Interesting*.

She ignores my question, so I continue. "That was the plan, but he wanted to stay out later."

"So you got wasted?"

I set my plate down with an exhale. "Why are you pissed at me for coming back after a few too many at my brother's bachelor party? I didn't hurt anybody but myself."

She's trying not to look at me, but her eyes keep flicking to my exposed skin. "I was worried when you were gone for so long, and I didn't have a way to check in with you."

"Do you want my number? I'll give it to you right now."

"No." She scoffs and gets to her feet and stands in front of me with a slight tremble in her stance.

It is pure torture to keep my hands in my lap and not pull her closer to where I'm seated. "What do you need, Sienna?"

She bites the inside of her cheek, her eyes tempests of emotion. "Why are you so nice to me?"

I shrug and take a sip of coffee. "I'm not feeling particularly nice right now, so it may not be the best time for that question."

Her gaze bounces erratically down to my mouth. *Very interesting.*

"But, in general, I'm nice to you because I like you. And we're friends, right?" I watch her as I take another long drag of my beverage.

She swallows. "We're friends, but you don't have to be so kind all the time. You were supposed to leave me alone when I started being a bitch to you years ago. But you—" She closes her eyes. "You're everywhere here. I can't breathe without seeing you or smelling you on my skin."

I carefully place a hand on the back of her thigh and tug her closer.

"What do you need, Sienna?" I slowly repeat my question as I reach to cup her cheek. "Tell me and I'll give it to you."

She shakes her head firmly, and I notice a glassy sheen in her eyes. "You should finish your food and lie back down. I'll check on Alex on my way downstairs to work."

She's gone so quickly I could be convinced I dreamt the entire exchange. The ghost of her haunts me as I sit on the bed, her perfume lingering in the air.

Chapter 22

Sienna

I dropped Sawyer like a bad habit this morning, and now my day is in disarray.

I ran out of the room so quickly that I forgot everything except my computer. I've been conserving battery and trying to tune out loud people without my headphones because I'm afraid to go back to the room in case he's there.

I'm a complete and utter mess. I waited up for him last night thinking I just needed to talk to him more and I'd feel better, and the later he stayed out the more I spiraled.

Do I have feelings for him, or is this just dredging up my old crush? Is this purely physical for him, or something more? Is he getting hit on at the bar right now? How awkward will things be between us after this? Am I ever going to be normal about a single thing in my whole life?

I try to distract myself by catching up with my mom. My dad's home and taking it easy, with Hazel checking on them every day between shifts at the hospital.

My laptop finally runs out of power in the late afternoon, and I close the lid with a sigh. *It's time to face the music.* But first, I gather my belongings and head to the café for some caffeinated liquid courage.

The space looks empty as I come around the corner, but a pair of voices catches me by surprise. The instant I hear Sawyer, I throw myself against the wall before coming into view. *I have absolutely zero chill.* I don't recognize the second voice, and I strain to make out the conversation.

"I was disappointed to see you re-signed with Buffalo. It's your seventh year in the league, and I would've thought you would sign somewhere you could make some actual money."

A flicker of protectiveness fans across my chest. *Who the heck is this jerk?*

Sawyer is slow to respond, and when he does, his voice is flat and emotionless. "Yeah, well, the Outlaws are always a winning team, and that's worth something to my job satisfaction."

"It's a shame your stats regressed last year. You were outscoring everyone two years ago. You would've gotten better offers in free agency if you hadn't backslid."

And then it hits me. Derek Lane has always been a bully, especially to his eldest son, and it seems not much has changed since I last saw him over a decade ago. I grit my teeth at his words.

"I had other offers," Sawyer replies. "But Buffalo's the best place for me right now."

Derek tsks. "Maybe it is, with the way you've been playing. Have you ever talked to Jamie Montour about improving your game? Now, *that* guy is a superstar, although he's lost some of his edge now that he's pushing forty."

"He's one of my best friends," Sawyer says quietly.

I'm consumed by a roar of anger I haven't felt in years. Sawyer may be a jackass sometimes, but he's *my* jackass and doesn't deserve to be talked to like this. I've never backed down from fighting for what's right, and I'm not about to start now.

"Hey." I stride towards Sawyer, whose faded eyes brighten with surprise. "I've been looking for you."

The hint of a smile pulls at his lips. "You have?"

I hook my right pinky discreetly around his and lie through my teeth. "I need a partner for the shuffleboard tournament. You in?"

His gaze is locked on mine, and it feels like being examined under a microscope.

"Is this Sienna Bissell?"

The hair on the back of my neck rises at Derek's tone. I squeeze Sawyer's finger before turning to face his father.

"Mr. Lane."

"Well, gosh. Haven't you grown into a pretty little thing?" Derek's eyes graze over the sliver of abdomen visible above my linen pants, and I'm incapable of hiding my disgust.

Sawyer wraps his hand around mine and tugs me closer. "I'll catch up with you later, Dad, OK?"

Heat radiates from our joined grip and into my torso. I can feel a warm flush spreading across my chest. Derek's departing response is muffled beneath the sound of blood rushing in my ears.

The tremor in Sawyer's palm is what brings me back to the present. I look up to find his eyes wild and his breathing erratic. He squeezes my fingers so hard that I wince.

"Hey." I shake his arm to get his attention, but he's lost in taking shallow gulps of air. "Sawyer?"

He looks right through me, and I respond the only way I know how, without overthinking.

I press my hand to his cheek and pull my body flush against his. "I'm here. You're safe."

His grip softens slightly, and I'm able to wrap my arm around his waist, continuing to cradle his face with my other hand. I lay my head on his chest and listen as his rapid heart rate gradually slows beneath me.

I squeeze him as hard as I can until his arms encircle me and I know the din of anxiety in his brain is quieting. His shoulders sink into mine, and for a moment I worry that I may crumple under the weight of this full-grown athlete.

"I'm sorry," he whispers. "That hasn't happened in a long time."

"When's the last time you saw your dad?" I ask.

"A couple of years ago. But we talk every so often."

"It's different in person." I move my palm from his cheek to his chest.

"This is really embarrassing," he whispers.

"It's not." I tilt my head up. "I'm glad I was here."

He buries his face in my hair. "You've still got the magic touch."

Everything is overwhelming: his shaky breath on my skin, the familiar beat of his heart, and the weight of emotion threatening to crush my ribs.

I've missed this. I've missed *him*. He may have broken my heart, but those shattered pieces never stopped caring for and worrying about him. Seeing that wounded boy underneath the bluster of this man is turning my world on its head.

Why have I been lying to myself all week?

"I never thought I'd hold you like this again." His words dance across the shell of my ear.

I slide my hand to the back of his neck. "That's what friends do, right?"

I want him to kiss me more than I want my next breath, and I know it's written plain as day on my face.

His eyes drop briefly to my lips, and he swallows. "Right. Friends."

"Sawyer." His name is a whispered prayer and a soft plea.

His heart pounds against my chest again. "Sen, I—" Pain flashes across his face. "I should go."

He pulls away and it physically hurts. His warmth leaves me with a whoosh, and my body feels empty.

"I'll see you later, OK?" His smile doesn't reach his eyes. "Thank you for getting me through that."

Once he leaves, I slide down the wall until I'm seated on the floor. *What have I gotten myself into, and how am I going to fix it?*

Chapter 23

Sawyer

"Cannonball!"

I wince as Alex's splash hits me square in the face, sending torrents of water down my sunglasses. The sun is hot and intense at midday. "Dude, enough already."

He grins and runs his palm over his face. "I get to marry the best woman in the world tomorrow, man. I feel like celebrating."

I smile. "Well, I can hardly argue with that logic." I glance behind him. "Speak of the devil."

Ellie swims up and hugs my brother from behind. "Good afternoon, gentlemen." She plants a kiss on his cheek before turning to me. "Sawyer, can I talk to you for a minute?"

Uh oh.

"Ooh," Alex singsongs. "Someone's in trouble. What'd you do?"

She rolls her eyes. "Nothing. I just need to get his opinion on something, so scram."

I swim backward until we have some distance from the rest of the wedding crew. "What's up, Elle?"

She grabs a pool noodle. "I keep meaning to tell you, I had a nice time chatting with Sienna earlier this week."

"You two seemed to really hit it off." I grin. "I'm impressed."

"She's lovely. Funny, caustic, full of interesting stories and questions." She watches me closely. "I think she just wants people to wholeheartedly choose her, not half-ass a connection to get something from her."

I nod. "You nailed it."

"Speaking of which..." She kicks her feet to float closer. "Are *you* choosing her?"

I swallow. "What do you mean?"

"The two of you are like magnets trying not to snap together. The tension is unmistakable."

I glance across the pool to where Sienna is, for once, not working. She's reading a book with a sun hat pulled low on her forehead, looking stunning, as usual.

"This is exactly what I'm talking about."

My gaze flicks back to Ellie, who looks at me with a smile. "Can I feign ignorance?"

She bops me over the head with the end of her noodle.

"She doesn't want me, Elle," I say with a sigh. "I'm lucky she's tolerating me enough to consider us friends again."

"The two of you are being so dumb." She adjusts her sunglasses. "Does she know how you feel?"

I bite my lip. "I mean, I feel like she should, based on some...things that have happened."

Ellie's eyes go wide. "Shut up."

I sheepishly scratch the back of my neck.

"OK, so some *things* have happened, but have you *told* her how you feel? She's a woman who likes things spelled out for her."

"I know." I float onto my back. "But I can't do that now. She told me she just wants friendship."

She smiles sadly. "You're a good man for respecting her wishes."

"But I'd rather die than be her friend and nothing else."

"OK, that's dramatic." She blows a kiss at Alex from across the pool. "Well, just in case *things* ever happen again, maybe you should take the opportunity to let those emotions out into the open. They're strangling you all bottled up inside."

"You're very wise. Alex was smart to lock you down."

"Here, let me help you." Ellie kicks her feet until she's away from me before cupping her hands around her mouth. "Sienna! Come hang out!"

Sienna looks up from her book.

"I want you to meet my sisters. They're just like me, so you'll like them." Ellie tilts her head towards the gaggle of Tremblay women floating on loungers in the middle of the pool.

Sienna hesitates, but visibly relaxes at Ellie's wide smile. "OK."

Ellie pumps her fist. "I'll go get you a floatie."

Sienna slowly walks towards the pool as she pulls her hair into a messy bun. She sits down on the edge, her long legs dangling in the water.

"Could you help me?" she calls to me, and I nearly take a digger in the deep end moving so quickly to her side.

The amount of down bad I am for this woman should be studied in a lab.

"Sure." I swim to her as casually as I can. "Can I..." I hold out my hands towards her, and she locks her gaze onto mine.

"Please."

I lift her by the waist and slowly lower her into the water. She grips my shoulders on the way down, and my heart pounds in response.

"Thanks." She doesn't move her hands, and I forget to breathe. "Could I talk to you later, if you're not busy?"

I force myself to let go of her hips. "Absolutely. Just grab me when you want me." I pause. "That came out wrong."

Her chuckle is low as she skates her fingertips down my arms on her way out of my embrace. "I'll keep that in mind." Her eyes dance as she fixes me with a half-grin that makes my soul leave my body.

Did she just...flirt with me? Sienna doesn't flirt, although I've always suspected she would be a freaking pro based on our banter.

"I'll see you later." I watch her swim away while my head spins.

Later that afternoon I haul myself out of the water, dripping with each step towards a towel rack. It's empty.

I walk a few paces towards the next one, but quickly see it's also lacking towels. I lift my sunglasses and scan the circumference of the pool. Every single towel rack is empty.

"There aren't any towels." Sienna appears at my side, water rolling down her skin and pooling on the concrete.

"Very observant, Nancy Drew."

She glares at me, and I grin.

"Sometimes I think you piss me off on purpose."

"Oh, I absolutely do. It's hot when you yell at me."

Her eyes drop down the length of me and back again.

I'm not going to survive this trip with my heart, or my dignity, intact, am I?

Alex swims by with Ellie hanging onto his back. "Are they out of towels?"

"It looks that way. We probably caught the staff between laundry cycles." I crane my neck and recheck some of the farther-flung racks.

"There's a little hut around the corner where they stock them, too," Ellie says while sipping an umbrella drink. "If there are any available, they'd be there."

"Good call. I'll grab some for everyone."

"Thanks, man," Alex says. "We're about to get out, too."

"I'll help you." Sienna chimes in.

My eyes slide to her.

She shrugs. "You probably won't be able to carry enough for everyone."

My pulse quickens. "We'll be right back," I say to Alex and Ellie while tossing my sunglasses on a table.

Sienna and I pad across the pool deck in bare feet. The concrete is hot and rough against my soles, and I'm eager to stretch out on a lounge chair in the sun.

The silence between us feels like a pot about to boil over. "I appreciate your help."

"No problem."

We approach the covered hut and find a full shelf of fluffy white towels. "Bingo," I say.

She reaches to take a handful at the same time as I do. Our hands brush against each other, and my stomach clenches.

"Excuse me," I murmur, making no effort to move my hand from hers.

She exhales and looks up at me. Her chest is rising and falling at an elevated pace.

"Can I help you?" I ask softly, wrapping my hand around hers.

I watch her closely, unsure how much I can push without igniting the powder keg.

Turns out she only needed a small spark.

She shakes my hand away and shoves my chest with two hands, backing me up until I'm flush against the teak wood wall. My breath leaves me with a *whoosh* before she's pulling my mouth down to hers.

Strawberries. Espresso. A blazing inferno wherein I happily succumb to the smoke.

"Is this what you wanted to talk to me about?" I mumble against her.

"You told me to grab you when I wanted you."

Her nails run up my back as I grab at her sides. Her skin is warm and slick from the pool, and there's so much of it to touch. "Is that what this is? You want me?" I cup her backside and press into her, desperate to be as close as possible.

"You know I do." Her voice is a raspy whisper.

Hearing her confirmation pours jet fuel on the fire. "I don't think friends do this."

"Then it's a good thing I don't want to be friends." Her tongue dips between my lips and I spin her to switch positions, pressing her into the wall so I can devour her mouth.

"Me either. That was a terrible idea." I'm kissing her so hard I fear I'll leave bruises.

"I'm so sorry I suggested it." Her words come out stilted between kisses.

My fingers graze the ties at the sides of her bathing suit. "This fucking bikini," I hiss.

"What's wrong with it?" She won't let go of my mouth.

"What's wrong is I can't stop thinking about untying these. It's driving me crazy."

She leans back. "You've been thinking about me?"

I firmly grip her waist. "Sen, I've been thinking of nothing *but* you."

She watches me, breathing rapidly. Her fingers press against the back of my head as she pulls my lips closer to hers. "Tell me what you've been thinking about."

Fuck me. "You want to know what I've been fantasizing about?"

She nods with eyes locked onto mine.

I exhale deeply. "You're dangerous."

"Tell me."

We're not coming back from this. Platonic friendship is out the window. My fingers tremble as they skate up her sides. "I've thought about how I'd untie these strings on top with my hand." I slide my flattened palm underneath the strap on her back, and her breath catches. "I'd take my time with each one, pulling so slowly until you begged me to hurry."

She squirms in my grasp and I dust my lips down her throat.

"Then I'd kiss my way down your body until I'm on my knees, and I'd untie the bottoms with my teeth."

"Oh, fuck," she gasps and a full-body shudder rolls through her.

"I've been dying to touch you again." My mouth wanders between her breasts. "Dying to taste you."

She trembles as I lower myself, trailing kisses along her abdomen.

"We can't do this here," she whispers.

"I'll behave." I nip along the edges of her bikini bottoms. "I'm just torturing myself."

She buries her hands in my hair. "No one's ever wanted me the way you do."

"Idiots, all of them." I kiss up her inner thigh. "I'm losing my mind from craving you."

She pulls my head back to look at her, and this is where I've always wanted to be: on my knees for this incredible woman.

"Come here." Her eyes are ablaze as she wraps her palm around my chin. "Come back to me."

I don't make her wait, scrambling to my feet and pushing her back into the wall.

She groans and rubs her hips against my obvious desire for her. Her hands grab the waistband of my swim trunks and fist in the elastic.

"*Fuck*, Sienna," I hiss, wrenching my mouth away from hers. "Do you want to go back to the room?"

She pulls me back. "We can't. People are waiting for us."

"Let's drop the towels off and leave. I'll figure out an excuse."

Voices drift into the hut, and they're getting louder.

"Dammit." I kiss her one last time before releasing her. I scan quickly for any obvious signs of our interlude. "Did I hurt you?"

She looks down and notices the pink marks where I had gripped her body. A mischievous smile breaks across her face. "Damn, Sawyer."

"I'll make it up to you later." I toss a towel at her. "Put that on."

She mindlessly wraps it around her waist but continues staring at me. "You've been craving me?" she asks quietly.

I look at her with exasperation while listening for visitors. "Where have you been the past week?" *Or the past eighteen years?*

"I thought maybe this was just physical for you. Nothing more."

I peek around the corner. Whoever had been nearby must've walked past the building. *Phew.*

"You're so much more experienced than I am, so I figured it wouldn't mean anything to you."

I look back to find her with arms crossed and gnawing on her bottom lip. Tendrils of hair have escaped her bun, probably thanks to me, and are curling around the nape of her neck.

I would laugh at the ridiculousness of this conversation if I weren't feeling so deadly serious about it. The idea that Sienna has no idea I've been yearning for her for years is laughable.

I pick her up and deposit her on a nearby countertop as she squeaks in protest. "You're infuriating."

"*Me*?" She glowers.

I untuck the towel from her waist so I can step between her legs. She sucks in a sharp breath as I tilt her head back with both hands.

"Do you think I'd kiss another woman the way I kiss you?" I ravage her mouth with my tongue, and she moans. "Like I'm dependent on you for my next breath? Like I'm starving for just a crumb of you?"

She tries to reply, but I swallow her words.

"So, yeah, I crave you. I can't get enough of you." I pull back roughly, and her labored breath washes over me. "I'm a dog on a fucking leash for you."

She stares at me with parted lips and flushed cheeks.

"And if you keep looking at me like that, I'm going to—"

The loud voices return, and this time they don't pass by. A gaggle of young guys pile into the towel hut, laughing and pushing each other around.

I back away from Sienna and pull her off the counter. Her towel falls to the ground, and the group begins to chatter.

"Sorry to interrupt," one of them says with a grin, watching Sienna bend down to retrieve the towel.

I step in front of him. "You were just leaving."

"What is this, a Jedi mind trick?"

I cross my arms and glower down at him from six-feet-three-inches in the air.

Another guy tugs his friend toward the door. "We were just leaving."

She's quiet as we make our way back to the pool.

I stop her before we get to the gates. "Let me see your face." I turn her jaw from side to side and swear. "I scratched you up with my beard. I'm sorry I manhandled you."

Light dances across her eyes. "I'm not."

She's a goddamn minx and I won't survive her. "I can't have you go back to our friends like this." I run my thumb against her swollen bottom lip. "It's not exactly subtle."

Her grin is wicked. "I don't mind if they know."

I groan and pull her mouth to mine for a quick kiss. "We need to actually talk."

"We do. Tonight?"

I cringe. "I've got the ceremony rehearsal and dinner afterwards. Not sure when I'll be back from that."

"I'll wait up."

I squeeze her hand. "OK. We'll talk then."

Chapter 24

Sienna

I sigh heavily as the door closes behind Sawyer.

He dressed in a hurry once we got back to our room, leaving with promises to have a real conversation once he returned from the rehearsal dinner. I thought he might kiss me as he left, but he hesitated before squeezing my shoulder and ducking out.

Me: How are things at Three Sisters?

Noah: Busy! We're getting backed up since we reduced the hours, but we're working through it

Me: Thank you guys for covering for me

Noah: No problem, Boss Lady. The school laptops are done, and Vinny's got us caught up on voicemails. Enjoy your last few days of vacation! *palm tree emoji*

Me: You're the best. Keep me posted

The truth is, I haven't thought much about work in the past day, not since my encounter with Sawyer and his dad. The clouds have parted, and I've been able to see him for who he still is. And he feels like *mine*, like he always should have been.

I've gone from wanting to crawl out of my skin anytime he's nearby to feeling like I might die if I don't crawl inside *his*. My heart wanted to burst out of my chest when we were in the towel hut earlier, and all I want is to give this a chance. To give *us* a chance. But that feels like betraying the insecure girl who promised never to let a boy hurt her again.

It might be time to come clean to the one person who can talk some sense into me.

I put my phone on speaker mode while I wash my face.

"Long-lost sister! Have you decided to relocate to Jamaica instead of coming home to drizzly Western New York?"

I chuckle. "Don't joke, because it's tempting."

"So, how are things on the island?"

I fill Hazel in on the various activities over the past week, including seeing the ocean for the first time and trying ackee and saltfish, the national dish of Jamaica.

"Well, aren't you having a proper vacation for once?" she teases. "It sounds like you've actually been relaxing and taking a break."

"I have." I fiddle with the cap on my night cream.

"What's the reason for that?"

"What do you mean?"

"You don't just *relax* for no reason. You're allergic to relaxation."

"Don't be a jerk." I tap eye cream into my skin. "The shop is in good hands with Noah and Vinny. I know you're checking on Mom and Dad, and that gives me a lot of peace."

"Mmm hmm. You looked peaceful in the pictures Alex has been posting on social media."

The low hum of a warning siren begins in my gut. "What pictures?"

"He's been posting about the wedding week. I've seen some lovely sunsets, lots of drinks with umbrellas, and you looking quite comfortable on Sawyer's shoulders."

Busted.

I clear my throat. "I was peer pressured into playing pool volleyball."

"You don't even like going in the water."

"There was an intimidation campaign."

"I mean, if a hunky jock offered to put his hands on me, I'd jump in the pool, too."

"*Haze,*" I hiss.

"I'm just saying, you two seem pretty friendly with each other after getting stuck together on the flight down."

I sigh. "I was hoping to talk to you about that."

"For real?" I hear her sit up in bed and rearrange the pillows. "I was mostly joking because you wouldn't know a vacation fling if it hit you in the face, but *tell me everything.*"

"There's no *fling.*" I pad back to the bed and flop down. "I don't know what to call it."

I told her everything: enjoying our time together on the flight down, the hotel losing my reservation, and the bet. Well, a watered-down version of the bet.

"Sienna Bissell, you absolute hussy."

My cheeks are flaming. "I don't know what came over me."

"I do: hot guy, one bed. This is a spicy Hallmark movie."

I pull a pillow over my eyes. "Stop it."

"Well, don't leave me hanging. Who won the bet?"

I pause. "He did."

Hazel shrieks, the sound getting further away as her phone falls to the ground. "Oh my God!"

I giggle. "You're ridiculous."

There's a racket as she scrambles to retrieve her device. "*I'm* ridiculous? You're finally getting laid—by *Sawyer*, might I add—and haven't uttered a peep to your darling sister."

"Well, we haven't...done *that.*"

"Just—? OK, less detail is probably best in this situation, but I have to know..."

I brace for the question I see coming a mile away. "Yes. He knows what he's doing."

"I knew it. Maybe I *do* want the details."

"I'm so confused, Haze," I whisper. "I'm starting to really like him again, and that scares me. He humiliated me years ago. He's a ladies' man. He's egotistical, and—"

"Hold up," she cuts me off. "I know how much that birthday party incident fucked you up at the time, and I was fully with you on cutting him out of your life. But are you still feeling hurt about it now? I figured your personalities were just oil and water once you grew apart."

I squirm. "Well, yeah, I'm still hurt. He broke my heart, and clearly wanted someone else who was the complete opposite of me."

"Is it possible you're feeling more embarrassed than angry about what happened?" she asks gently. "Teenage boys make all kinds of bad decisions, but you've held this one against him for over a decade. Have you talked to him about it to hear his perspective?"

I bite my lip. "No."

"Never? You've never brought it up?"

My silence is deafening, and I suddenly feel very, very foolish. I should have opened up to Hazel about this a long time ago, instead of digging in my heels and ignoring the problem.

"What am I going to do with you?" She sighs heavily. "Sawyer's not a bad guy. I think he puts on a cocky playboy persona, but he's a big softie. And he's never forgotten where he's come from."

My jaw ticks because I know she's right. I saw it when he interacted with the kids he coaches, when he paid for Noah's Junior Outlaws registration, and when he revealed he's learning my tribal language so he can converse more with my parents.

"So, are you two just fooling around for kicks, or is this becoming something?" she asks when I don't respond.

I swallow. "He said something to me earlier, and I'm not sure what to think about it."

"What'd he say?"

"Well, we were kissing, and—"

Hazel chuckles. "Just some casual making out between two people who have zero romantic interest in each other."

I ignore her. "I told him I'd assumed this was purely physical for him, given his dating history, and—"

"I really need to teach you how to talk to boys."

"—and he said he'd been craving me. That he was starving for a crumb of me."

"Holy Bridgerton moment," she gasps. "He said that?"

"I've never watched that show."

"How are you so brilliant and yet so dumb?"

I blink. "What?"

"It's pretty clear he's had a thing for you for years. You couldn't stand him until this week, but he hangs around you like a kicked puppy."

I bite my lip. "He said it's hot when I yell at him."

She laughs so loudly that I pull the phone away from my ear.

"So, yeah, I think he likes you. It was the clothes I packed, wasn't it?"

"What am I going to do?" I groan.

"Oh, I'm sorry, one of Buffalo's most eligible bachelors can't breathe without you. Whatever will you do?"

"I want to forgive him," I whisper. "Is that weak of me?"

"Forgiveness isn't weakness," she says gently. "Maybe there's another story waiting to be told about you and Sawyer, maybe not. At least talk to him about what happened to make you pull away. He deserves to know and give his side of the story."

My sister may be younger than me, but she's always been wiser.

"I think you may be right, unfortunately."

"I know I'm right. And you better keep me posted about the next forty-eight hours, because this is a romance novel and I'm on the edge of my seat."

Chapter 25

Sawyer

The bride and groom are bickering, my parents are avoiding each other, and my stepdad and I are sharing some whiskey in the back corner. *Pre-wedding nerves are getting the best of everyone, I suppose.*

"You doing OK, kid?" Rich asks, nodding towards my father.

I sip my drink. "Better today. I was surprised he actually showed up yesterday."

"I knew he wouldn't turn down a free meal or two."

My eyebrows shoot up. "He's not helping to pay for the wedding?"

Ice tinkles in his glass as he swirls it. "Nope."

I swear under my breath as I watch my father chatting up one of Ellie's aunts.

"I really don't understand how you and Alex came from his genetics," Rich says. "You couldn't be more different."

I clink my glass against his. "That's because you're more of a father to us than he ever was. We learned from you how to be men."

He smiles softly. "I appreciate that. I hope you know how much I love you two, as though you were my own."

"We definitely do."

My mom taps a glass with her fork and signals for everyone to take their seats for the rehearsal dinner. I slide into a table with my immediate family and the other groomsmen, sighing with relief when my dad finds a chair elsewhere.

"What's up with you?" Alex asks.

"We're having dinner?" I furrow my brow.

He takes a rough swig of his beer. "You're off. Not yourself."

I shrug. "I'm fine, as far as I know."

He watches as Ellie and her bridesmaids giggle and open a bottle of wine at their table. "You and Sienna were gone for a long time getting towels earlier."

I bite the inside of my cheek to keep from swearing. "You would not believe how popular that little hut is."

"Two peas in a pod this trip, the two of you."

I set my drink down with a sigh. "What do you want to ask me, Alex?"

"If you're cruising to get your heart broken."

I look over at his searching eyes.

He raises an eyebrow.

"She's been staying in my room since the first night."

"No fucking wa—" His jaw drops and I clap my hand over his mouth.

"Not in front of Mom and Rich," I hiss.

He nods, and I pull my hand back. "Are you two—?"

"The hotel messed up and canceled her reservation," I explain. "They're booked solid, and she didn't have a room, so I offered mine."

"What a gentleman."

I glare at him. "No ulterior motives. We had that travel day from hell, and after the first night she seemed able to tolerate me, so we just kept the arrangement."

"Are you sleeping on the floor?"

I scratch the back of my neck. "I offered to, but she said not to."

He grins. "And?"

"And nothing. That's all."

He looks at me.

I stare back.

"You think I don't know when you're lying?"

I tightly grip my icy cold glass of whiskey.

Alex's face softens. "It's killing you, isn't it? Being so close to her?"

I swallow. "Yes."

"Do you want to sleep in my room tonight? It might actually cut the tension between me and Ellie."

I chuckle. "You two need alone time to work this out before tomorrow. What the heck is going on with you?"

He sighs. "She's been pissed at me since I stumbled home after the bachelor party. I thought we were cool yesterday, but this morning she woke up swearing at me in French, so I'm giving her some space."

I cringe. "In French? That's bad."

"You're telling me." He takes another sip. "I think she's just stressed about everything going perfectly at the wedding tomorrow."

Food begins arriving, and my mom elbows me from the other side to get my attention. "You should bring some of this to Sienna. I'm sure there will be leftovers, and she always works through dinner. Do you know where her room is?"

I fidget with my watchband. "Uh, yeah. I can do that."

She peers at me as she cuts into her steak. "It's been nice to see you two spending time together again this week."

"Don't get your hopes up, Mom." *Too bad I already am.*

She holds her hands up in innocence, a smile tugging at her lips. "Just making a comment."

"I'll see you in the morning?" Alex claps me on the shoulder. "We've got a photographer coming to watch us get ready, or something."

I chuckle. "Just let me know when you need me. I've been getting up earlier this week."

"I bet you have." He waggles his eyebrows at me and I narrowly avoid dropping leftovers as I aim a kick at his ankle.

I slowly open the room door a few minutes later, taking care to balance the containers of food. "It's just me," I announce as I come around the corner. She's lying on her side in bed, fast asleep. And she's wearing my t-shirt and a tiny pair of sleep shorts. A smile tugs at my lips, and I put the food in the fridge for another time.

She fell asleep on top of the sheets, and I debate whether to risk waking her by covering her. I gently pull back the covers and slip into bed next to her. She stirs slightly, and I dust a kiss across her forehead.

"Sawyer?"

"I'm here." I brush a piece of hair from her cheek. "You're wearing my shirt again."

"Sorry," she says without opening her eyes. "It's comfortable."

"Keep it." I pull her closer and tug the sheets out from underneath. "It looks better on you, anyway. Do you want some dinner?"

"Too tired. I tried to wait up for you."

"It's OK. I got back late."

"Talk tomorrow?" she murmurs.

"Tomorrow."

I kiss her softly on the cheek and watch as her breathing slows while she descends back into sleep. I trace her shoulders beneath my shirt, trying to commit every angle and curve to memory in case she disappears like a mirage once we leave in two days.

"What are you doing to me, Sen?" I whisper, placing my forehead against hers.

Chapter 26

Sawyer

I feel her before I see her, as something warm and soft wraps around my torso. I crack an eye open to find Sienna resting her head against my bare chest with her arm flung across my stomach.

My breath stills as she settles back into sleep. A quick glance at the clock tells me it's long past the time she normally wakes. I slowly wrap my arms around her and cradle the back of her head. Some wisps of hair have escaped her long braid, and I tuck them behind her ear.

She stirs, and I curse myself for waking her. Her dark eyes meet mine, and I see a flash of surprise flicker across them before she visibly relaxes.

"Hey," I say softly.

"*Čwé:'n.*"

"I was here first, you know."

A sleepy smile tugs her lips upward, and I very much would like to kiss it away.

"What time is it?" she asks.

"You don't want to know."

"...why?"

"It's nine."

"*Nine*?" She attempts to sit up, but I tighten my grip on her. "I never sleep until nine!"

"I know, but it's Saturday. You can indulge." She tries to wiggle out of my grasp, but I easily hold her in place. "If you're wanting to keep my ego in check, then a beautiful woman trying to bolt out of my bed is a pretty effective way to do it."

"Ugh." She beats a defeated fist weakly against my chest.

I brush a kiss against her forehead. "Since you're stuck here, how about we have that talk?"

She sighs and slumps in my arms. "That's probably a good idea."

"You seem reluctant." I try to read her eyes, but am left with no answers.

She catches her lower lip between her teeth. "I suppose I am."

"Why's that?"

"Because it's hard for me to talk about. But it's important."

"How can I hel—"

Pounding sounds at the door, jolting us apart.

"What the hell?" I mumble.

"Maybe they'll go away?"

"Sawyer!" Alex's voice rings out. "Open up!"

I swear and begin untangling from Sienna. "Have I mentioned how much I wish I were an only child sometimes?"

She smiles and watches me hastily pull on a shirt.

"Don't go anywhere." I lean over and kiss her softly on the cheek.

I yank the door open with a huff. "This better be goo—"

Alex pushes past me into the room. "Why aren't you answering your phone? The photographer will be here any minute, and—" He stops abruptly at the sight of Sienna.

She gives him a small wave. "Hi Alex."

He spins to look at me and I fix him with an annoyed stare. "We talked about this last night. She doesn't have a room."

"Yeah, but—" He clears his throat and turns back around. "Good morning, Sienna. How are you?"

"What do you need, Alex?" My voice is terse until my half-awake brain puts everything together. "Oh, shit. The photographer."

"Yeah, man. The photographer. I've been blowing up your phone for the past hour."

I grab the device from my nightstand and see all the missed calls and texts. "I guess I slept through all that somehow. I'm sorry."

"Well, grab your stuff and get your ass over to my room before Mom notices you're not there and comes here next." His raised eyebrow elicits another glare from me.

"You're lucky it's your wedding day, so I have to be nice to you." I start shoving clothes and toiletries into a bag. "Can I shower over there?"

"Yes. Now *go*."

I pop my head around the corner to look at Sienna. "I'll see you at the ceremony?" I hope my expression conveys the disappointment and reluctance I feel at leaving so unexpectedly. "I'm sorry," I mouth silently.

She waves me on. "I'll see you there. Have fun."

I'm adjusting my maroon bowtie in a mirror when my eyes dart to Alex in the reflection.

"That's a great shot of the brothers looking at each other. Stay just like that," the photographer says as her shutter snaps in quick succession.

"So," Alex says, "I see things are going well with Sienna."

"Buzz off." I smooth the edges of my collar.

"I just didn't expect to see her freshly woken up and wearing your t-shirt, is all. Very domestic."

I ignore him and go in search of my shoes, with my brother in pursuit.

"Are you ever going to tell me what's going on?" he asks.

"Sure, if there's ever anything to report."

He hovers as I tie my laces. "The woman who hates you is suddenly sleeping in your clothes, and there's nothing to report?"

"Nope."

He crosses his arms, and I pat his cheek on my way to the other side of the room.

"Alex!" Ellie's mom pokes her head into the room. "Do you have the garter? Ellie needs it for photos, and it's not in her bags."

"Oh, crap. Yeah, let me look for that and run it down to her." He begins digging through some nearby bags.

Mrs. Tremblay shakes her head. "You can't see her before the wedding."

"I'll do it," I volunteer, happy for the opportunity to shake my brother for a few minutes. "I'll be right over."

"Mike!" Alex calls out to his college roommate. "Have you seen Ellie's garter?"

Mike jumps in place, clearly startled. "Um, I think I saw it in the box with the rings."

"You're a good man, Mike." I rifle through the box in question and pull out the scrap of blue ribbon and lace.

My brother grabs my arm as I head towards the door. "Tell her I said hi." His lips quiver in a smile.

"I will, you big sap."

My knuckles rap loudly on the door of the honeymoon suite a few minutes later.

Amélie, Ellie's oldest sister and Maid of Honor, peeks out. "Is Alex with you?"

"Nope. Just the better Lane brother." I twirl the garter on my index finger. "Special delivery for the bride."

"Mellie, is that Sawyer?" Ellie's voice rings out from the room. "I need to talk to him."

Amélie swings open the door and gestures grandly for me to enter.

"You look beautiful, Mel." I smile, and she spins around in her silky maroon dress that matches my tie.

"Thank you. Now get in and get out so we can finish the photos." She shoos me away.

I find my future sister-in-law pacing around the bed, looking utterly resplendent in her wedding gown.

I stop in my tracks, struck by the realness of this long-awaited day for our family. "Oh my goodness, Elle. You're stunning."

A smile warms her features, and she gives me a kiss on the cheek. "Thanks, Sawyer. And thank you for bringing the garter. I needed my 'something blue'."

I feel an unexpected prick of tears behind my eyes. "No problem. Alex is going to lose it when he sees you." I tilt my head to the side. "Speaking of your delightful groom, are you two cool? He said to say hi."

Ellie chuckles. "We're fine. I slept here last night, for tradition's sake, and we texted each other for hours." She waves toward the bed. "Sit."

The mattress dips under me. "What's up?"

She resumes pacing. "Have you talked to Sienna yet?"

"You're spending the hours before your wedding worrying about my love life?"

"It's more fun than worrying about the caterer or the flowers." Her dress swishes behind her as she passes. "So?"

I exhale. "Not yet. We keep getting interrupted. Your lesser half was the most recent cause."

"I'll talk to him about that later," she mutters. "OK, so run me through what happened with you two when you were younger."

"Beats me, truly." My leg starts bouncing up and down. "We were closer than ever, and then one day she completely retreated."

"What happened right before that?"

"She came over to my dad's place to watch a movie for my birthday. He made me invite all of my old friends from when we lived together in Hamilton, even though I hadn't talked to them in years. I had to beg him to let me invite even one person from my new life, so I picked Sienna."

Ellie shudders. "I honestly cannot stand that guy. Sorry. He makes my skin crawl."

"You're not alone in that."

"Continue."

I run my palm over my freshly shaved face. "Things were awkward from the start, because I barely knew, or even liked, most of these 'friends,' and I could tell Sienna was uncomfortable with a room full of random people. But then she sat with me during the movie and we almost kissed."

She spins around. "Why didn't you?"

My fingernails dig into the back of my hand. I've relived this moment countless times over the years, wondering what could've been and how I managed to screw it all up. "I was about to. Her lips were right there, Elle." I close my eyes and take a breath. "But then the movie ended and someone turned the lights on, so the moment was gone."

"And you never tried again?"

"I was going to, but just a few minutes later she left, claiming she wasn't feeling well." My jaw ticks. "Something was wrong; I could tell immediately. But she's never wanted to talk to me about it."

"Ellie!" Amélie calls from the living room area of the suite. "We need you for pictures!"

Ellie huffs. "One minute!" She grabs her bouquet and points it at me. "Well, what the hell happened between the almost-kiss and her running away?"

I throw my hands up. "I don't know what happened. I went to the kitchen to wash the popcorn bowls, and when I came out, she was gone. She'd been collecting the rest of the bowls for..." My voice trails off as something tugs at the edges of my memory.

"What is it?" She nudges my foot with her sparkly heel.

I blink. "I found a stack of bowls outside the kitchen when I came out. On the floor, like someone had left them there in a hurry."

"Sawyer." She fluffs out her wide skirt and crouches in front of me. "What happened in the kitchen?"

I cannot believe I didn't string these obvious pieces of evidence together before this, but the answer is staring me plainly in the face.

I lick my lips. "One of my worst former friends had been flirting all night, and she was bad-mouthing Sienna to me. I tried to change the topic, but then she kissed me and I pushed her away. *Ow!*"

Ellie smacks my arm. "You absolute dolt."

"She saw it, didn't she?" A tsunami of realization and horror crashes into me. "Oh my God, Elle. I didn't put it together, because that was such a brief moment and I couldn't wait to get out of there and find Sienna again."

"You're lucky I have photos to take, or I'd be beating you over the head with this bouquet." She puts her hands on her hips. "How can you be so tremendously oblivious?"

My head falls into my hands. "This is a nightmare. I cannot believe this is what sunk us."

"*Éléonore!*" Mrs. Tremblay's voice is sharp from the next room.

"I've got to go." Ellie places a comforting hand on my shoulder. "But Sawyer, you have to talk to her tonight. Grovel. Beg. Tell her what actually happened, and how much you want to start over. I think she cares about you enough to listen."

"Thank you." My voice is muffled by my palms.

She gently peels my hands away. "I love you, but get out of here." She squeezes my wrists. "Go get your girl."

Sienna

Sawyer enters the room while I'm putting on mascara in the bathroom mirror.

"What are you doing here?" I ask, hovering with my wand. "I thought I wasn't seeing you until later."

His gaze travels down my body, taking in my satin robe. "I wanted to walk my date to the ceremony."

Flip. Flip. My stomach does a cartwheel. "You look...nice." He looks downright edible in his tan suit with the jacket draped over his arm.

He rests his hip against the bathroom doorway. "Just nice?"

It's my turn to drink him in. "Are you fishing for compliments?"

His eyes smoulder. "Yes."

I set the mascara on the counter and take two steps to where he's leaning. I wrap my hands around his suspenders and pull myself close. His breath hitches, and it sends a zip of delight down my spine. Knowing that my presence has an impact on him is intoxicating. "Keep dreaming," I whisper before pushing him away and closing the door with a smirk.

I hear his heavy sigh and then a distinct *thunk* on the other side of the door. "Sen."

A smile tugs at my lips as I re-open the barrier. "Yes?"

His head hangs forward from where he'd rested it. With eyes full of yearning, he raises a hand to cup my cheek. "Let me know if you need any help getting ready."

The type of help I'd like would mean we'd miss the wedding. "I will."

He brushes his thumb up and down my jaw. "I promised Alex I'd be down in a few minutes. Think you can be ready that fast?"

I nod. "I just need to get dressed. I'll be right out."

He reluctantly retreats, and I fly into action: pulling on my dress, fastening some abalone shell earrings, and spritzing perfume. Hazel packed heels that are far taller and sexier than I would pick for myself, and I gnaw on my lip as I consider them. *Here's hoping Sawyer doesn't mind the extra height.*

He's seated on a chair, bent at the waist and scrolling on his phone when I emerge. "Alex is absolutely going to kill me if we don't—" He looks up and the device slips in his hand.

"Would you help with my shoes?" I ask, dangling the sparkly heels from my index finger.

He blinks slowly before his gaze roams down the silky column of my navy slip dress.

"You look..." His eyes are everywhere all at once. "Sensational."

"Thank you." I slide one heel on, brace myself against the dresser, and plant my foot on his chest. "Now, be a good boy and buckle these, please."

He stares at my heel for a few seconds before looking back up at me.

"Do I need to reboot you?" I hop on my stationary leg. "I can't hold this position for long."

"Sorry," he mumbles, blowing out a weighty exhale. He cradles my foot in his hand, gently turning it over for inspection. "What needs to happen here?"

"You can take apart a car engine but can't figure out how to buckle a shoe?"

He glances up with an amused smile playing at the corners of his mouth. "I could say the same about you and your ability to disassemble a computer."

I pin my lower lip between my teeth and watch him wrap the straps around my ankle. He's gentle, holding the back of my calf as he slides through the buckle.

"Does that feel OK? Not too tight?"

"It's perfect."

"Good." He kisses the top of my foot and lowers it to the ground. "Hit me with another one."

There's something in the air between us, something different from even this morning, and I can't put my finger on it. There's an urgency and a reverence in the way he's looking at me and touching me.

"There you go." He sets my second foot down. "Ready?"

"Yep. Let me just grab my lipstick and we can head out."

I spin and begin walking towards the bathroom. My dress has an open back, and cool air swishes against my skin as I hurry. I've only taken three steps before Sawyer's strangled groan gives me pause.

"What's the matter?" I look over my shoulder to find him burying his head in his hands.

"You are so gorgeous it hurts." His voice is muffled. "It physically hurts to look at you."

I turn back around, moving at a snail's pace as I approach where he's sitting. I thrust a hand into his hair and slowly drag his head up and back until he's looking at me.

His gaze locks onto mine, and the devotion in his eyes steals my breath.

"What do you need, Sawyer?" I ask quietly.

"A chance," he whispers. "I'll give you anything you want if you'll just give me another chance to earn your trust. Please, Sienna."

Desire, power, and a flicker of hope race through my veins.

"You're begging," I murmur in surprise. "Why?"

"I've been begging for years." He runs his fingers down my sides before dragging my hips towards him. "You just haven't been listening."

A pang of confusion laced with a dawning certainty hits me in the chest, as though something I've always known was below the surface is finally bursting through the dirt.

"I'm your date tonight," I say. "Isn't that enough?"

"It's not enough." His fingertips dig into my waist. "I need you to be mine."

"Sawyer," I whisper. "What is this?"

"I've been in love with you for years, and touching you the way I've been is exquisite torture. I'm about to explode, Sen. I need to know if you feel anywhere close to the same."

My eyes pop wide open in shock. "You're...what?"

"I love you."

I push his shoulders back into the chair, my other hand still buried in his hair.

"No, you don't." My voice is rough and laced with panic.

His dark eyes don't look away from mine for an instant. "I've loved you since we were kids. I've spent my life praying that maybe, one day, you'd change your mind about me. I've measured every woman I've met against you, and they come up short every single time."

"How is that possible?" I choke back a sob. "I thought I was only a friend to you."

"You've always been the only one I've ever wanted." He's looking at me like he's worried I'll either kill him or kiss him, and honestly, that feels like an accurate assessment of the situation. "I didn't read the signs the night of my birthday, and I let you leave thinking I'd rejected you, didn't I? I feel sick just thinking about it."

I stare at him. I've spent years unpacking the embarrassment of throwing myself at him, only for him to kiss someone else right in front of me. *How could I have possibly misinterpreted that situation?*

"I'll spend the rest of my life making it up to you. Please, Sienna."

I've never seen him like this. So desperate, beaten, and regretful.

"Please," he repeats softly. "I've never wanted anything more than I've wanted you."

"You're serious." I state it as a fact rather than a question because I already know the answer. I trace his neck with my fingers, enjoying the way his pulse flutters quickly beneath my touch.

He swallows. "Please put me out of my misery. Let me love you, or cut me off completely. I can't bear—"

I hike up my dress with one hand and straddle him in the chair. His strangled moan as I sit fully sends me to the stratosphere.

I want to climb him. Consume him. I settle for kissing him with so much force that I nearly knock both of us backward.

I grind against him, needing more. I scratch at his skin, wishing I could crawl inside him. My head is spinning with no hope of stopping.

His hands are everywhere: palming my back, grabbing my thighs, winding into the hair at the nape of my neck. His teeth pin my lower lip, and he groans with need.

"You cannot fucking love me," I pant between kisses. "You barely know me anymore."

"I've missed out on years of your life, but I know who you are." He holds me steady, staring deeply into my eyes. "I love your sharp edges and dry humor. I love how you move heaven and earth to take care of people. You're fire and ice, and I want to drown in the thaw."

My brain is scrambled and incapable of processing this avalanche of new information. For all the over-analyzing I've done, I never once considered that he'd been pining for me since we fell out.

Someone pounds on the door, and I gasp in surprise.

"Sawyer!" Alex yells. "Where the hell are you? You're fucking late, and my soon-to-be wife is about to kill you."

Sawyer holds me against him as I draw in deep breaths to calm my racing heart. "Sorry, man. Had a bit of a wardrobe mishap. I'll be down there in two minutes."

"If I don't come back with you, Ellie's going to put my balls in a vise," Alex huffs. "I'm not leaving here without you."

"Goddammit." Sawyer cradles my face and kisses me firmly. "Can I meet you down there? I don't like leaving you like this."

I bury my face in his neck as my breathing begins to slow. "That's fine. I need to pull myself back together, anyway."

"How do I look?" he asks, running a shaky hand through his disheveled hair.

I give him a once-over. "Annoyingly sexy."

"Fucking hell, Sienna." He rubs his face. "How am I supposed to leave you?"

Alex pounds on the door again.

"Cool your fucking jets, bro!" Sawyer yells. "I've got one more minute."

I stand and quickly brush the wrinkles from his shirt and pants. "You're going to have some explaining to do. At least I hadn't put my lipstick on yet."

"I can live with that." He pulls me close. "So, what is this? Is this a chance?"

"Maybe."

"Maybe." He tilts my chin up and kisses me softly. "I can work with 'maybe'."

"Sawyer!" Alex snaps.

"I'm going to charm the hell out of you tonight." Sawyer gives me one last tender kiss.

"I'd like to see you try."

"Challenge accepted."

Chapter 28

Sawyer

"What the hell happened to you?" Alex gapes at me as we stride down the hallway.

"I told you. Had a wardrobe mishap. I'll send a bottle of champagne to your room tonight to make up for it."

"You—wait. Sawyer." Alex tugs at my sleeve insistently enough that I stop and face him.

"What?"

He looks me up and down. "Did you have a girl in your room?"

"Yeah, Sienna. You know this."

"No, I mean—" He grabs my face and turns it for inspection. "I'm not sure if she tried to murder you or fuck you, but you've got scratches on your neck. And you smell like strawberries."

I bat him away. "Get out of here. Let's go before Ellie cancels the wedding."

"*Sawyer.*"

I'm biting the inside of my cheek to keep from beaming, but I can't hold out much longer.

"Are you late because you were hooking up with her?" Alex's eyes light up. "Is she the girl you were talking about the other night, the one you can't have?"

I cough.

"Oh my God. I'm not the only one getting lucky tonight."

I shove him forward, and he laughs it off. "Don't talk about her like that."

"I'm seriously so happy for you." My brother throws an arm around my shoulder and squeezes. "Ellie's going to flip. She loves Sienna."

My grin continues to break through. "Don't get ahead of yourself. I haven't locked anything down yet. We'll see how tonight goes."

"Your *hair*, man." Alex smothers a smile as he looks at me.

I frantically comb my fingers through it with a sheepish smile. "She likes my curls."

He laughs heartily. "OK, Romeo. Let's go."

The ceremony is beautiful, but I only have eyes for the Indigenous siren in the fifth row.

Sienna catches me watching her no fewer than a dozen times over the course of the twenty-minute event. I looked away briefly to wink at Ellie as she walked towards Alex and to hand the rings to the officiant, but otherwise I fought not to flat-out stare at the woman of my dreams.

I offer my arm to the Maid of Honor at the conclusion of the vows, and we follow the new Mr. and Mrs. Lane up the aisle. As I walk by, I grab Sienna's hand and quickly kiss the back of it.

"I'll see you soon," I say with a final squeeze, loving the flush that creeps into her cheeks as I do so.

Ordinarily, I would enjoy the endless socializing that comes with a wedding, but at the moment I'm climbing the walls to talk to Sienna. I'm desperate to know how she feels about me, especially in light of my declaration earlier.

But first, we have to take more pictures, in every variety of pairing, position, and location imaginable. Then I dance into the reception hall with Ellie's sister, just before the happy couple is introduced. There are first dances, toasts, and the Best Man speech. I struggle to keep my voice steady as I talk about my brother, who is my lifelong best friend, and the woman who was made for him.

Dinner is next, and at this point I'm about to claw my eyes out with anticipation. Sienna's seated at a table with my mom and Rich, and it brings a smile to my face to see her so at ease with them. Mom admires her earrings, and Rich tells some sort of long-winded story with lots of hand gestures while she laughs.

I'd nearly forgotten how natural it felt to have her be part of my family. She slots into our dynamic as if she's been born for it.

Waitstaff are clearing our plates when I elbow my brother to get his attention. "Can I bounce from the wedding party table now that dinner's over?"

Alex frowns. "Don't you want to eat cake with—"

"I love you, man, but I want to eat cake with my girl."

He opens his mouth to respond, but Ellie leans across to cut him off.

"Go," she says to me with a wide smile. "We've kept you apart long enough."

She doesn't have to tell me twice. I jump out of my seat and make a beeline for Sienna's table. My mom gives me a knowing smile as I approach.

"So sorry to interrupt." I wrap my arms around Sienna's shoulders from behind, and she brings a hand to rest on my forearm. "Do you mind if I steal my beautiful date away for a few minutes?"

"Not at all." Mom's eyes dance as she covers Rich's hand with her own. "We'll save you some cake."

My stepdad gives me a wink as I help Sienna to her feet, and I covertly cross my fingers in his direction.

"Where are we going?" she asks as I intertwine my fingers with hers.

"Not sure yet, but we'll figure it out."

I lead her through the exterior doors in search of a quiet place to talk. Her stilettos click against the concrete as we wind past the pool and towards the beach. There's a gentle breeze coming off the ocean, so I stop to shrug off my suit jacket.

"Put this on. It's getting chilly." I wrap it around her shoulders, and she slides her arms through the sleeves with an amused smirk.

"You're being bossy again."

"And I haven't heard a single complaint about it." I kick off my shoes and socks.

"What a beautiful sunset tonig—*Oh*!"

I scoop her into my arms with the hand not holding my shoes and proceed to carry her across the sand.

"Did you just…pick me up with one arm?" She grabs my collar to steady herself.

"What, like it's hard?"

She makes a sound low in her throat that warms my insides. "It's unfortunately very hot."

I make my way towards a covered seating area facing the water. "Sounds like I need to do it more often."

"No one's ever picked me up before. I'm too tall."

I gently set her down on a wicker couch. "Well, you're the perfect height for me."

"Even in heels?" Her eyes appear genuinely worried as she looks up at me, and this just will not do.

"Especially in heels." I dust a kiss across her forehead before sitting next to her. "Tower over me, please."

She leans into me, and I wrap my arm around her shoulders. For a few minutes there's only the sound of our breath and the waves crashing on shore as we share space.

I slowly run my fingers up and down her arm. "This is nice." My voice is quiet as I conjure the memory of our first almost-kiss thirteen years ago.

Sienna tilts her face up and cradles my cheek. "It is."

I wish I had a time machine and could go back to change what happened. In the absence of that technology, all I can do is pray she lets me rewrite our story going forward.

I kiss her softly, taking my time to savor her. Nearly every other kiss has been frantic and driven by need, but I want this one to be a new beginning. I can taste her strawberry lip gloss, and it is just as glorious as the first time.

She pulls back and rests her forehead against mine. "You've loved me all this time?"

"I have no expectations that you feel the same way, but yes." I trace along the edges of her jaw. "I always have."

She swallows. "But I heard you tell Tori we were just friends, and then I saw you kiss her."

I inhale deeply, the heartbreak hitting me anew as she confirms what I suspected. "Tori is petty and mean-spirited, and I was trying to get her off your back. I saw how she acted around you that night, and I was furious. I should've addressed it more directly with her, but I took the easy way out."

Her fingers tangle in the hair at the nape of my neck. "You kissed her."

I shake my head. "*She* kissed *me*, and it was completely unexpected. I was so stunned I didn't move for a few seconds, but then I pushed her away. I never saw her again after that. You can ask Alex; I told him about it the same night."

"That's what I saw?" she rasps. "I looked into the kitchen in those exact seconds?"

"You must've." My hands tighten on her shoulders. "I didn't realize what happened, and I never could figure out why you suddenly couldn't stand to be around me. I can't tell you how much I regret not fighting harder to get you back."

She closes her eyes, and tears spill from beneath her lids. "We could've been together all this time, but instead I clung to this hurt and resentment that didn't even need to exist."

I kiss the tears from her cheeks. "Sweetheart, don't cry. You'll make me cry, and I am not a cute crier."

"I'm so sorry," she whispers. "I never even gave you a chance to defend yourself. I thought you'd grown tired of me. That my feelings were one-sided, and I'd only imagined you felt the same."

"Sen, I was out of my mind for you. That missed kiss has haunted me ever since." I wipe away more wetness from under her eyes. "But we can make up for lost time, if you're willing to take a chance on me again."

She pulls my mouth back to hers for a salty kiss. "Please be mine, Sawyer. Please."

"I always have been."

Chapter 29

Sienna

"So this is...it? You just repeat these same steps over and over for the entire song?" I blink in bafflement.

"I knew you'd be a natural with your dancing background."

Step, step, step, clap.

"Wait. Why is half the group on the wrong beat?"

"My people can be rhythmically challenged. Don't hold it against them."

As promised, I somewhat-willingly came out on the dance floor with Sawyer once we returned from the beach. My anxiety about being visible among so many strangers was quickly diminished by his comforting presence and lightheartedness.

The Electric Slide ends, and he pins me against him with an open palm on my back. "Stay out here with me," he implores as the DJ shifts to Pitbull. "I'm having fun dancing with you."

I push a damp curl from his forehead. "I regret to inform you that I am also having fun."

"It's almost as though you like me or something."

I tug him closer with the undone ends of his bow tie. "I find you tolerable."

"That's quite an escalation from hating me." His lips brush against mine as he speaks.

"It helps that you look good in a suit."

"Is that so?"

"Especially with your shirtsleeves rolled up like this." My fingers skate down his chest and across to his bare forearms. I run my thumb over the small strawberry tattoo nestled amongst the rest of his ink.

"Do you like my tattoos?" he asks with a smile. "Because I really like yours."

"My—oh, that old thing?" The pads of his fingers skip down the notches of my spine. "I got that in college. It's from the Tuscarora Thanksgiving Address."

"I'd love to see it up close sometime."

I wrap my arms around his neck and move in time to the upbeat music. "You can see it tonight, if you'd like."

"I'd like that." His voice is low against my ear, and now I'm wondering if anyone would notice if we left early.

Someone bumps into us, and I look up with a jolt.

"I'd tell you two to get a room, but I know you already have one," Alex teases as he spins by with Ellie.

She flashes me a smile, and I giggle with delight.

The lights begin flashing in bright colors as "Single Ladies" by Beyoncé begins pumping through the reception hall. Two women at the table next to ours gasp in delight and jump to their feet.

I look over at Sawyer. "What's this?"

He runs a hand over his mouth, smothering a grin. "Bouquet toss."

"Bou—? Oh." I groan.

Rich leans over. "More white people nonsense," he says, and I chuckle in reply.

Sawyer raises an eyebrow. "Have you never participated in one?"

"I told you, Native weddings aren't like this." I watch as women from across a range of ages make their way to the dance floor. Some run eagerly in their heels, while others slowly march to the front as though they're facing a firing squad.

"Well?" His chestnut eyes dance over the water glass he sips from. "Get up there."

Panic jumps up and nips at my stomach. "Oh. Oh no. I don't think so."

Sawyer leans forward on his elbows. "It's a requirement. Ellie's going to haul you over there if you don't go."

My heart stops. "She wouldn't."

"Oh, she would." He curls his pinky around mine as he leans close to my ear. "I hope you catch it."

"And why's that?

"Because it means you're next to get married." *Creator, help,* because I can feel the feminism leaving my body from the way he's looking at me.

"Sienna! Get over here!"

Ellie's voice rings out, and I close my eyes to gather strength.

"I told you." Sawyer clinks his glass against mine. "Take a drink for courage, and get out there, baby."

Ellie appears at my side with a beaming smile. "Come on, girl! I'm about to throw the bouquet, and I need you there."

I send her brother-in-law a distress signal with my eyes and he smiles.

"She's coming, Elle. One second." He tucks a stray piece of hair behind my ear as his gaze clicks back over to mine. "I'll be right here when you get back, OK?" He kisses me softly, and my stomach begins to unclench. "Now, get out of here before I ruin your lipstick."

"I'm going to get it all over you later," I whisper against his lips.

His grip tightens on my jaw. "God, I hope so."

Ellie bops him on the head with her bouquet. "Let go of her, please!"

He chuckles and releases me. "Sorry, sorry. Can't be upsetting the bride on her big day."

"I'm throwing this right to you," Ellie says as she drags me onto the dance floor.

"Please don't," I reply weakly.

She looks back at me with a smile. "Sawyer hasn't taken his eyes off you all night. He's smitten."

"I would like to die now, please," I announce five minutes later as I sink into a chair in the middle of the dance floor. Ellie's bouquet is clenched in my hands.

"Don't you dare." Sawyer gets to his knees in front of me, a blue lace garter snug on his bicep. "We didn't get this far just for you to pass away from embarrassment."

I did everything I could to avoid that bouquet, but it bounced off several bridesmaids before landing squarely on my feet. Alex flung the garter directly to his brother afterwards, and now we're being forced to perform some sort of hyper-sexualized wedding ritual before I can slink back to our table.

Raunchy music with horns plays as Sawyer slides the lace over my knee.

"Are we done?" I ask while shielding my face with the flowers.

"Not even close."

"Sawyer!" I squeak as he pulls the garter up another several inches.

He grins up at me. "Need to get credit for all those bonus years of good luck."

"I'm guessing we'll be seeing you around our house on Six Nations again soon?" Sawyer's mom asks me with a warm smile.

Sawyer winds an arm around my shoulders and pulls my chair closer to his. "I sure hope so."

If I could have seen the future a week ago when I hastily booked this trip, I would have shrieked in horror. I'm on a completely different path than expected, but somehow it feels like the one I should've taken originally.

I smile at my sweet, thoughtful, devastatingly gorgeous date. "Yeah, I imagine I'll be back in Six from time to time." I squeeze Sawyer's thigh under the table, and he drops a kiss on my temple.

"Final song of the night, folks," the DJ announces. "I need everyone out here on the dance floor to celebrate Alex and Ellie one last time."

Sawyer holds out his hand to me. "May I have this dance?"

My lip quivers upward as I place my palm in his. "Is this part of your charm offensive tonight?"

"Absolutely."

The soaring notes of "Unchained Melody" fill the hall, and Sawyer pulls me close with an arm at my waist.

"You're the most beautiful woman here, you know that?" He laces his fingers through mine and slowly sways us from side to side. "I'm the luckiest man in the world."

I toy with the hair at the nape of his neck. "I bet you say that to all the girls."

He draws me against him even more tightly. "Do you want to know the real reason why I wasn't interested in that flight attendant?"

My eyebrow inches upward. "Why?"

His breath skates across my ear. "Because she wasn't you."

My knees liquify. "You're laying it on thick."

"It's true." He kisses my jaw. "I don't think you realize how serious I am about you."

I smile into his neck. "I do. And I feel the same way."

"Do you really?" His intense gaze makes my heart race.

"Yes." I rest my head on his shoulder. "I'm all in with you."

He kisses my cheek. "Ditto."

The music approaches its crescendo, and I breathe in his cologne. "Do you know if the Best Man is single?"

His chuckle rumbles against my chest. "He's taken."

"Darn. I was hoping to go home with him tonight."

The hand at my waist clenches the fabric of my dress. "That can be arranged."

"Do you think he puts out?"

I squeak when he squeezes me firmly.

"Depends how nicely you ask."

"I can be very nice when I want to be."

He dusts a kiss across my lips. "As long as you're still mean to me from time to time. Keep me in line."

"I can't imagine that'll be much of a hardship."

"Glad we're on the same page."

Chapter 30

Sawyer

Sienna kisses my neck and giggles as I carry her back to our room.

"I can walk, you know."

"Not on my watch. Grab the key out of my front pocket, would you?"

She scans us in and I take her straight to bed, gently depositing her on the mattress.

"How are your feet?" I kneel and draw one of her heels into my hands.

"Sore." She watches as I gently unbuckle the golden straps.

"Can't have that."

Her eyes run over me as she leans back on her arms. "I think I like you on your knees."

I grin and carefully slide the shoe off her foot. "That's good, because I plan on being here for a while."

She makes a low sound and offers me her other heel.

"These are really sexy." I repeat the process, dropping a soft kiss on her ankle between steps. "*You're* really sexy."

"Thank you. You make me *feel* sexy."

"Glad to know I'm doing something right."

My thumbs knead her aching soles, and she murmurs happily. "Are you going to help me with the garter while you're down there?"

"It's next on my list." I run my hand up her leg until I feel fabric on her upper thigh. "I can't believe you let me put it all the way up here. Very risqué."

She kicks at me with her other foot. "You didn't give me a choice."

I part her dress along the high slit until the lacy adornment comes into view. She exhales, and I kiss along her thigh until I reach the garter. I take it between my teeth and tug downwards.

She growls my name and I look up. "You're such a tease."

I tug further, and she takes in a sharp breath.

"I assure you, I always follow through on my teasing." I kiss every inch of skin I can find as I pull the garter down. She's already squirming and I haven't even gotten to my favorite part yet.

"Can I use my tongue on you?" I get the lace past her knee, and it falls to the floor.

"Only if you really want to." She watches me from her forearms, her eyes heated and her dress increasingly askew.

"Let me show you how much I want to." I drape her exposed leg over my shoulder and pull her hips closer.

She swallows. "You've done a lot for me this week. I want to return the favor."

I kiss a path up her inner thigh. "Later. Trust me, I'll enjoy this as much as you will."

Her breath picks up as I move to the other leg with my lips. "I don't want to be selfish."

"Be greedy, sweetheart." I hook my fingers into the sides of her panties and tug. "I'm begging to worship you. I'll keep you awake all night if you let me."

"I'm not sure it'll be enough." She gasps as I lower my mouth to her.

"It definitely won't be." My tongue flicks over her. "We're making up for lost time, remember?"

I push her dress up to her waist and pull her other leg over my shoulder. She collapses fully onto the bed with a moan that unleashes any remaining restraint I had left.

I devour her. Licking and sucking and breathing over her like a starving man at an oasis. She tugs at my hair and writhes beneath me as I lose track of time in this unlikely heaven I've found myself in.

"How are you so good at everything?" She moans while covering her face with her hands.

"Because I've been dreaming about having you in my bed for years." I throw an arm across her hips to keep her from wiggling clear off the mattress. "I know exactly how lucky I am to be here."

She curses when I slide my fingers inside her as I suck on her clit.

"Does your grandmother know you swear like that?"

"Do you ever shut the fu—"

"There's my feisty girl."

She clenches and falls to pieces around me a few minutes later, her legs shaking on either side of my head.

I ease her further onto the bed, kissing her thighs and abdomen as she trembles.

"Thank you for making my dreams come true," I murmur against her skin. "You were worth the wait."

Her chest heaves as she looks at me. "As soon as I recover the use of my limbs, you're going to be in so much trouble."

"Oh no, that sounds terrible."

She tugs me closer, and I roll on top of her, bracing my weight onto a forearm. My erection presses against her, and her eyes widen.

"Are you turned on from going down on me?" she asks incredulously.

"Mmm hmm." I kiss her languidly, and she rolls her hips against mine with a needy groan.

"You are unbelievably hot." She traces up my length with her fingers, and I suck in a breath when she wraps a hand around me.

I rest my forehead against hers. "Find something you like?"

"Creator couldn't give you *one* thing to keep you humble?"

"He did." I dust a kiss across her cheek. "He gave me you."

"How the hell does that fit anywhere?"

My body rumbles with barely repressed laughter. "Wouldn't you like to know?"

She squeezes. "Let me up. You're wearing entirely too many clothes."

"Let's do something about that."

Chapter 31

Sienna

If this man doesn't get inside me immediately, I'm going to lose my sanity.

I get to my knees on the mattress and wrench him towards the headboard. Well, he helpfully scoots where I want him, because there's no way I'm actually capable of moving his large frame on my own.

I straddle his lap, push the suspenders off his shoulders, and get to work on his shirt buttons.

"You always were a woman on a mission," he murmurs, watching me undress him with amusement.

I kiss him and keep unbuttoning. "And right now that mission is getting you naked."

He groans into my mouth. "How the hell did I land you?"

I yank the shirt out of his waistband. "You're irresistibly charming and good with your hands."

"Heck yeah, I am."

I sit back and admire the view after tossing his white button-down. "It's disgusting how gorgeous you are."

"Speak for yourself." He pulls my hips closer.

I grind against him. "These pants need to go next."

"Just a second." Sawyer's hand trembles as it skates down my bare back. "I want to look at you."

"Are you nervous?" I ask, running my thumb against his cheek.

He swallows. "I am."

"First time? I'll be gentle."

He barks out a laugh and kisses my forehead. "It's my first time with you, so it might as well be."

"You're not what I expected." I comb the hair away from his eyes. "You're soft and romantic."

His lips dust across the back of my hand. "I'm a loverboy at heart. Especially for you."

"So I've got you wrapped around my finger?"

"And I couldn't be happier about it."

My dress unzips easily beneath his fingers. Sawyer gently slides the thin straps down my shoulders, and the fabric pools at my waist. He draws a deep breath, and my nipples harden under his gaze.

"You. Are. Breathtaking."

I'm used to attention from men, but this is something else. This is being treasured, adored, *cherished*.

I didn't believe it when he told me, but it's beginning to sink in. This is the way a man looks at the woman he loves. My stomach flutters at the thought.

"Do you want to take down your hair?" he asks softly. "That can't be comfortable."

I raise my arms and begin to grab pins. "You just want to see it cascade over me while I'm topless."

He follows my every movement, a slow smile developing on his lips. "I can't argue with that visual."

Hairpins collect in my hands as I work across my head, and pieces of hair begin unfurling around me. Sawyer brushes them away before his hands drift across my breasts. He rolls a nipple between his fingers and I pause, pleasure blooming in my veins.

"Pretend I'm not here." His second hand gets in on the action, and now I'm fully distracted. He pinches me lightly, and I sharply intake a breath, my fingers digging for the remaining pins.

"Keep going, or I'll stop." He sits up and takes a nipple into his mouth with a groan. "You're so fucking perfect."

Bobby pins fall around us as I moan. "I can't."

"You can." His teeth graze against me and I squirm in his lap. "Let me see that beautiful hair come all the way down."

I grumble and steel myself to finish the job. Pins softly thump on the carpet as the last of my hair comes tumbling out.

"My God." Sawyer's eyes darken as my tresses fall unabated to my waist. "Sen." He grips a hand in my hair and pulls me to him for a rough kiss. "I'm going to take such good care of you."

"I know you are. I've sampled your work."

He chuckles against my lips.

"I need you. Now," I remind him.

"Understatement of the century." He flicks open the button of his pants, and I take the opportunity to slide my dress all the way off. "Do you want to be on top? That way you'd control the pace."

"I want you to be in control. I trust you."

"Say that again so I can record it."

"You're the worst."

He grabs me around the waist and flips me onto my back. "You're still the boss, OK? Hand me my wallet."

I reach for it on the nightstand. "Tell me you didn't travel with condoms."

He pulls one out with a sheepish smile. "You wouldn't be very happy right now if I hadn't," he points out. "But, in my defense, I only have one. I didn't expect any extracurricular activities on this trip."

"Guess you're going to the store in the morning."

"The instant they open." He runs his length over me, and I whimper.

"Please."

"I'll go slow." His soft gasp as he begins to sink into me unravels my self control.

I tug at his hair, desperate for him. "More."

"I don't want to hurt you." His shoulders quiver from holding himself back. "You feel so good, it's unreal."

"I can handle you."

I'm quickly humbled as he presses further inside.

"*Fuck*, Sawyer." I tilt my hips to make room for him, and he slides deeper with a moan.

"My girl is such a fucking champ," he breathes. "You were made for me."

"I feel so full," I whisper, feeling every delicious inch of him stretching me.

He kisses me with a groan. "You're never getting rid of me. How am I supposed to ever look at another woman after you?"

Each slow thrust elicits a gasp. "You're not. I'd kill you."

"Goddamn." His breath is warm on my neck as he drops his head. "You got a possessive side, baby?"

I wrap my legs around his waist and nip at his earlobe. "I don't share well."

"Good thing you won't need to. I'm obsessed with you."

"I've noticed."

His shoulders shake with laughter. "You're not in a position to be roasting me right now."

"I'm in exactly the position I want to be in."

"How are you still a brat even when I'm inside of you?" He hooks my right leg over his arm, and my eyes roll back at feeling him even deeper.

"What are you going to do about it?" My breath comes out ragged.

His gaze pours over me, and a smirk lifts the corner of his mouth. "Baiting me again?"

I nod. "You're not the only one who likes it when we're mean to each other."

He raises an eyebrow. "You want me to be mean?"

I bite my lip. "You were a little mean when you had me on the desk."

"I noticed you were into that."

He pulls away and I whine at the loss.

"Lift your hips."

"Bossy." I do as he requests, and he slides two pillows under me.

"You told me to be mean. I'm giving you what you asked for." His grin is unholy, and I may be regretting my statement.

He slides back inside me, and I don't recognize the primal groan that tears from my throat.

"You like that angle?" He bends low to kiss me, and I can barely breathe from the fullness and pleasure flooding through me. "You're taking me so well."

I'm flat out whimpering underneath him. "Sawyer, please."

He catches my wrists in his hand and pins them above me. "I need you to know something."

I'm not above begging, and if he doesn't start moving inside me I'm going to lose my ever-loving mind.

"You're it for me, Sienna." He alternates between slowly nailing me into the mattress and kissing me deeply. "There's no one else."

I couldn't respond if I tried; my breath taken by my rapidly peaking orgasm and the ache in my chest.

"If you're finally mine, then I'm never letting you go. I'm yours, in every way possible."

His thumb starts insistent circles against my clit, and it's the extra stimulation that I've been craving. I shatter into a thousand pieces, my body quaking and hot tears spilling from my eyes.

Sawyer kisses me, holding me through the climax until his own hits. He buries his face in my neck, and I have never been so thoroughly, transformatively loved in my life.

He releases my wrists and gathers me into his arms. "Are you OK?" he asks, wiping away my tears.

My heart pounds as I nod. "That was really intense."

"It was." He kisses me gently. "I love you so much, Sen. I know it's probably overwhelming to hear that, but I want you to know you mean everything to me. I don't know what I've done to deserve you, but it's a damn miracle I won't be taking for granted."

I thread my hands through his hair. "You're not the only one grateful for a second chance. Thank you for being so patient with me."

His dark eyes lock onto mine, and he slides a palm beneath my jaw. "I can't promise that I'll be perfect, because I know I'm not. But I'm going to do everything I can to be the man you need for a long, long time."

I wrap my legs around his waist and pull him closer. "I want you tattooed on my heart and in every crevice of my world. I don't want you to be perfect. Just be you."

"I'll remind you of that the next time you're about to throttle me."

"Deal."

Chapter 32

Sawyer

I thread my fingers through Sienna's as we stroll through the Buffalo airport. Being with her back on home turf feels incredible, like walking through a dream.

My phone buzzes from my back pocket and Jamie's picture pops up on the screen.

"Do you mind if I take this?" I ask her.

"Go right ahead."

I grin. "Can I tell him?"

"About...us?"

"Yeah. Us." I squeeze her hand.

She shrugs. "Go ahead."

"I'll make this worth your while." I swipe to answer the call and tap to switch it to video.

"Hey Jammer."

The screen is black for a few seconds before Jamie finally appears. "Did you mean to turn this into a video call?"

"Oops. How'd that happen?" I throw my arm around Sienna's shoulders and pull her into the frame.

He blinks. "Oh, hey Sienna. I didn't realize you went to Alex's wedding."

"It was a last-minute trip." She looks up at me with a smile, and I grin from ear to ear.

"A very fortunate one." I tilt her chin up, and if she keeps looking at me like this, we're not making it to Baggage Claim.

He clears his throat. "How'd everything go in Jamaica?"

"Perfectly." I rub my thumb across her jaw and lower my mouth for a gentle kiss.

Jamie sucks in an audible breath, and I chuckle against Sienna's lips.

"Is he going to be OK?" she whispers and tugs the collar of my t-shirt to bring me closer.

"Eventually."

"Um, I'm going to need you two to come up for air, because I have some fucking questions!"

She giggles, and it lights up my insides.

"Sienna?"

She turns to the phone with an easy smile. "Yes?"

"Blink twice if you need help. Did he drug you?"

Another giggle. "He did not."

I kiss her cheek and wrap her back under my arm, smiling widely at Jamie.

He's openly gawping at us. "Are you—? Is—?"

"I don't think I've ever seen you speechless, Jammer," I say.

"There's a first time for everything," he mutters. "So, you two are—?"

"Together? Yeah. We are." I look back down at her, and she's gazing at me.

"You're going to need to publish a book, Lanes, because this would have taken historic levels of delusion to pull off. How the hell did this happen?"

"What was it you said, Sen? That I'm irresistibly charming and good with my—"

She slaps a hand across my mouth, and I laugh heartily.

Jamie groans. "He's never going to let us hear the end of this, Sienna. You've unleashed a monster."

"Don't worry, I'll take him down a few notches." She fixes me with a stern look, but I see the edges of her lips fighting a losing battle against a smile.

"Please humble me anytime you want, baby." I nip at her thumb and her eyes darken.

"I'm still here, you know."

We both turn to look at Jamie, who grins wolfishly.

"Get the hell out of here, creep. I need to make out with my girl."

"When can I see you again?" I breathe against her lips, my hand winding into her hair as I press her into the side of her car.

How the hell am I going to be away from her? I've quickly gotten addicted to being with her every day this week, but I know that's not sustainable as we jump back into real life.

"If you've got a computer that needs fixing, you can come see me at work." Her hands slide up my back beneath my corduroy jacket.

"I've got a hard drive you could work on."

"Solid state or hard disk?"

I nibble her lower lip. "I'm shamelessly hitting on you, Lady Einstein."

"Oh." Her head falls forward into my chest as she chuckles.

I wrap her in my arms. "I have training camp the next four weekends, but during the week I can be available whenever you need me."

"I might need you a lot."

"Consider me at your service. Have I done enough to earn your number, finally?"

"I suppose so."

"Gimme your phone, gorgeous."

I pin her to the car as I enter my information into her contacts. She kisses me and I snap a photo to save to my profile.

"I've got a lot of work to catch up on in the coming days, but maybe you could come over for dinner one night?"

"You'll need to file a restraining order to keep me away." I slide the device back into her pocket. "Just say when, and I'll be there."

"I'm going to like having you at my beck and call." She pulls me close with a saucy grin.

"That sounds like heaven."

Jammer: I need to tell you something, and I recommend you sit down for this

Z: Is everything OK?!

Jammer: Oh shit, sorry to worry you, Zeke. Everything's OK. It's about Sawyer

Wes: Go on

Me: Why are you sharing my business, man?

Jammer: Don't pretend you don't love being the main character

Me: You're right. Proceed

Z: Are you sure everything's all right? You're making me nervous

Jammer: Sawyer has a girlfriend

Wes: I literally just needed to sit down

Z: Like, a real one?

Me: *picture of me and Sienna kissing in the airport parking lot*

Wes: NO FUCKING WAY

Z: Isn't that the girl who hates his guts?

Me: Gentlemen, I've peaked at age 29. I will never pull off anything as remarkable as this ever again

Jammer: Career season loading in 3, 2, 1…

Wes: Chelsea's screaming and demanding an immediate debrief when you get home

Z: We might be joining you. Genny wants to drive up

Me: Can I shower first, or…

Wes: NO

Z: NO

Jammer: Could someone video chat me in?

Chapter 33

Kuhserhęháh

Early Winter / November

Sienna

"Is this really necessary?"

Someone bumps into me while perusing a rack of Outlaws jerseys in the crowded arena store.

My sister fixes me with a stern look. "This is your first time watching your boyfriend play professional lacrosse. Yes, it's necessary to wear some team gear." She flips through the hangers and hands me a jersey with Sawyer's name and number ninety-one.

I stare at the garment as if it's laced with poison oak. "I've never worn a jersey in my life. What do you even wear with that?"

She pushes it into my chest. "Sometimes I fear you're hopeless."

The woman next to us cranes her neck to see the jersey number in my hand. "You're dating Sawyer Lane?!"

A sinkhole would be appreciated right now. I give a small nod, and her jaw drops.

"Lucky," she mutters as she walks away.

Hazel giggles and tosses an orange and black beanie at me. "You're breaking hearts across the Buffalo-Niagara region, sis."

Tonight is the Outlaws' home opener, and my first time watching Sawyer play since high school. My family loves lacrosse; it's part of our Tuscarora culture, but I've always been the odd one out. I appreciate the game given to us by the Creator, but sports have never been an interest of mine. I've sat through games here and there, but almost always under duress.

"This is cute." Hazel holds out a t-shirt version of Sawyer's jersey. "Great for warm weather, or to sleep in. Though you might not get much rest if you wear this around him." She elbows me forcefully until I duck away into another aisle.

"Knock it off." I chuckle and grab a generic team sweater. "I like this. I could wear it with my black corduroy skirt tonight."

"Boring." She yawns. "You're lucky that 90s fashions are coming back. Your old lady wardrobe is passable at the moment." She piles some more items into my arms. "Get it all. Sawyer gave you his credit card for this, right?"

I groan under the weight. "This is too much. And I'm not using his card. I'm pretty sure I make more money than he does. The NLL barely pays these guys."

"Excuse me. I didn't mean to eavesdrop…" A beautiful woman with a long, dark braid peeks around the stack of clothes I'm holding, and I instantly feel at ease because I can tell she's Native. A pair of beaded corn earrings glimmer at her ears, and her large brown eyes are warm and friendly. "Are you Sienna?"

"I am."

Her face lights up. "You looked familiar and sounded like you knew Sawyer. I'm Genny Skye." She darts forward to catch a rogue shirt that falls from my grasp, and a sparkly stone flashes on her ring finger. "Soon-to-be Jacobs. I'm engaged to one of Sawyer's teammates."

"You're from Cattaraugus." I nod towards the East Lake Elementary School lanyard around her neck. It's the closest primary school to the nearby Seneca Nation territory.

Genny looks down and scoffs. "Oh geez. I can't believe I forgot to take this off after school." She yanks her ID off with a chuckle. "Yes, Zeke and I are both Seneca. And you're Tuscarora, right?"

"I am. My sister, Hazel, is around here somewhere, too."

"Big fan of your fiancé," Hazel pokes her head around the aisle with a grin. "He's such a fun player to watch."

"I'm so glad I ran into you. Sawyer asked us to find you and bring you over to our section." She walks with us towards the checkout. "I'm here with my friend Chelsea John, who dates another of the players. We have a little Indigenous WAGs group going. She's Oneida."

My memory lights up at the name. "I've met Chelsea, I think. At the Tuscarora picnic last year." I turn to my sister and quietly ask, "WAGs?"

Hazel rolls her eyes with a grin. "Player wives and girlfriends. Keep up!"

Genny chuckles. "I'm so excited to meet you. I've heard so much about you from Sawyer that I feel like I already know you. We're going to have a blast tonight."

My smile is genuine, even though we've just met. "I'm looking forward to it."

Hanging out in all-female groups is not something I do often. I'm socially uncertain in the best of situations, and after spending years working with guys, I'm usually at a loss about how to behave around women. Men are easy: bring something to eat, smile at their jokes, and occasionally roast them. It's a winning strategy that's worked well for me in technology spaces.

But I'm immediately relaxed around Genny and Chelsea, and quite frankly, it's a relief.

"Who's the little one?" Hazel tosses popcorn into her mouth as we watch the team warmup. "He's cute."

"That one's mine." Chelsea's eyes twinkle. "But if you like shorter guys, Jamie's still single."

"We really need to find him a nice girl," Genny says. "He's been on his own for a long time."

Hazel frowns. "He's not with Connor's mom? I just assumed they were a couple since I've seen them together at summer festivals."

I shake my head. "No, they split up years ago after the accident."

Genny looks over. "Accident?"

"Yeah, when Jamie was—"

Sawyer scans the stands, and my pulse does something inconvenient when his eyes find mine in the crowd. A grin explodes across his face, and Chelsea gasps next to me.

"Look at him!" she squeaks before turning to me. "Look at *you!*"

"Oh my gosh." Genny looks between the two of us as I cover my flushed cheeks with my hands. "I've never seen Sawyer look that happy to see someone."

Hazel crunches through some more popcorn. "I've seen the way he looks at her for years, but she never wanted to hear about it."

Chelsea passes me an icy cold beer. "Tell us everything."

My sister snatches the drink from my hand. "She won't. I'll tell you what you need to know."

I have to admit, lacrosse is more enjoyable when it involves watching Sawyer run around in shorts. And he's *good.*

He was wound so tightly in his first few years playing in Six Nations. He beat himself up for not being creative enough, not anticipating the ball, and being consumed by how others thought of him. He worked his tail off to overcome his mental demons, and clearly it has paid off. Seeing him play now is the realization of his teenage dreams, and emotion wraps itself tightly around my heart as I watch him fly around the floor.

Sawyer muscles a defender toward the net using his considerable leg strength. Zeke yells for a pass, but he's too heavily guarded. Sawyer glances down, and Chelsea sucks in a breath.

"He wouldn't—" she begins, just as he throws the ball under his left leg.

It bounces between the feet of the defender, catches the goalie unaware, and catapults into the net.

"What the hell was that?" Hazel laughs as the arena erupts into cheers while the goal horn blares. "He's a psycho for trying to score on a shot like that."

"He *is* a psycho," Chelsea says with a chuckle. "That's what makes him so dangerous near the net."

The opening guitar riff of "Layla" rings out through the loudspeakers, and Genny tilts her head in confusion.

"That's not Sawyer's goal song," she says.

Chelsea frowns. "He must've changed it for the new season."

Sawyer jumps and crashes against Zeke in celebration as the team congratulates him on his goal. Immediately after he turns, finds me in the crowd, and points my way with a big, cocky grin. And then the jerk *winks*.

"Oh, hot damn," Genny says while my stomach flips into the next dimension. "How come Zeke never acknowledges me after he scores?"

"I know, right?" Chelsea agrees. "Wes needs to up his ga—"

"Oh my God." Hazel grabs my forearm. "You're his Layla."

"His what?" I blink at her.

"His Layla!" My sister's thumbs fly across her phone screen. "Look at the lyrics."

Genny and Chelsea peer over my shoulder as I scroll.

Hazel's leg bounces up and down. "He said he's loved you from afar all this time, right? And he begged for another chance?"

"He did?!" Genny's eyes shoot up to mine. "*Sawyer?*"

I nod and re-read the words on the screen. *That...absolutely could be about us.*

"He changed his goal song for you!" Chelsea squeals. "This is exactly the type of romantic bullshit I suspected he was capable of."

I gnaw on my lip as I watch Sawyer grab some water on the bench.

"You should join Spicy Book Club." Chelsea nudges me. "I think you'd enjoy it."

"Ooh, yeah! You totally should!" Genny says. "I tried to talk Zeke into it, but he'd rather sketch than read in his spare time."

I raise an eyebrow. "What's Spicy Book Club?"

"Wes and I read romance novels and talk about them," Chelsea says. "It's really fun, and it's honestly great for communication about...bedroom stuff."

My cheeks warm. "Sounds intimate."

She giggles, but tries to hide it behind her cup. "It is, but we can adjust for a mixed group." She pulls up an ebook on her phone and hands it to me. "Here's a dark romance we read early on, if you want to check it out."

I skim the description. *Whew.* "This seems intense."

She smiles. "Don't worry. I'll start you off with something much more tame. Maybe a slow burn with lots of yearning."

"I'll give it a try." I hand the phone back to her. "I like to read."

"Sawyer is going to eat this up." Genny chuckles.

"You'd better pass along all your recommendations to me," Hazel adds. "I don't have time for an actual man, so I need some book boyfriends to keep me occupied on my breaks in the ER."

The friends and family room is packed following the game. Freshly showered players trickle out into the waiting arms of their loved ones, and my foot taps with nervous impatience.

"Whoa." Hazel scrolls on her phone. "Sawyer's going viral for that ridiculous goal he scored earlier."

"Lemme see." Chelsea leans over to look. "Is ESPN posting the replay?! They almost never cover indoor lacrosse content."

"No way!" Genny squeezes between the two of them.

"Is that...good?" I ask, peeking over the top of my sister's phone.

Chelsea smiles. "Definitely. Box lacrosse is a minor sport in the U.S. compared to football and hockey. This type of exposure from national media helps grow the game to people who don't typically follow it."

Hazel gestures behind me with her chin. "There's the man of the hour."

Warmth floods my extremities as the familiar scent of Sawyer's shampoo hits my senses. His arms envelop me and I sink into his chest.

"Hi." I tip my head back and smile up at him.

"Hey." He slides a palm down my jaw as he bends over for a kiss. "I could get used to you waiting for me after games."

"They're *hot* together," Chelsea says to a just-arrived Wes as he dusts his lips across her forehead. "We're not that hot together anymore."

"I disagree." Wes grins and pulls her close under his arm. She giggles when he whispers in her ear. "You're making me look bad in front of my girl, Lanes."

"I'm inviting Sawyer and Sienna to Spicy Book Club," Chelsea says to her boyfriend.

His eyebrow cocks. "We're expanding?"

"No fucking way!" Sawyer straightens. "I've been dying to join but didn't want to be a weirdo shoehorning in on your, uh, romantic thing."

"You'll fit right in." Chelsea winks at me, and my cheeks flush at the memory of Hazel revealing entirely too much about the Jamaica trip.

Wes looks between the two of us. "Do I want to know?"

"Absolutely not."

"So, what's the next book selection?" I ask.

Chelsea looks at Wes. "I don't think we've picked yet, have we?"

He shakes his head. "We got off track with training camp. Maybe we could all pick together?"

She claps. "Tell me the tropes you're interested in, and I can throw out some suggestions."

I cringe. "I fear that is an advanced question. I'm a complete newbie to romance."

She whips out her phone and leans back into Wes' chest. "This is going to be fun! How about sports romance? A bit of art imitating life." She looks at me with a saucy grin.

I groan. "I have too much sport in my life already, I'm sorry to say."

"Sorry about that," Sawyer murmurs.

Chelsea swipes her phone. "Enemies to lovers?" Another wicked grin thrown in my direction.

"Sounds hot." Sawyer kisses my cheek and *oofs* when I elbow him in the solar plexus. "Are there any nerdy IT romances?"

Wes and Chelsea look at each other. "Workplace romance!" they suggest in unison.

I look up at Sawyer. "Are they always this adorable?"

He wraps his arms around me. "Pretty much, yeah."

Chapter 34

Kuhserhęhé·θuʔ
Late Winter / December

Sawyer

*T**hump. Whack. Thunk.*

The sound of rubber bouncing off plywood rattles inside my head with every fling of the ball. Each shot is different: forehand, backhand, one-handed, behind-the-back. All possible ways I can think of to shoot, I practice over and over. It's tempting to think that creative playmaking comes from spontaneity, but in reality, it requires endless work and familiarity with stick skills and your teammates. It's how my childhood friend, Neil, finally broke through to me with trick shots. We practiced them until my stick felt like an extension of my body. Until I recognized the way his shoulders twitched before he let loose a behind-the-back pass and was ready before the defender knew what was coming. Neil had been practicing them since he was a toddler, and taking me back to basics was exactly what I needed when my family first moved to the rez.

"What did that board ever do to you?" Wes asks before squirting water into his mouth. "Does it owe you money?"

I chuckle and whip a low shot at the panel propped against the wall. "I didn't like how it looked at me."

Our motley crew of practice players looks a bit different from usual. Wes and I rent time at a local facility twice a week to keep sharp between games, and Chelsea typically joins us to stay in shape during her offseason. Zeke and Jamie are joining us today, as well as Lauren Powless, a friend of Chelsea's from her days playing college ball. The atmosphere is warm and animated, but a nagging malaise has settled around my thoughts.

"You're off to a hot start this season," Lauren says as she scoops a ball I missed. "You're all over my social media feed."

I snag her pass. "I'm not lighting up the scoreboard as much as I should be, though. My overall goals are down."

Zeke wipes his face with a towel. "I have no doubt you'll be taking the leading scorer mantle from me any week now, Lanes. You're unstoppable lately."

"You're showing up for the team in new and important ways." Jamie taps my shin with the head of his stick. "You're playing looser and more confidently, and that helps the new players settle in and find their flow. You're turning into a real leader."

Chelsea elbows me. "I'm guessing that has something to do with how happy you are in your personal life."

My stomach warms and a smile breaks through. "I am really fucking happy at home, that's for sure."

Having Sienna in my life again still feels unreal, as though one day I'll wake up to find this has all been a dream. I make the thirty-minute drive to see her in Niagara Falls as often as she'll let me, content to simply spend time in her space while she flutters around saving the world one broken computer at a time. Tonight I'll bring her dinner, rub her feet while she works on the couch, and try to get fresh with her while we watch a show before bed. My non-lacrosse hours are pretty freaking perfect, if you ask me.

"Happy at home, but not at work?" Wes asks quietly as we pack our bags at the conclusion of practice.

I stuff my rib pads into the duffel with a sigh. "I don't know what my problem is. I'm finally dating the woman of my dreams, I'm getting some looks from national media, and yet I feel…restless. Like something is missing."

He nods. "You mentioned this during free agency. But you decided to stay in Buffalo."

My phone buzzes, and I give it a quick glance.

> **Dad:** Your one-handed dunk shot made ESPN's top plays of the week. It's good to see you finally getting the attention you deserve, since the Outlaws clearly won't give it to you

> **Dad:** You should be the face of that franchise, not stuck on the second line or killing penalties

I pocket the device. "I did. It felt like the right decision at the time, and maybe it still is. I just feel like I need something more if I'm going to keep playing for another ten years, you know?"

Wes pushes a hand through his sweaty hair. "And what's that? What does 'something more' look like to you?"

The question sits heavy in my gut like locker room silence after a loss. "I want to make my family and friends proud. They've invested a lot in me, both financially and emotionally, and I want to be worth that."

He crouches next to me, his green eyes flashing with concern. "Do you really think they're not already tremendously proud of you? You're a hell of a human, Sawyer, not to mention your success on the floor."

I brush him off. "I'm sure they are. Well, my dad will never be happy, but I really need to not let that bother me so much."

"It sounds like that guy wouldn't be satisfied if Randy Bissell was his son."

"I'm sure there's a championship somewhere that Randy hasn't won in his storied career." I smile. "Can you imagine if I married Sienna? The Bissells are lacrosse royalty."

Wes raises an eyebrow. "Thinking ahead already?"

"With that girl? Always."

"You are so gone for her." His laugh is warm as he gets to his feet. "Well, I think you should figure out what *you* want from your playing career." He hands me my duffel bag before grabbing his own. "If you don't get clear on that, life has a way of making decisions for you."

Chapter 35

Kawę́ʔkye

Time for Cold Air / January

Sienna

I pick at a chef's salad and tuck myself under a fleece blanket on the couch. The Outlaws are winning late in the fourth quarter, and I have the game on in the background while I work on my laptop.

I keep an eye attuned to the audio while responding to emails in the shop's inbox and creating support tickets for next week. My phone buzzes on the coffee table a few times, but I keep my focus on the task at hand so I can finish before bedtime.

The buzzing comes closer together and becomes impossible to ignore, so I set my computer to the side and reach for the phone.

The WAGs group chat has exploded.

> **Chelsea:** That no-look goal by Sawyer was GROSS in the best possible way

> **Genny:** He definitely pointed at the camera for you afterwards, Sienna! I hope the TV feed caught it

> **Genny:** Wish you were here! Games are more fun when we're all together

> **Chelsea:** OH MY GOD he did it again. Sawyer is sick. Certifiably insane.

> **Genny:** I'm sorry, did he score one-handed while FALLING DOWN?

I smile as I skim their in-person game commentary. I would have loved to have been at the Hideout tonight, but I knew I'd be twitchy about leaving so much work to be done before Monday.

Sawyer and I haven't seen much of each other since the NLL season began. Work keeps me busy, and he's either traveling or playing on the weekends. It doesn't bother me too much, since we used to spend years maintaining a friendship with infrequent visits, but I do miss him.

Things have gotten serious quickly, as we've already exchanged keys to each other's places and drop by when our schedules allow. He's coming over after tonight's game, and we'll finally get a day off together tomorrow.

I'm not sure I'll let him out of my bed.

I continue scrolling through my messages until a flurry hits.

> **Chelsea:** Sawyer's going viral online again for his goals tonight, but this time people are tagging Rocco Stone!

> **Genny:** You're deeper in the sports world than I am. Who's that?

> **Chelsea:** He's a former NBA player with a popular talk show on ESPN. Kind of a shock jock with a big personality. People pay attention when he talks about someone on his program.

> **Genny:** Maybe he'll show some clips of the Outlaws on his show!

I glance up as the closing horn sounds on the television. The Outlaws have won the game, and my stomach flips to know Sawyer will be here soon.

My phone vibrates yet again.

> **Chelsea:** Sisters.

> **Chelsea:** Rocco Stone just posted asking if he should have Sawyer on his show!

> **Genny:** !!!!!!!!!!

> **Genny:** SIENNA, WHERE ARE YOU??

Warm lips dusting across my forehead pull me languidly from a dream.

"Sawyer?" I ask, finding the contours of his cheek as I blink the sleep from my eyes.

"Yeah." His beard grazes my jaw as his kiss travels down to my mouth. He smells warm and woodsy from the shower, and desire curls in my belly at his nearness.

I tug him closer as his tongue gently parts my lips. "Sorry. I watched the whole game, but fell asleep updating tickets."

He kicks his shoes off and settles his torso between my legs. "A likely story." His hand tangles in my hair. "Did you eat dinner?"

"Mmm hmm."

"Drink water? Take your vitamins?"

I giggle and squirm as he kisses the side of my neck. "OK, Mom."

"Say that again, but call me Daddy instead."

I roll my eyes and push his patterned blazer down his arms. "You're incorrigible."

"Oh baby, talk dirty to me with your big dictionary words." He trails kisses between my breasts as a wandering hand slides underneath my sweater. "You take terrible care of yourself when you're in work mode. I want to make sure you're getting what you need."

My breath catches when his lips glide across the skin of my abdomen. "Are you going to take care of me, then? Because I need *you*."

He chuckles with a low moan. "Please let me take care of you, sweetheart." The button on my jeans opens with a flick of his fingers. "Please."

"I've missed you." I lift my hips to make his job easier. "So much."

His mouth brings my body to a simmer. "This is all I've been able to think about for days. You're a goddamn distraction."

The sight of him stretched out between my legs while still dressed in slacks and a button-down is so hot I nearly combust on the couch.

I grind against him, and he groans. "I saw women at the arena tonight with signs for you. They seemed like...fans of yours."

He chuckles. "Jealous?"

My hands tug roughly at his hair. "No, because I knew you were coming home to me."

"You're damn right." He slides his fingers inside me, and I see ancient constellations. "I belong to you."

I clutch him to my chest a few minutes later as I drift back down to Earth. "Give me one minute, and then I'm getting on top of you."

"Thank God." He rolls his hips against me. "I'm close to death over here."

"Oh, you poor thing." I push him into a seated position and undo his shirt buttons while he glides a hand up my back to unclasp my bra. Clothing piles on the floor below us as we undress each other with desperation.

I straddle his lap and slowly sink down onto him, pausing to collect myself.

"Relax for me, baby," Sawyer murmurs in my ear. "You're so tight."

I exhale a shaky breath and lower myself fully.

"There you go." He moans against my neck and wraps his arms around my torso. "You're so perfect for me, Sen. Do you feel how well we fit together? How perfectly we balance each other?"

Oh, I feel it. My pace is unhurried as I move against him. "You feel so good," I whisper.

He pulls me even closer, resting his forehead against mine and holding me tightly. It's so clear that he loves me, and it's become increasingly harder to deny that I feel the same way. Emotion throttles my heart and my throat. It's so much. It's too much.

"Sawyer," I rasp.

"Yeah?" His lips brush against me.

"Are you trying to make me fall in love with you?" I attempt to keep my voice light and teasing, but it comes out as a tearful plea.

He moves a hand to cup my jaw. "Is it working?"

I choke on my reply, feeling torn in half by overwhelming emotion and physical sensation.

"Sienna?" he asks in a hushed tone. His eyes search mine, and I'm about to fall over the metaphorical edge.

"Loving you is the most natural thing in the world," I breathe. "You're so easy to love."

His lips part and he slides his palm to the nape of my neck. "You—"

My thighs quiver as the spark catches inside of me. I cry out his name, and he slams his mouth against mine. I feel consumed, burning up from the inside as well as the outside. Sawyer roughly grips my hips as we fall apart together.

We stay wrapped up in one another for a while, unwilling to let the moment end.

"I love you so much," I mumble against his neck.

He dusts kisses down the side of my face. "I love you, too, but you already knew that."

"I've always loved you. I just hated you for a while."

He chuckles. "Sex so good you're confessing your love for me. Just like I planned."

"Not a humble bone in your body."

"You love me."

"Unfortunately, I do."

Chapter 36

Sawyer

"Are you sure I need this big microphone?" I ask with a frown. "The one on my laptop works fine."

Wes shrugs and leans over my desk chair. "Chelsea insisted. She uses this for recording her podcast with the history museum and says the sound is way better than her computer."

I tap the top of it. "I don't care how good it sounds if I can't get it to work."

"If only you knew someone in tech support," he deadpans.

I brighten. "You're a genius."

My phone rings as I prop it against the participation trophy from my first lacrosse tournament as a kid. Noah's face pops into view.

"Hi Coach," he says with a smile. "What's up?"

"Is the boss available? I need some IT help."

"Yeah, let me get her." He gets to his feet. "Do you need me to leave so you two can be all sweet and gross together?" he faux whispers.

I chuckle. "No, I legitimately need help with my computer."

Sienna comes into view looking delectable in a white sweater, glasses, and her hair pulled up in a ponytail. She tilts her head. "Why are you calling me on Noah's phone?"

"Because you never have yours at work, Mrs. Flintstone. Could you help me real quick? I'm calling into ESPN in twenty minutes and can't get my microphone to work."

"Is it turned on?" she asks.

"Yes, it's turned on." I roll my eyes and discreetly flick the power switch I hadn't noticed along the side. "Oh, it's asking to pair with Bluetooth."

"Mmm hmm." She glances at me pointedly over her glasses. "So go ahead and click to pair."

"It's very hot when you tell me what to do," I murmur. "Especially when you're wearing those glasses."

"Yuck, I heard that!" Noah gags from across the room.

Her lips edge upward. "Is it working now?"

She talks me through verifying that the microphone is correctly set up in the videoconferencing software, and we are officially in business.

"*Nya·we̜,*" I sigh with relief. "You're a lifesaver."

"*Čeḣ.* Call me once you're done, OK? I love you."

"Joining us today from the frozen hinterlands of Buffalo, New York, we have professional lacrosse player and all around goal scoring sicko, Sawyer Lane!"

Rocco Stone is a bombastic talk show host for the biggest and most influential sports network in the world. His outlandish antics and easygoing interview style have made him popular among younger fans, but he's also earned a begrudging respect among sports journalists for his breaking news sources. It's a really freaking big deal to be on his program.

I laugh. "Hey Rocco. It's great to be with you today. Thanks for having me on."

"Man, I just cannot believe some of these goals you're scoring lately," Rocco says. "I admit, I don't watch much lacrosse, but these replays people have been sending me are unreal. Talk me through what's happening here."

We watch some plays and chat for a few minutes, which helps me settle into a rhythm and calm my nerves. Rocco's casual but intense, bouncing around topics at a rapid pace infused with humor.

"Have you always played like this?" he asks. "Lacrosse is the national sport of Canada. Are they pumping out tons of trick shot Canucks up there?"

I chuckle. "I've been playing lacrosse since elementary school, but I used to be a much more conservative player. I moved to Six Nations Reserve in middle school and learned how the Haudenosaunee people play the Creator's Game, and that completely changed how I approach the sport."

Rocco sits forward. "The Creator's Game, what's that?"

A wide smile blooms across my face at the opportunity to discuss one of my favorite topics. "Lacrosse was given to the Indigenous peoples of present-day New York State by the Creator. The game originated with them, and the rest of us are given the honor of playing alongside them. Lacrosse is more than a sport. It brings communities together, it heals our bodies and our minds, and we play for those who no longer can."

"Wow! I had no idea lacrosse came from Native Americans." He whistles. "I'd love to talk to you more about that sometime, along with what you've learned from that tradition. We're out of time, but could we have you back next week?"

"Absolutely. I'd love to." My leg bounces against my chair.

I close my laptop lid and blow out a weighty exhale once the call ends. I did it.

Everything happens at once. Wes flings open my bedroom door, my phone starts ringing, and text notifications begin chiming.

"You did so well!" He gives me a high five before pulling me in for a hug. "You came across as really chill and knowledgeable."

"Thanks, man." I tap my phone screen. "Hey Rich."

"Sawyer!" My stepdad's voice booms into the room. "Your mom and I just watched your ESPN interview. You did great, kid. We're so proud of you."

"*Nya:węh*," I thank him in his Cayuga language. "I hope I represented the game well."

"You're an excellent ambassador for the Creator's Game and Haudenosaunee people." Rich sniffs. "Our community is lucky to have you."

"Everything I know, I learned from you," I say softly.

A text from Sienna pops up on the screen.

> **My Girl:** You were fantastic. Noah, Vinny, and I watched in the shop

> **My Girl:** Can I pick up some takeout and come celebrate with you over dinner?

> **Me:** There's nothing I'd like more

Another call comes in while Wes fetches us some celebratory beers, and I put it on speaker without looking.

"Hello?"

"You were made for TV!"

I cringe and accept an icy cold bottle from Wes. "Hi, Dad. You saw the interview?"

"I did. I'm telling everyone I see that my son is a natural on ESPN. They should hire you as a regular guest!"

I chuckle and take a sip. "I wouldn't go that far."

"Next time, make sure to focus more on your skills and accolades you've earned, like the gold medal with Canada at the international tournament last year." My father pauses. "It was nice of you to mention the Indian stuff, but that's not what Rocco Stone wants to hear about."

Wes raises an eyebrow from across the kitchen island, and I mouth "sorry" to him.

"That wasn't the impression I got," I reply. "And the Haudenosaunee need people to amplify their voices, especially right now when they're fighting to be included as their own nation in Olympic lacrosse."

My dad scoffs. "Your mother got you caught up in all that stuff when she remarried, but your home is still here in Canada. You don't need to fight for them."

"Yikes, man," Wes says once I hang up. "That's your father?"

I swig some beer. "Unfortunately, yes. Hopefully, you never have to meet him."

"And that's whose career opinions you care about?" He shoots me a sharp look.

"All right, all right. Point taken."

He sets his bottle down with a clatter. "You're good people, Sawyer. We're lucky to have you as an ally."

Sienna enters the kitchen bearing plastic bags from a nearby Italian restaurant. "What are we talking about?"

Wes gives her a squeeze before I sweep her into my arms. "I'm so happy you're here." I kiss the top of her head. "My phone's been blowing up all afternoon. I just talked to my dad."

Her disgruntled noise makes me chuckle.

"Well, in happier news, I picked you up some extra garlic bread." She begins unpacking the takeout containers.

I moan. "My favorite."

"Is Chelsea joining us?" she asks.

Wes nods. "She'll be home from work any minute."

"Great. Then we can all congratulate Sawyer while making sure his head doesn't get too big."

She gives me a peck on the lips, and I sit back into a barstool to contemplate how magnificent life feels at the moment.

Chapter 37

Kęnęhteh

February

Sienna

"Does anyone have Valentine's Day plans?" Vinny asks as I make some final notes in a support ticket.

Noah straightens the small table and chairs in the shop's waiting area. "I'm making my mom pancakes before she heads out to work tonight. I found some red food coloring in the back of a cabinet."

"That's adorable," I say with a smile.

Vinny laughs. "That bottle's probably from the Obama administration."

Noah frowns. "Food coloring doesn't go bad, does it?"

"I'm sure it's fine." I glance at the wall clock. "You guys can head out if you'd like. Sawyer's picking me up soon, so I'll close everything down."

A chorus of *ooooh's* fills the room.

"Is he taking you out for a fancy dinner?" Vinny asks.

"I actually have no idea." I close my laptop lid. "It's a surprise."

Noah gasps. "What if he's going to propose?"

I bark out a laugh. "We've been dating for four months."

"Boss Lady, if Sawyer freaking Lane ever asks you to marry him, *you say 'yes'*. He's famous!"

I guffaw. "Don't ever let him hear you say that. His ego doesn't need any more feeding."

"You have to be talking about me." The door jingles as Sawyer enters with a grin.

I look over my glasses at my employees. "See? I told you."

He casually leans against the wall with his arms crossed. *The man is a damn snack, and he knows it.* "Just about ready to go?"

"Yeah. Let me change real quick."

"I'm going to head out," Vinny announces. "See you tomorrow."

"Bye, Vin." I set my glasses on the counter.

Noah shoves his hands into his pockets. "Do you want to shoot around while Sienna gets ready?"

An easy smile spreads across Sawyer's face. "Sure. I always have a couple of sticks in my car. You'll just have to be a good shot, because I'm not doing a ball hunt in the mud."

I head to the back room to change out of my work clothes. We've had a few unseasonably warm days, so I opened a window earlier to air out the stuffy space full of tech repair equipment. The blinds are closed, but I can hear Sawyer and Noah's voices carrying from the parking lot.

"Can you teach me some more *Skaru꞉re̜'?*" Sawyer asks.

I hear a distinctive *whoosh* as someone throws the ball. "Sure. What do you want to say?"

"Well, it's Valentine's Day." Sawyer clears his throat. "How about 'I love you'?"

My stomach goes warm and gooey as I button a sleeveless corduroy dress over my white top.

Noah's smile comes through in his voice. "And this is just hypothetical, right? You're not trying to rizz up some Tuscarora girl?"

"I am absolutely trying to rizz up a Tuscarora girl."

Noah chuckles. "I love to see it. 'I love you' is *Ke̜nure̜hkwa'.*"

"*Ke̜nure̜hkwa',*" Sawyer repeats. "Like that?"

Hearing him speak my Native language never gets old and never fails to turn me all the way on.

"Yeah." The ball bounces on the blacktop. "She'll know that one. Everyone uses it."

"Give me one that'll stump her."

Noah's quiet for a few seconds. "*Skwáhye̜.* It means 'you're cute', in a flirtatious way."

Sawyer repeats it quietly under his breath. "Got it."

"Do you want to know how to say 'my wife'?" Noah's tone is playful, and I roll my eyes as I pull on some black tights.

"I'll come back to you for that one. She's not ready for it yet."

"But you are?"

"I'd marry your boss tonight if she'd let me."

Thunk. My boots slip from my hands and fall to the vinyl floor. *Did he just...*

"It's that serious?" Noah sounds as shocked as I feel.

"I'm as serious as a heart attack about her."

My heart races, and I lean against the workbench to take a few deep breaths. Surely Sawyer is joking, but he doesn't sound like he is. For as easily as we've slipped into familiarity with each other again, there's still so much we need to learn. I don't know how he'd respond in a crisis, or whether he wants kids someday, or what he wants to do with his life once he retires from lacrosse. Little things, too, like whether cookie dough is still his favorite flavor of ice cream, or how he folds his laundry, or where he'd travel if he had unlimited funds.

Marriage? That was something that enters the conversation once you've been together for at least a couple of years. That seems like a responsible amount of time to get to know the other person.

The front door dings again, and I scramble to step into my shoes.

"You don't have to rus—" Sawyer runs out of breath when I emerge in a flurry. "You look fantastic."

I pull out my hair tie and fluff my hair. "I hope this is OK for wherever we're going."

"Yeah." His eyes trace up and down my body. "It's perfect. You're perfect."

"*Nyaꞏwe̦*," I peck him on the lips and move towards the door, but he pulls me against him.

"Come here." He nuzzles my cheek. "I'm so lucky to be spending today with you."

"Ditto." I close my eyes and breathe him in.

He runs his index finger along the neckline of my dress. "This is going to be fun to unbutton later."

"Aren't you presumptuous, Mr. Lane?"

He nips at my ear with a low sound. "Are you going to make me work for it?"

"Always."

"You're serious?" I blink at Sawyer.

"I figure you probably still have some leftover aggression towards me, so it would be good to get that out."

"This seems dangerous."

"Only if you miss. So, don't miss."

The Throwing Pit features a plethora of entertainment options, with axe throwing at the center. My stomach clenches at the idea of dropping a weapon on my foot or accidentally injuring someone else.

"I really don't know about this," I say as an employee hands me a trio of small axes.

"You'll get the hang of it, I'm sure." Sawyer smiles and positions his body as we were shown in training: feet planted, arm back. I drink in the sight of his bicep flexing as he pushes his left arm forward and releases the axe with ease.

"Nice job!" the bespectacled college student says. "Your first throw is already close to the center."

His next two throws land similarly, and he retrieves them with a pleased glimmer in his eye. "Your turn."

I stagger my feet and nervously reach for an axe.

"Do you want some help? It would give me an excuse to touch you." Sawyer gently skims my waist with his hands.

"No, you'll distract me." I shake him off, and he steps back with a chuckle.

"All right, Miss Independent. Let's see what you've got."

I drop both arms behind my head and breathe out a shaky exhale. "Are you sure I'm not going to hur—"

"Throw the axe, Sen."

Thwack. Relief washes over me as I manage to hit the wooden target. And then I realize *where* I'd hit it.

"Have you done this before?" asks the kid with glasses.

I shake my head.

"Damn. OK." He looks at Sawyer. "You might want to hide the knives when you get home, bro."

"Jesus Christ, Sienna."

My blade sank into the middle of the bullseye. I smile and reach for the second axe. "Beginner's luck. Stand clear of the upcoming disaster."

Thump. Another bullseye, this one just to the right of the last.

"Do you play darts, maybe?" Glasses Guy asks. "Or softball?"

"She fixes computers for a living," Sawyer says.

Glasses frowns. "Well, that skill set shouldn't translate to this at all."

"Are you kidding me, Lanes?"

The three of us whip around to find Zeke standing with his arm draped around a beaming Genny.

Sawyer embraces his friend with a wide smile. "Hey man. What are you doing here?"

Zeke claps him on the back. "Getting my creative Valentine's date idea shamelessly stolen by you, apparently."

"Not true. We absolutely did not talk about this." Sawyer kisses Genny on the cheek, and I exchange warm hugs with them both.

"Do you mind if we crash your date, or would you prefer we keep to ourselves?" Genny asks.

I wave my hand. "Come hang out. We were just getting started."

"Correction: Sienna was absolutely kicking my ass. She's a shark." Sawyer tucks me into his shoulder.

Genny tugs on my arm. "I call dibs. Two teams: girls versus boys."

"No way." Sawyer pulls back. "You're not getting her away from me."

Zeke talks over both of them. "Good luck to Sawyer, but I know better than to challenge Genny on anything."

I smother a smile, feeling warmed from the inside by the friendships I've managed to form in the past few months.

Genny and I mop the floor with the boys and retire to a nearby booth to play cards while Sawyer and Zeke face each other.

I deal a game of UNO after we order a round of drinks. "So, when's the wedding?" I ask, nodding towards her engagement ring. It's beautiful and simple, like her, with an oval diamond in an antique setting.

Genny stretches her fingers to look at it with a smile. "July. It's not easy finding free weekends with professional athletes."

"I'm starting to see that." I take a tentative sip of my wine and find it palatable. "How did you know your relationship was heading towards marriage?" Her eyes widen and I panic. "I'm sorry, that's probably too personal. You don't need to answer that."

"No, no." She waves me off. "It's not. I'm just surprised you're asking." A sly smile lifts her lips. "I'm wondering *why* you're asking."

A blush creeps into my cheeks, and I manage a shrug. "None of my close friends have gotten married yet, so I was curious. It's such a big decision."

She chuckles around her glass. "Well, it's complicated, to be honest. Zeke and I have been close friends since birth, basically. There was mutual romantic interest once we were older, but we were both afraid to make a move and ruin the friendship."

This is a familiar story. I nod and lay down a card on top of hers.

"We were finally getting our acts together to give things a try when his dad passed away unexpectedly," she continues.

I gasp. "I'm so sorry. I didn't know."

"It's OK. It was shocking, and it completely devastated Zeke. His relationships with everyone fell apart after that, and we went through a long period of not talking." She smiles sadly. "When we finally reconnected, I was so angry and hurt about how things ended, so it took a lot of trust to get past that."

"I can relate," I say. "Sawyer and I have had a similar dynamic."

She circles the rim of her glass with her index finger. "I thought everything would be perfect once we were together, but it wasn't. We went through some really, really tough times and, frankly, I'm shocked we made it through." She glances up. "I can tell you that open and honest communication is *so* important. It's easy to ignore warning signs because you don't want to see them. It took you so long to get to this point, and the idea of losing each other again is just..." She shakes her head. "It's unthinkable."

I draw four cards. "I can imagine. I feel like Sawyer and I have done a good job communicating so far, but there's still a lot we haven't covered yet."

"You'll get there." Genny plays a card. "He's utterly besotted with you, from what I can see."

I smile. "Trust me, the feeling is mutual."

Chapter 38

Kanęharę'kye
Corn Planting Time / March

Sawyer

The Hideout is eerily quiet. A few cleaning personnel pass me on my way to Coach Travis' office, but otherwise the space is still. It's a big change from practice and game days, when the arena bustles with equipment managers, athletic trainers, and the crew prepping the turf.

Coach had texted asking me to come by, which was beyond unusual for a Tuesday. I knew better than to ask for details, so I showered and headed over immediately. My sneakers squeak on the freshly mopped linoleum as I come around the corner. Coach takes off his glasses when I enter, setting them down next to the tablet where he's reviewing game film.

"Lanes. Glad you're here. Sit." He nods towards a flimsy folding chair across from his desk, and I pray I won't break it. He winces when I carefully lower my large frame. "Sorry. I don't get many visitors here. I'd rather be on the floor drawing up plays."

"It's no problem." I attempt to cross one ankle over my knee before thinking better of it. "You wanted to see me?"

"Yeah." He runs a palm across his face. "This is usually a GM conversation, but I wanted you to hear it from me."

Icy tendrils shoot across my chest. The General Manager would only be involved if we were talking about...

"Am I being cut?" I ask, hoping he doesn't notice how my voice shakes around the edges.

Coach barks out a laugh. "Cut? You're a dynamo, Lanes. No one is cutting you." He shuffles through a disheveled stack of yellow Post-it notes until he pulls one out. "The team is being offered multiple draft picks for you."

My pulse hammers chaotically, trying to find its rhythm. "A trade?"

He smirks and taps a pencil against the desk. "Today *is* the trade deadline. Look at you using your context clues."

I narrow my eyes at him while a smile threatens to break free.

He slaps a Post-it in front of me. "Miami wants you for their playoff push, and they're willing to move heaven and earth to make it happen." *Tap tap.* "A first-round pick this year and a second-round pick next year, plus a practice squad player we don't really need."

I stare at the figures in his handwriting. "Is this finalized?"

"No. That's why I brought you in." He leans back in his chair. "Would you be interested in playing for Miami this season?"

"Why does it matter? It's the team's decision, not mine."

"Yeah, but you're not just any player." He slides the pencil behind his ear. "It would hurt like hell to lose you, Sawyer. As a player, certainly. I'm not sure we can sustain a deep playoff run without you. But as a person, as a leader?" He shakes his head. "The loss would be incalculable."

I look up to find a softness in his eyes. We're used to seeing Coach have it all together, always focused on the next shift. He looks more uncertain than I've ever seen him at this moment.

"I just—I don't understand." I try to relax my shoulders, but they seem stuck. "I'm a second-line guy. I'm not the top scorer. I'm—"

The words die on my lips as Coach fixes me with a withering look. "I'm too old to talk you through a self esteem crisis. But the reason you're on the second line is because you can make something out of every play, no matter how stunted or messy. You can set up Zeke for a flashy goal, or turn a loose ball into the filthiest backhand pass I've ever seen. You don't need the best players around you to make things happen."

I smother a grin.

"You make everyone around you play better because you clean up their messes and elevate their game. You're a goddamn force on the floor. Opposing teams have to stretch their best defenders to cover our top line, and then come back to deal with you. It's a huge advantage for our offense. You're the most creative, flexible, and downright disrespectful player on the Outlaws. And that's really saying something, considering Jammer's here, too."

A laugh bubbles out of me. "Should I take that as a compliment?"

The pencil gets tossed next to his keyboard. "I'd rather cut off my shooting arm than lose you, especially to fucking *Miami* with their speedboats full of cash." Coach scowls. "But your contract is up after this season, and I know they made you an offer in August."

I nod slowly. "They did."

"This would be a way for you to try them out and see if it's the right fit for you. And Buffalo would get some draft capital for the future." He folds his hands behind his head. "Selfishly I hope you'd go play with them for a few months, get it out of your system, and then come back to us on a long-term deal next season. But you have to do what's right for you."

I wipe my sweaty palms on my thighs. "How much time do we have to make a decision?"

He glances at the wall clock. "Two hours. I thought you might want to talk to some people before you decide."

"They'd want me down there for this weekend's game, I assume?" My mind races with the logistics this would entail.

"Yeah." He pauses. "And they want you to relocate to the area for the remainder of the season. They've made a big push to keep their players local to cut down on commuting costs and build camaraderie."

My stomach drops. "My whole life is in Buffalo." *Sienna's in Buffalo, and we've missed out on so much time together already.*

"I know. It's a big ask, and I'm pissed they're making it." He leans on his forearms. "You can say no and we'll turn down the offer. The owner and GM gave me the right of refusal on this, because it's you."

"OK." I get to my feet and hope my legs hold up under me. "I'll get back to you before the deadline." I extend my hand to him. "Thanks, Coach."

His grip is tight. "Good luck, Sawyer."

My brain feels like I took a hard hit into the boards as I pull away from the arena. I'm scrambled, mixed-up, and confused. All I know for sure is that I need to get to Sienna as quickly as possible.

She doesn't keep her phone on her while she's working with clients, so I merge onto the highway and head north towards Niagara Falls. I don't have much time to figure this out, and her input is essential.

Thoughts are flying through my head too fast to process. Will she and I be OK if I move to Miami for the next three months? I'll need to move out of my apartment with Wes, since it's Outlaws player housing. Where will I live? How will I get back and forth to home games and to the Miami airport for away games?

What if I get down there and mess everything up? What if I'm not good enough to carry a team, and their ownership regrets trading away so many valuable assets? What if the fans and the other players hate me?

Sienna looks up when I pull open the door to Three Sisters Tech. Her lips lift in a smile, but she cocks her head in confusion.

"Hey, Coach Lane!" Noah pops up from the nearby table where he's working on a computer. "Are you here to see Sienna?"

"Yeah, once she's available." I shove my hands in my pockets and glance to where she's showing an elderly client how to pay his electric bill online.

"Is it important?"

I shuffle my feet against the thin carpet. "Yeah, it is."

"Let me help." He approaches the counter with a smile. "I can take over with Mr. Rickard, if you'd like."

"Thanks, Noah," Sienna smiles gratefully before nodding her head towards the back room where she stores equipment.

The door clicks quietly behind me. "I'm really sorry to bother you at work."

"It's no problem. Is everything OK?" She squeezes my hand.

"Yes. No." My anxiety rises rapidly to the surface now that she's with me and I can let down my guard.

She wraps herself around me against the door. "What's going on?"

I bury my face in her hair and inhale deeply. "I'm being traded to Miami."

She freezes. "What?"

"I have the option to refuse it, but it makes a lot of sense for me and the Outlaws to agree."

"What does this mean? I'm not—" She shakes her head, as though trying to jostle the pieces into place in her brain. "I don't understand."

I tug her towards the workbench and lift her onto it so we're eye-to-eye. "If Buffalo trades me to Miami, they get some high draft picks to use in the next two years. They can select some great rookies for the future, in exchange for me playing for the Storm for the remainder of the season." I hesitate. "I almost signed with Miami in the off-season, so it's a place I've been interested in."

"Wait. Wait." She rubs circles on her forehead. "This is a lot."

"I know. I'm sorry." I squeeze her thigh. "I have an hour to consider the offer and let Coach Travis know, otherwise I wouldn't have thrown everything at you like this."

"So, you would fly to Miami or wherever on the weekends?"

I bite the inside of my cheek. "I'd move there until June or whenever they're eliminated from the playoffs. So, it could be six weeks, it could be three months."

"Oh." She swallows.

"If this creates a problem for us, then my answer is immediately no." I tilt her chin up. "I'm not willing to jeopardize our relationship for any reason."

"A three-month separation isn't a huge deal. I'd miss you, but we're adults and can make that work." She tightens her grip on my waist. "But if you've been considering signing there long term, is that still on the table? Would you move there permanently next season?"

My eyes flutter closed because it's a question I'm afraid to answer. "It's a possibility. I can't pretend it's not an appealing option if I like it down there. It's a chance to challenge myself with an emerging team, and to be a leader in a way I can't be in Buffalo."

Sienna sniffs, and I open my gaze to find her eyes watery.

"Baby, don't cry," I whisper. "That's a problem for another day. We don't need to think about that now."

"Why didn't you tell me you've been thinking of leaving the Outlaws?" she asks with a tremor in her voice. "This feels like it's coming out of nowhere, but you've been sitting on it for months."

I haven't let her in all the way, and I know it. "I should have. I'm sorry." My forehead rests against hers as I wrap her in my arms. "I've been trying to ignore my feelings, and that hasn't done me any favors."

"I can't move to Florida," she says quietly. "My business is here. My community is here. *Your* community is here."

"I wouldn't see my parents and Alex as often, but we'd be OK."

She shakes her head. "Not just them. All the people here who love you, including your Native communities. You've blossomed as a person and a player because of the people who have raised and coached you in Six Nations and Tuscarora. You're loved and accepted here."

Something twists in my insides. "That means a lot. Thank you."

She scans my face. "You want to do this, don't you?"

I nod. "For this season, yes. After that, we'll re-assess."

"Then we'll get through it together." She smiles, but it doesn't reach her eyes. "I'll come visit when it makes sense."

Relief floods my veins, but it doesn't feel like I expected. "You probably won't even have a chance to miss me."

"Yeah." She kisses me with trembling lips. "I'll come over after work and help you pack."

Chapter 39

Sienna

Climbing the steps to Sawyer's apartment feels like walking into a funeral.

I'm a mess. I tried to hold it together for him at the shop, but the reality of him leaving is hitting hard. It feels wrong to think of him moving away, even if it's theoretically temporary. The possibility of a permanent relocation weighs heavily on my heart, and I can't shake the dark clouds that have taken up residence around me.

Wes opens the front door, and he looks like I feel. His green eyes are dull, when they're typically full of life. His hair is disheveled as though he's been shoving it out of his face without regard for aesthetics, and he never changed out of his gym clothes.

The barest smile ghosts over his lips when he sees me. "Hey."

"Hey." I shift from foot to foot, uncertain how to proceed. We've spent time together since Sawyer and I have been dating, but I have to assume that's coming to an end now that they'll no longer be playing for the same team.

He holds out an arm. "Do you need a hug? Because I do."

Relief washes over me. I nod silently and step into him.

He squeezes me tightly. "We'll get through this. You still have a family here, even if Sawyer is in Miami. We still want to see you. You know how the Oneida adopted the Tuscarora into the Five Nations in the 1700s? Consider this a similar situation."

I choke out an emotional laugh. "How are you so nice?"

He smiles. "It's my superpower. Come on in and join the packing party."

The living room is bustling with activity. Moving boxes litter the floor alongside piles of lacrosse equipment. The kitchen island is taken over by flipped-open boxes of pizza, a twelve-pack of beer, and a bottle of wine. Sawyer's friends—*our* friends—are scattered throughout the apartment.

Chelsea stops mid-bite of pizza to pull me into a hug. "How are you doing?" she asks quietly.

I swallow and plaster on a smile. "I'm OK."

She fixes me with a look. "You don't have to pretend for me."

I glance over to Sawyer, who's sorting through equipment with Jamie and hasn't noticed me yet. "No, but I should for him."

She squeezes my hand. "That's fair. But let's make plans to get together this weekend so you can talk, OK?"

I nod and move further into the room, where I'm intercepted by Genny. She hands me a glass of wine and steers me towards one of the kitchen stools.

"I'm making him a packing list to get through the next four weeks. I figure you'll probably see him by then, either in Florida or here, so we just need to take it one month at a time." She slides a pad of paper toward me. "What should we add to this? Does he take any medications, or have hobbies, or something you know he uses daily that he wouldn't want to forget?"

I blink at her neat handwriting filling the page. "Um, I'll have to think about it." I jump in my seat at the sound of packing tape being peeled loudly as Zeke closes up a box.

Genny leans closer. "Or would you rather pack his clothes? There are suitcases in his bedroom. I know it's really loud out here."

"That might be best," I say quietly. "I'm feeling kind of overwhelmed."

She pushes my glass towards me. "Take all the time you need. We've got things under control out here."

I touch Sawyer's shoulder as I walk by. "Hey. I'm here."

His face lights up, and he scrambles to his feet. "I'll be right back, Jammer."

Jamie nods, his jaw tight and his eyes hollow. He returns my smile, but it's superficial.

Sawyer closes the bedroom door behind us. "Thanks for being here. Everyone is helping so much, and that's eased my anxiety a bit."

"I'm glad." I kiss his cheek before turning to the open suitcases on his bed. "I'm assuming you'll mostly need workout clothes down there? Maybe a few options for going out with teammates?"

He watches me. "Yeah. That sounds good."

I open his drawers and start pulling out clothes. I carefully count out pairs of athletic shorts, shirts, and socks. "You'll need to do laundry once a week, but I'll pack you a few extras of everything in case you get busy."

"Sen."

I fold and roll each item, tucking them into the corners of a roller bag. "I'll put your gym stuff in this one, and regular clothes in the other. That'll make it easy to find what you need in case you're not able to unpack right away. Is the team putting you up in a hotel?"

"I can stay at the team house near the arena." He approaches me, and I zip around him towards the closet.

I grab hangers full of suit pieces and lay them on the bed. "You'll need arrival outfits, too, I suppose? I'll see if Chelsea can help put a few together for you. I'm hopeless at that stuff."

"Sienna." Sawyer lightly grips my upper arms. "Stop for a minute."

"I can't," I whisper.

A tear leaks from the corner of my eye, and he brushes it away with his thumb. "Talk to me. I know this is hard. And sudden."

I swallow past the lump in my throat. "It's OK. Don't worry about me. I just need a little time to adjust to the new normal, and then I'll be fine."

He cradles my face in his palms. "I don't want you to just be fine. I want to support you through a tough situation that I'm directly responsible for putting you in."

I wipe away my tears with annoyed fingers. "The best thing is to get you to Miami safe and sound so you can start settling in. We'll figure everything else out along the way. When is your flight?"

He scans my eyes with the ghost of a frown. "Early tomorrow morning. Wes said he'll take me to the airport."

"I'll take you. I can drop you off and then head into work." I press a soft kiss against his lips. "I want to see you off."

He flexes an open hand on my back. "Thank you. I'd like that."

I rest my head against his heart for a few seconds before summoning the will to continue. "Let's finish packing so you can get some sleep."

"Let me know when you get in," I whisper against Sawyer's lips.
"I will."

We're on the curb outside the Buffalo Airport, stretched over each other like second skins. The sunrise softens his brown eyes, and the last thing I want is to leave him here.

"I'll check the team schedule and find a weekend to come down there." I thread my fingers through his hair.

"I can't wait." He manages to pull me even closer. "We'll see each other soon. You'll be sick of seeing my name on your phone."

I nod. "I'll keep it on me more often. *Kęnuręhkwa'*."

"I love you, too." He kisses me reverently, and a nearby passenger whistles in approval.

I wave and smile as he hauls his bags through the sliding doors and into the terminal, making sure to keep the tears at bay until I'm back in my car and out of view.

Thirty minutes later, I park and lay my forehead on the steering wheel. The shop doesn't open for another two hours, and the last thing I want is to be alone right now.

It doesn't take long before a familiar blue sedan pulls up beside me in the lot. I wipe away my remaining tears and exit my car.

Hazel stops in her tracks, her eyes wide with surprise. "What are you—What happened?" She drops her work bag and jogs to me.

"Everybody's OK," I choke out. "But I need to talk."

"Of course. Come inside and I'll make coffee." My sister drapes an arm around my shoulder and steers me towards her apartment building.

"I'm so sorry to bother you after work." I sniffle and wrap myself in a fuzzy blanket. "I know you must be exhausted."

Hazel hands me a steaming ceramic mug, and I gratefully wrap my hands around it. "It's no problem. I'm too amped up to fall asleep, anyway. Rough night in the ER. Lots of dumbass college students making bad decisions on spring break."

I smile weakly and take a welcome sip before updating her on the changes in the past eighteen hours.

"Ho-ly." She sets her cup down with a clatter. "I had no idea. I haven't checked the news since before I went in for my shift." She squeezes my kneecap. "Tell me what you're feeling. What you're *actually* feeling," she clarifies when I open my mouth to respond.

I pause. "Honestly?"

She nods.

I inhale deeply. "I didn't even know he was unhappy with the Outlaws, and it scares me that he was keeping it from me. I worry that he's listening to the wrong voices in his life, like his father, instead of the people who know and love him the most. His continued insecurities about his career reek of Derek Lane. And what if this leads to him signing a long-term deal down there? We can deal with a short separation, but to live apart seven months out of the year would not be a great foundation for a new relationship." I catch my breath. "I'm afraid to lose him after everything we've been through to get to this point. And I'm worried that I may not know him as well as I thought."

Hazel exhales. "That's a lot. And I'm really proud of you for being able to put words to all of these anxieties. That's not easy for anyone, especially you."

"Is that a...compliment?"

"We'll call it a compliment, yes."

I smile around my coffee mug.

"OK, first order of business: Sawyer needs some better communication skills." She reaches for a notebook on the coffee table and starts writing.

My lip twitches. "Are you...making me a to-do list?"

"I know how you operate." Her pencil flies across the page with gusto. "So, you'll need to have a conversation with him about why he wasn't open about this stuff. The Outlaws discontent, the previous offer from Miami, all of it. I think there's room in that discussion to bring up your concerns about his dad, but maybe feel that one out. You might need to wait a bit for that."

She scribbles some more notes while I watch.

"The long-term deal thing…that's going to be a wait and see situation, unfortunately." She looks up. "Miami will have to approach him to ask to sign an extension, or to re-sign him during August free agency. So, that may not even happen."

I swallow. "OK."

"He may play for them for the next few months and discover it's not the right fit, for any number of reasons. Maybe the coach is a jerk, maybe the owner is cheap, maybe his teammates can't find the back of a net to save their lives."

A soft chuckle rumbles in my chest, and it's a relief to feel some unexpected joy.

"A question I have for you is: Do you trust him? And do you trust *yourself* to read the situation as it develops?"

I sigh. "I thought I did. I thought we got past the old anxieties and mistrust back in Jamaica."

Hazel taps her pencil on the paper. "You worked through a lot, but you've probably been in a honeymoon cocoon. Shit has, unfortunately, just gotten real, and it's normal to experience some growing pains together."

"That's a good point." I gnaw on my lower lip.

"And one more thing." She scrawls more. "You should take this time to get your life back in balance. Don't think I don't notice how many hours you work every week, when there's nothing in that shop of yours that couldn't wait for the next business day."

I frown. "You know I have to work three times harder than anyone else to be taken seriously in my industry. It's hard to earn trust from clients, especially men."

"I love you, but you're full of shit."

My mouth pops open. "Haze!"

"Well, you are." She sits back against the couch with crossed arms. "You work yourself to the bone and wind up becoming a hermit. How many of Sawyer's games have you been to? How often do you go out with friends?"

I cringe. Both numbers are extremely low.

"You love to read. How many books have you read this year? How often do you park your butt on the couch and just *relax*?"

I itch the back of my neck. "OK, I see your point."

"You've made time for Sawyer, but if your entire life is work and a man, no matter how dreamy he is, you're going to burn out and lose sight of yourself."

Yikes. I hadn't thought of it that way.

Hazel's face softens. "Sawyer's trade could be an opportunity for you to reconnect with yourself and the people around you. That'll help distract you while he's gone."

I fall forward and rest my forehead on her shoulder. "Thank you."

She hugs me tightly. "Go home, take a nap, and show today who's boss. Text me and let me know how you're doing, all right?"

I nod and give her a shaky smile. "I promise."

Chapter 40

Sawyer

I step outside the airport and immediately begin sweating.

The March temperatures in Miami are pleasant, all things considered, but I'm absolutely roasting coming from still-wintry Buffalo. I lug my bags to the side and begin stripping off layers until I'm cooler. I plop down onto a steel bench to figure out my next move.

I call an Uber to take me to the team house before tossing off a message to Sienna.

> **Me:** Landed. Can't wait to get you down here. It's warm enough to wear your bikini *lip bite emoji*

My Girl: You realize that's Hazel's, right?

Me: I'm assuming she'd gift that to you if she knew all the action that thing saw in Jamaica

My Girl: I'll see what I can do.

Me: Send pics *eyes emoji*

A text comes in from a Miami number as my driver arrives.

Unknown: Hey Sawyer! I'm with the Miami Storm's social media team. Could you stop by the arena this afternoon to get fitted for your gear and take shots with the team photographer? We want to feature you in promos for this weekend's game. Thanks!

"I guess we're hitting the ground running," I mutter.

"Hey man. Welcome to the house." My new teammate opens the front door just as I'm raising my hand to ring the doorbell. "I'm Chauncey. Come on in."

I flip through my mental team roster as we walk into the sprawling ranch. *Chauncey Bradford. Face-off specialist and second-year player from Towson, Maryland. He posts a lot of trending videos on TikTok, based on my in-flight research.*

"Nice place." I look around at the stucco walls full of bright artwork.

Chauncey shrugs. "It's all right. Not bad for a free place to live during the season." He gestures vaguely toward the living room. "You can put your stuff over there."

"Do you go home in the off-season?" I make my best attempt to neatly stack my pile of luggage in a corner.

He flops onto the brown leather couch. "I work for my dad's investment firm in Manhattan when I'm not playing here." An Xbox controller is thrust in my direction. "Wanna play Madden? I was just about to start a new game."

"I appreciate the offer. Maybe later." I smile hesitantly. "Is there a bedroom I should—"

"Sawyer, right?" A shirtless blond behemoth emerges from the nearby kitchen. "Aidan Ross. Hot Pocket?"

He holds out a plate, and I tentatively grab one. "Thanks, I'm starving. And yeah, I'm Sawyer." I immediately wince as blistering hot cheese squirts into my mouth on the first bite. "Mmm, ham and cheddar," I manage to choke out.

Aidan Ross. Third-year defenseman from Mooresville, North Carolina. His Instagram page is full of brand-sponsored posts for protein powders and creatine, along with gratuitous weightlifting videos.

"Has Chaunce shown you around the place?" Aidan asks, starting on a second Hot Pocket.

"Not yet. I was wondering where I—"

A toilet flushes, and a slender guy, who can't be more than twenty-two, materializes from the bathroom. "Do *not* go in there for a while," he says seriously.

"Seriously, Keegan?" Chauncey retches while thumbing through defensive formations on his controller. "Not cool, bro."

"Oh, hey." Keegan strides over and outstretches his hand. "You must be the new guy."

Keegan Finch. Rookie forward from Chatham, New Jersey. He posts videos making kombucha and talks about his comic book collection on YouTube.

I grit my teeth through the overwhelming desire to immediately wash my hands. "Sawyer Lane. Nice to meet you."

"We've got another roommate, too, but he's never home," Aidan says.

"I thought Matt was around today?" Keegan asks.

Matt Henderson. Fifth-year goaltender from Syracuse, New York. A complete ghost on social media. I couldn't find a trace of him anywhere.

"Nah. He's out doing whatever weird shit he does on a daily basis," Chauncey replies.

I'm in the entirely wrong age group and socioeconomic bracket for this living arrangement.

"I'm sure I'll meet him soon." I shift on my feet. "Is there a particular bedroom I should move my stuff into?"

"Bedrooms are full," Chauncey says without taking his eyes off the TV.

"...what?" I tilt my head in confusion.

"Chauncey's sitting on your bed right now." Aidan pounds his chest and burps. "That couch is really comfortable, though."

What in the actual eff? I rub my forehead. "I need to get fitted for my equipment at the arena. Does anyone need anything while I'm out?"

"We're good, man," Chauncey says.

"See you around." Aidan wipes his hands on his sweatpants. Keegan drifts out of the room without saying anything.

Get me out of here.

I'm twitchy by the time I arrive at the Eye, the arena where the Storm play. So far I'm loving my first impressions of Miami, even if my housing leaves something to be desired. The city is alive with vibrantly colored storefronts, Latin music blasting from cars, and the hum of pedestrians rushing to and fro. I have every intention of lying in the sun at every opportunity and working on my tan. I've spent my entire life living in cold climates, but have never felt made for them. My body and soul drink in sunshine like water.

The situation at the team house is...unfortunate. I'm an extrovert, but even I need some occasional quiet time without people around. Not to mention, I'm hoping to talk Sienna into the occasional spicy video chat. I plan to keep myself busy, but it's going to be tough to manage. Especially if Chauncey insists on playing video games in my "bedroom" every day.

I can make this work. It's only for a few months. Everything else will be great.

I meet with the Equipment Manager, who sets me up with my new uniform and team-branded gear. The social media team is ready to take official photos as soon as I'm fully kitted out. I dump everything into an empty stall in the locker room and take in the space as I get dressed.

It's the nicest locker room I've ever been in. Everything feels brand new, which makes sense since the team has only been in the league for three years. The stalls are spacious, the team logos on the carpet and walls are pristine, and there are bins of extra supplies available throughout. It even *smells* new, which is a major upgrade over the eye-melting mustiness of a typical locker room.

I could get used to this.

Neil: Heyyyyyyyy teammate!! I saw the trade news late last night!

A grin breaks across my face as I set my shoulder pads down to respond to my friend's text. He signed with the Storm during free agency in August, and I'm elated to be on the same team with him.

Me: YOOOO brother! Can't tell you how pumped I am to play with you again! I bet we can still make some magic together on the floor

Neil: That's right. Six Nations' finest, reunited at last! I'm flying in on Friday, so let's meet up before practice and I'll show you around the neighborhood

I buckle my helmet in place and open my phone camera to get a look. My stomach drops at the sight of myself in a new uniform. I look pretty snazzy in gold and black, but it hits differently than the classic orange, black, and white of the Outlaws. I snap a photo giving a thumbs-up sign and send it to my group chat.

Me: New threads

Wes: Sick

Wes: And by sick, I mean I'M sick that you're wearing another team's jersey

Z: Do you have to rub it in our faces that you're cheating on us?

Me: You should see this facility. It's like a Ritz-Carlton

Wes: The Hideout might be a Best Western, but she's loyal and reliable

Z: Unlike you

Me: Hey! Rude

Me: You alive over there, Jammer?

I fiddle with my gear for a minute, hoping to get a response from Jamie before I head into the photographer's office, but my phone stays quiet.

"It's good to fucking see you, Lanes." Neil claps me on the back two days later as we hug in the lobby of his hotel. "It's been a while."

I grip him tightly, more emotional than expected at the sight of him. "I'm really glad you're here." I hold the embrace longer than usual, and he gives me a pat.

"You doing OK, man?" he asks, concern etched on his features.

I smile tightly. "Yeah, I'm all right. No worries."

His eyes narrow slightly, and I know he sees right through me. "If you say so. Let's head down to the Riverwalk. It's not far, and it's a great way to see a bit of the city."

"Let's do it."

Miami weather is pretty freaking perfect today. Warm without being too hot, and an appreciated lack of humidity. Bayfront Park beckons us with its spacious greenery and sparkling fountain as we leave behind the busyness of downtown.

"So, how have your first few days been?" Neil asks. "Are you settling in?"

I bite the inside of my cheek. "Things are good. I'm living at the team house and feeling like a dinosaur next to all those young guys."

He stops walking. "You're at the team house? That was full, last I heard."

I scratch the back of my neck. "Yeah, it is."

His jaw ticks. "Are you sleeping on an air mattress or something?"

I cringe. "The couch."

"Oh, what the—" Neil runs a hand over his face. "I can't believe this. The richest team in the league is making its new star player sleep at a frat house rather than pay for a hotel or long-term rental? It's not hard to provide basic accommodations."

"Whoa there, killer," I joke and jostle him with my elbow. "I'm a big boy. If I'm miserable, I can talk to the GM, but I'm making it work for now."

"It shouldn't be like this." He starts walking again, but his pace is faster and his steps heavier.

I adjust my stride to catch up, which isn't too difficult since I have a few extra inches on him. "How did you manage to be a commuter? I wish I could've flown in for games and continued living in Buffalo."

His long, dark braid swishes as he stomps along the picturesque path hugging the Miami River. "They were more open to it because it was a condition of my free agency. I help take care of my mom in Six, and I don't like to be away from home for too long."

I nod. Sherry Jonathan is a pillar of the community, and she's beginning to struggle with the effects of multiple sclerosis. "That's reasonable. I'm glad the team was flexible."

"They have been. But I'm planning to sign elsewhere next season," he says. "The travel is too much with my family obligations, and I want to be more involved in the community, too." He glances over. "What about you? Think you might sign an extension and stay here?"

"It's a possibility, depending on how the rest of this season goes. But it would complicate my personal life, and I'm not a huge fan of that."

His smile is slow and easy. "Do you have someone special back home?"

A grin splits my face. "Do you remember my friend Sienna?"

Neil's eyes go wide. "Hell yeah, I do. You had a huge crush on her."

"Well, I still have a huge crush on her." I flip through my phone until I come across a picture of us.

He whistles. "You're dating up, Lanes."

"And I know it." I navigate to the website for Three Sisters Tech. "She owns a computer repair business on the Tuscarora rez now."

"Haven't your people stolen enough?" he teases. "Now you're taking our best women, too."

We laugh and continue along the path to Biscayne Bay. Hours pass in what feels like minutes, and I feel more like myself than I have in days.

"I want you to consider staying with me on game nights," he says once we return to his hotel. "I can request a room with two beds, so you could sleep like a real boy on the weekends."

I open my mouth to wave him off, but think better of it. "I might take you up on that. Thanks for the offer."

"You can thank me by teaching me how you managed to pull a Native baddie. I need some help in that department."

I chuckle. "You've got the charisma, man. You don't need my help."

"Just wait until you hear about my miserable dating life." He claps me on the shoulder. "I'll see you at practice tonight? Pack an overnight bag, and we can have a sleepover afterwards."

My eyes crinkle with laughter. "You've got it."

Chapter 41

Sienna

"Have a nice day."

I smile tightly at the customs agent as I cross the Canadian border. It's always nerve-wracking, and it's been months since my last trip so I'm feeling rusty.

My phone rings from its dashboard holder, and I blindly answer while navigating multiple lanes of traffic to get to the correct highway. "Hello?"

"How's my favorite sister-in-law?"

I grin. "Don't you think you're jumping the gun a bit?"

"Not at all," Ellie says. "Sawyer's going to wife you up in no time at this rate."

"Do I get a say in the matter?"

"Not really, no."

A chuckle rumbles from my chest. "What's up, Elle?"

"Just checking to see where you're at so I can time dinner. Your parents are already here."

"I just got on the QEW, so I should be there in an hour. Do you need anything?"

"Just your lovely self. Can't wait to see you."

I hum happily as I cruise towards Hamilton, Ontario, where Ellie and Alex have a home. I'd been tempted to beg off due to work when she invited me for dinner with our families, but I'm taking Hazel's advice and pushing myself out of my comfort zone.

My phone rings again, and I smile widely when Sawyer's name and picture light up the screen.

Well, the name and picture *he* chose when he entered his number. He snapped a photo of us kissing on the way back from Jamaica, and it warms my insides every time I see it.

"Hello World's Best Boyfriend," I answer.

His laugh is low and gravelly, and my stomach flips in response. "Nice to see you've kept that name in your contacts list."

"Hopefully it helps you aspire to greatness."

"Absolutely. What are you up to? Sounds like you're driving."

"I'm on my way to Alex and Ellie's for dinner." I flick my turn signal on to change lanes.

"Without me?" He gasps with feigned outrage.

"Believe it or not, I do occasionally have a life." *Very occasionally.*

"I know, and I love it." The creaking of wood and twine tells me he's settling into the hammock in his backyard. "I'm so happy that you and Ellie have become close."

"She's great. It's like having another sister." And I mean it. Ellie has been the best surprise, and that's helped me open up more readily to the rest of Sawyer's friends. "Are you tired? You sound sleepy."

He yawns. "Yeah, a bit. I pushed myself extra hard at the gym earlier."

"Are you sleeping all right? I never sleep well in a new place."

"You slept just fine in bed with me in Jamaica." His voice slides over the words like velvet, and I grip the steering wheel at his tone. "You were so comfortable that you even overslept a few times."

"Yeah, I was exhausted from dealing with you."

"Or from fighting your overwhelming attraction to me."

I roll my eyes. "You're avoiding the question. How are you sleeping? You haven't told me much about your house."

He clears his throat. "I'm sleeping fine. The house is really nice. The backyard's beautiful, and I wind up spending a lot of time out here."

"Your room must be empty, unless it came with some decor already?"

A pause. "It's OK. I don't mind living out of suitcases. It reminds me that this is temporary, and I'll be on my way back home to you soon."

"I miss you." I feel incredibly lame for feeling that way, but his absence gnaws at me. I pride myself on handling things on my own and not being reliant on anyone else, especially not a man. But *this* man makes me want to break all my rules.

"I miss you, too," he says softly. "You'll be down here in two weeks, and I'm going to smother you."

"I can't wait."

A comfortable silence falls between us as the countryside rolls by my window.

"What are you up to this week? Anything fun?" he asks.

"Wes and Chelsea invited me over to watch *Smoke Signals* tomorrow night. Apparently everyone will be there."

Sawyer groans. "Dammit. I wish I was, too. I miss that crew so much."

"Speaking of Wes and Chelsea, have you been keeping up on your Spicy Book Club reading?"

I hear the smile in his voice. "I have. And we're going to re-enact a couple of those scenes while you're down here."

I bite my lip. "Which ones?"

"The shower scene, for sure."

I murmur in approval. "You won't mind getting your clothes wet?"

"My clothes won't be the only thing getting we—"

"Sawyer! I'm driving!"

His laugh reverberates through my car. "Flustering you is my very favorite pastime."

"Don't distract me."

"Does Wes have a new roommate yet?"

"No. It's late in the season, so the team is holding off until the summer. I think they're hoping you come back, to be honest."

"I might," he says quietly.

I swallow. "You can't say things like that and get my hopes up."

"Sen..."

I shake my head to clear it. It wouldn't benefit either of us to discuss the future right now. "I should probably let you go. I need to start paying attention to exit signs soon."

"OK. Drive safe." He pauses. "Say hi to Jamie for me tomorrow, would you? He's been hard to get a hold of lately, and I really miss him."

"I will. Want to video chat tonight, and I can pass you around to your family?"

"I'd love that. I love *you*."

"Love you, too. I'll talk to you later."

Chapter 42

Nakahę̀·re·t

It carries it away / April

Sawyer

I'm playing stiff and I hate it.

There's always an adjustment period when playing with new teammates. They don't know your tells and your rhythms, and you're still learning theirs. But at the moment I feel like I'm thirteen years old again and playing with all the flexibility of a robot.

I'm on the floor with my roommate, Keegan, and three other offensive players. Keegan has good instincts, but as a rookie he's not seeing plays develop as well as a veteran, so he keeps missing passes and not being in position to throw to. I just kicked a ground ball to him from the corner and it whizzed right past his stick.

"Sorry, Lanes." His breathing is fast and rough as he squirts water into his mouth once we return to the bench. "I don't know how I keep missing you."

"Don't worry about it. We'll link up on the next shift." I bop him on the head with my glove.

Neil leans over from a few seats down. "He's squirrelly. You'll find Lanes in the places you *least* expect a player to be, so look there first."

Keegan gives him a weak smile. "You two used to play together?"

"Yeah, as kids." I take the water bottle from him and drink.

"Does Coach know? He should put you two on the same line," Keegan says.

I shrug. "I've mentioned it, but he didn't seem interested in mixing up the groupings."

"Jonathan! You're up." Coach calls down the bench and Neil immediately leaps over. "Don't get too cute out there."

I blow out a weighty exhale as I watch our offense scramble to make something happen. It's been hard to score all night, and it's not because the other team's goalie is on fire. We're missing chances and just can't seem to get things going.

By the fourth quarter, the entire bench is cranky. We're somehow only down by three goals thanks to Matt bailing us out in the crease, so the game is still within reach if only we could get some scoring.

Coach tosses his whiteboard on the ground. "We're not doing shit out there, so we're shaking things up. Lane, Jonathan, Finch. I want you heading out the door as soon as the transition guys head this way."

Neil, Keegan, and I bump fists as we watch our defenders shut down the other team yet again. Matt nabs the ball with his large goalie stick and tosses it out to a Storm player.

"Here we go." I smack the railing, and the three of us jump to our feet. Three defenders come off the floor, and we hightail it out the bench door and onto the turf.

Keegan brings the ball into the offensive zone while Neil and I jog up the sides. The kid looks nervous, so I catch his eye and he passes to me. We've done this a thousand times, so I know Neil's going to be in the slot on the right. I fake out my defender and send the ball lasering over to Neil, who stops to size up the defensive configuration.

He's buying time for me, so I quietly sneak closer to the goal, taking a few shoves to the back from the other team. But they're focused on Neil.

His right shoulder twitches, and I'm ready for it. He casually tosses the ball behind his back, his braid swinging from the force, and it lands directly in my stick.

It's in the back of the net before the goaltender can react, and the Eye explodes with cheers.

"That's the way to fucking do it!" I launch my body into the air, and Neil meets me halfway to celebrate.

He taps me on the helmet with a grin. "We gave 'em the ole Six Nations razzle dazzle."

"Nice pass from the line, Finchy." I throw my arm around Keegan's neck. "You read that well."

"Thanks, man." Keegan smiles widely. "Hell of a goal."

Coach raises his eyebrow as we pile back onto the bench. "Nicely done. Stick together for the rest of the game, you three."

The goal seems to light a fire under the rest of the team, and suddenly we're flying all over the floor creating chances. On our next shift, I assist on Neil's goal, a tricky behind-the-net dunk shot he wedges past the goalie. We manage to tie the game with thirty seconds remaining, and we have one last chance to score before time expires. If we win, the Storm secure their very first playoff berth in team history.

"I'm going to draw a few defenders and then pass you the ball, OK? Get yourself to the net and I'll find you," I say to Keegan.

He nods. "Got it."

Neil taps my shin with his stick. "Let's go entertain the stardust out of Creator."

I laugh as I walk to my position near the midfield line. Everything hinges on Chauncey winning this face-off, which he does easily.

Neil comes up with the ball and tosses it to me as time ticks down. We've got one shot at this, and the timing has to be perfect. I jog slowly into the zone, killing seconds and watching for Keegan out of the corner of my eye. He slowly steps towards the slot, his movements so slight that no one notices. The kid has stealth, I'll give him that.

Ten seconds remaining. I start moving faster and looking towards my left. Two defenders follow. I push towards the net and meet a brick wall of bodies, drawing another defensive player.

Five seconds. I throw the ball blindly to the right, praying the rookie is where he said he'd be.

Sneakers slide on the turf as everyone turns, and I see the dawning horror hit the defenseman across from me as Keegan winds up and sends an absolute rocket over the right shoulder of the goaltender.

The team bolts off the bench and piles onto Keegan until we're a mass of sweaty gear on the floor.

"Finchy's our hero!" Aidan yells from somewhere at the bottom of the pile. "We're going to the playoffs!"

Keegan's grin could be seen from space, and for the first time I really and truly feel part of this team.

"We're going out for drinks to celebrate," Chauncey says as I towel-dry my hair after my post-game shower. "You coming with us, Lanes?"

"Sure. Just let me check in on my girl first." I dig in my locker for my phone, and I'm surprised to find it already vibrating.

"You're whipped." He jostles me playfully with an elbow.

"Joyfully so." I slide to answer the call without looking. "Hello?"

"My boy! You looked good out there tonight. Big win, taking them to the playoffs for the first time!"

I grit my teeth and balance the phone on my shoulder while I pull on pants. "Hi Dad."

"How does it feel to be on a team that actually appreciates you?" His voice is lightly teasing, but my stomach curdles in response. "I notice they're including you on all the game promo graphics. They know you're a money maker."

I roll my eyes. "I'm not so sure that's the case."

"Buffalo only featured you occasionally, is all I'm saying."

"I know, I know." I toss my bag over my shoulder and wave to the guys on my way out of the locker room.

"How are you liking it down there? You looked better tonight once your coach mixed up the lines."

"Uh, it's good. I'm starting to click with some of the other shooters."

Neil jogs to catch up with me and points to the Uber app on his phone. I give him a thumbs up to indicate I'm willing to split a ride back to the hotel.

"Well, keep it up," my dad says. "This upcoming playoff run could determine the rest of your career."

Neil looks up at me with a raised eyebrow. "Your dad?" he mouths.

I nod and he wrinkles his nose.

"And don't get distracted by things at home," my father continues. "I know you're sweet on that Bissell girl, but there are plenty of beautiful women in Miami, and—"

"Trust me, she's irreplaceable," I cut him off. "I've got to go, Dad. My ride is almost here."

"I see Derek is just as delightful as always," Neil says a minute later as we pile into the Uber. "You've learned to tune him out, I hope?"

I shrug. "He has some good points. But yeah, I try not to let him get to me."

He scoffs. "I've never heard him make a single good point. You're an amazing player, Sawyer, and you have a really good head on your shoulders. Trust your instincts, not his."

"Thanks, man." I smile and type out a quick message to Sienna.

> **Me:** Can't wait to see you next weekend. Missing you like crazy tonight

> **My Girl:** I'm counting down the days

"You've been great with Keegan, you know. He's been playing small all season, but you got through to him tonight." Neil adjusts the stick in his lap. "You've come so far. You used to be the anxious new guy, and now you're the one doing the encouraging and guiding."

"I was lucky enough to have a friend who made a huge difference for me at a young age." I throw an arm around his neck. "Thanks for always believing in me, man."

"Right back at you." He bops me on the head.

Chapter 43

Sienna

I touch down in Miami determined to keep an open mind.

The city is a rollicking ball of energy, which Sawyer must love, although I'd much rather find a quiet spot on the ocean. The weather is perfect, as the heat and humidity of summer have yet to set in, and I allow myself to imagine my life here if Sawyer were to stay.

The idea of possibly giving up my business makes me ill, but I've decided that's Future Sienna's problem to worry about.

I barely have time to get to my seat before the game begins. I closed Three Sisters Tech early so I could hop on a flight, but there was a tight window to get here before opening face-off.

The arena is luxe, gleaming, and sterile. It's missing the history and character of the Hideout, like a middle schooler wearing a brand-new Nirvana t-shirt. Everything is *too* perfect.

Sawyer looks good on the floor. He's not flowing with the play quite as well as he did in Buffalo, but I chalk that up to getting used to different teammates. Some passes miss, ground balls squirt away, and players run into each other. It's as though there's sandpaper on the turf adding a bit of resistance to everything he does, but he still manages to score a hat trick and assist on several goals.

And the fans love him. It's clear from the loud cheer he receives when the team is introduced, and the crowds of people clamoring for his autograph between halves. I see quite a few "I like my goals scored on SICKO MODE" signs go up each time he touches the ball, in an apparent nod to his goal song here.

It suits him, but I miss "Layla."

I wander the concourse after the Storm win, my thoughts streaming as quickly as the Niagara River. I can see how this could be a place that makes him happy. If the team and the fanbase adore him, then it's hard to ask for anything more. Sawyer deserves so much love and recognition for what he brings to an organization, and I find myself thawing at these early signs of his acceptance.

I don't want to lose him. I don't want to keep up a long-distance relationship for more than half the year. But if he's thriving here, I won't stop him.

I skid to a stop in front of a familiar food vendor. I've walked in a circle and have yet to find the freaking friends and family room.

I take a deep breath and blink back the prick of frustrated tears. I spin to walk in the opposite direction and run straight into a wall of muscle.

"You're here." Sawyer sweeps me into his arms and nearly crushes me. "I'm so glad you're here."

He's holding me so tightly I can barely get a word out. "I couldn't find the—"

"It's OK. I found you." He buries his face in my neck, and I deeply inhale his clean scent.

He doesn't let me go, and that's when I feel his shaky breath against my skin. "Hey." I rub circles on his mid-back. "I'm right here. I'm not going anywhere."

I expected a happy and flirtatious Sawyer after a month apart, so this is disorienting.

I remain pinned in his arms as we sway together. He sinks a hand into my hair and gently tips my head back. His kiss is full of urgency and need, but lacking heat. It feels like he'd rather climb inside my skin than rip my clothes off.

A discreet cough reminds me that we're in public. I drag my mouth away from his and glance over his shoulder to find a sheepishly grinning Neil.

"Sorry to interrupt," he says, his warm eyes dancing.

I physically peel Sawyer off of me and throw my arms around Neil. "You're a lot taller than the last time I saw you at fifteen."

He squeezes me. "You're about the same height. *Ow*."

I step on his toes, and he laughs.

"It's so good to see you again, Sienna."

Sawyer pulls my back against him and wraps his arms around my shoulders. "Do you mind if we give Neil a ride back to the hotel?"

"Not at all. Do you need to stop by your house for anything?"

"Nope, I'm good." His smile is a little too bright, and his words a little rushed.

A flicker of concern licks at me, but I push it to the side. "Then let's head out."

"I'm going to drop my bag off in your room." Sawyer gives me a quick kiss as we enter the lobby. "Grab a drink at the bar, and I'll join you shortly."

"I'll order you something." I squeeze his hand, and he heads in the direction of the elevators.

"I'll miss my roomie tonight." Neil smiles warmly and holds a chair out for me in the hotel restaurant. "It's been fun having him around."

I cock my head. "You room together for road games, right?"

His smile falters slightly. "Well, because of his housing situation, I offered..."

A low rumble of alarm rolls through my stomach. "His...housing situation?"

He swallows. "What has he told you about the team house?"

"What's going on?" I ask quietly.

He sighs. "I didn't realize he hadn't told you. All the rooms are taken, so he's been sleeping on the couch. I told him to stay with me on home weekends, too, so he could get some rest occasionally."

I rub my temples. "He's told me about his roommates, and he calls me from there all the time." I frown. "Come to think, he's almost always calling from the backyard or walking back from the gym."

Neil scratches the back of his head.

"This makes no sense. The team wanted him down here so badly, but they had nowhere to put him?" I ask.

His jaw ticks. "They didn't want to *pay* to put him up somewhere. Ownership is loaded, but they're cheapskates about anything the public doesn't see." He takes a sip of his just-delivered mojito. "Arena, uniforms, even player salaries are well funded because those are visible. Everything else?" He shakes his head. "It's disappointing."

"I had no idea." I stare into the minty depths of my drink.

"I'm sure he didn't want you to worry," he offers with a half smile.

Ice clinks against the glass as I stir with my straw.

I hate being the last to know what's going on in his head. And it scares the heck out of me that he has such a hard time being honest with me, especially after the trade to Miami caught me unaware.

And if the Storm won't give him a place to sleep, how much do they really value him?

"He's lonely," Neil says softly. "He doesn't want to admit it, but he misses his people. You, of course, but also his family and friends. I think this experience has been a mixed bag for him, but he doesn't want to complain. Especially since you're sacrificing for him to be here." His eyes flicker behind me, and I know Sawyer is approaching. "You'll be good medicine for him this weekend."

"*Nyaꞏweˌ,*" I give his hand a quick squeeze.

"*Nyoh,*" he replies in Onondaga.

Sawyer kisses my cheek as he pulls out the chair next to mine. "What did I miss?"

We wave good night to Neil on our way towards the elevators. Uncomfortable thoughts swirl through my mind as we walk in silence.

Why would he continue to keep things from me? Everything seemed to be going well down here, but it's clearly not. How can I ever trust him if it seems he doesn't trust me?

"You OK?" Sawyer folds his arms across my chest as we wait. "You're quiet tonight."

I grind my molars and debate how to approach this. *"It's easy to ignore warning signs because you don't want to see them,"* Genny had told me a couple of months ago. She's right: the idea of Sawyer and me not working out after everything we've been through is unthinkable. I'm not leaping to that conclusion at this point, but it's growing more difficult to ignore our obvious communication difficulties.

"I'm tired," I finally respond, like a coward. "It's been a long day between work and travel."

He softly kisses my shoulder. "Thank you so much for making the time and effort to come down."

"Of course." I lean into his torso as I watch the floor numbers tick down.

His lips ghost down the side of my neck and goosebumps spread like wildfire. "I've missed you. So much."

"I've missed you, too." I reach behind and slide my fingers through his hair.

He runs his palm down my tricep. "I've been thinking a lot about the first time we fooled around on the desk."

"Is that what we're calling that now?"

"And there are so many hot moments I replay in my head, but do you know what my favorite part was?" He nudges me forward into the open elevator, and I pull him close to me as the doors close.

"Was it when I told you I hated you?"

Sawyer cradles the back of my head and just barely brushes his lips against mine. "You kissed me back."

"Did you expect me to sit there like a dead fish?"

"Kind of." His mouth quirks up in a half-smile. "Or push me away, and I would've deserved it. But you kissed me like you wanted it, and it gave me hope for the first time."

"I *did* want it." I grip his collar. "I would've rather died than tell you that, but I didn't want you to stop. I wanted you to consume me."

He groans and presses me into the wall, his kiss urgent and insistent.

"I need you," he rumbles. "I'm desperate for you."

"Me too." We should really have a conversation before we fall into bed together for the weekend, but damn it's hard to think straight with his hands on me.

His teeth drag along my earlobe and down my neck. "I want you on every available surface of that hotel room."

A shiver rolls through me, and I pull at his hair. "Tell me which ones."

He chuckles deeply against my chest as his fingers skate beneath the edge of my denim skirt. "Well, obviously the desk, for old time's sake."

"I packed the black bikini."

"Fuck yes." He grips the back of my thigh. "I'm going to show you all the things I wish I could have done to you last time."

I press against him with a quick glance at the elevator floor numbers as we come to a stop. "We should probably—"

"Get to the room as fast as possible?" His grin is wicked.

"No, I mean—Hey!" The carpet rushes up to greet me as he bends and tosses me over his shoulder. "I'm wearing a skirt!"

He tugs it down until I'm covered. "I've got you." He jogs down the hall, and I laugh as I bounce against his back.

"You're ridiculous."

He slides me down his chest and to my feet before pressing my body against the room door.

"Can you find the key?" he asks, tilting my head back for a deep kiss.

I frantically pat my pockets before pulling it out. "You don't play fair."

"Life's too short to play fair."

Fuck it. We'll talk later.

He scans us in and we stumble inside with me latched onto his lapel. My skirt and shirt hit the floor before we've taken more than a few steps. I shove his suit jacket down his arms and huff with frustration when it gets caught on his stupid muscles. He takes over so I get to work on his belt. A line of hastily discarded clothing trails behind us.

"First order of business." He scoops under my thighs and tosses me onto the bed. "Get the rest of these clothes off."

He reaches for my bra, but I push him off and roll us over until I'm straddling him. I flick open buttons as quickly as possible, but short of ripping his shirt off it's going to take me a minute.

"You need shirts with snaps," I grunt.

"I'll see what I can do." He traces his fingers down my shoulders and slides my bra straps down. "You are so fucking beautiful."

Once we're skin-to-skin, he pulls himself up to rest on the headboard and settles me against him. "Are you ready for me? I know it's quick."

I nod and he groans at the feel of me. "I love that you want me as much as I want you." He drops his head to my neck and exhales shakily.

"I do." My thighs quiver at the effort to slow down and adjust to him.

"I'm so glad you're here," he whispers. "I'm missing my gravity without you."

I flinch as he presses deeper, and he stops moving.

"I'm sorry, I shouldn't have—"

"Don't treat me like a delicate flower." I sink lower. "I just need a second."

"I've got all the time in the world, baby." He grips my hip as he holds himself steady. "And I want to spend every moment of it with you."

A few minutes later, I try to find my calm in the gradual slowing of Sawyer's heartbeat as I lay against his chest. I want to bury my head in the sand and pretend I'm not worried about him and worried about us. But something's wrong and it's haunting me.

He tenderly runs his fingertips through my hair. "Do you want to go to the beach tomorrow? I probably shouldn't hold you hostage in bed *all* day."

"Sure, that would be nice." I swallow. "Hey, so…"

"Hmm?"

I take a steadying breath. "Are you happy here? You seemed anxious when I first saw you tonight."

He continues to comb through my hair. "There's been a lot of change to get used to, but I'm settling in."

"How are things with your roommates? Are you comfortable there?"

Another pause. "They're good guys. I had my doubts at first, but we've gotten to know each other better."

I rake my nails through the hair on his chest. "Can I meet them this weekend?"

He kisses my forehead. "I hadn't planned on it. It's a bit of a frat house over there, and I'm looking forward to having some time away with you, is all."

I rest my cheek on his shoulder and let my emotions wash over me as he drifts off to sleep. We haven't seen each other in a month, and spending our limited time together having heavy conversations is the last thing I want.

Maybe he just needs more time to open up. Reconnecting this weekend will help.

Maybe if I keep telling myself that it'll become true.

Chapter 44

Kę́·ʔnęhs

It has mercy / May

Sawyer

*W*ell, shit.

That's exactly what I said when I realized who our playoff opponent would be.

I knew it would be hard to be back at the Hideout, but I completely underestimated just how difficult it would be.

The Storm weren't scheduled to play the Outlaws the rest of the season, so I thought I could avoid this. The lacrosse gods did not smile upon me, however, as we were promptly scheduled to play each other in the first round. It's a win-or-go-home scenario, and I'm not sure what would be worse: getting knocked out of the playoffs by my old team, or breaking their hearts by ending their season with my new one.

365

All in all, it feels like marching to my death as I enter the arena, exchanging handshakes and hugs with various building staff.

"We miss you, Lanes!" My favorite security guard gives me a high five and pulls me in for a bro hug. "You've got to come back to Buffalo!"

I smile tightly. "We'll see."

I come around the corner and nearly trip over a crouching Paige Bomberry, one of the Outlaws' athletic trainers, who is tying her shoe.

"Hey asshole." She grins up at me, her shoulder-length dark hair pulled back in a tight ponytail. "Who let you in here?"

"I know, right? You can't find good help these days." I extend my hand to help her up, but she bats it away and gets to her feet.

She fist-bumps me instead. "It's good to see you, Lanes. Staying healthy?"

"Fit as a fiddle."

"Well, no offense, but I hope you step on a thumbtack or something tonight. Hey!" She lands a soft punch in my midsection when I pull her into a headlock.

I laugh and release her. "It'll be a battle between these two teams, that's for sure. I'll see you on the floor, Dr. B."

Turning down the hallway towards the visitors' locker room feels wrong, as though I'm attempting to make the Earth spin in the opposite direction.

I can do this. It's just another game.

"Doing all right?" Neil asks softly as he straps on his pads in the stall next to mine.

I summon my Fake It 'Til You Make It persona and smile widely. "Never better."

"Hmm." He raises an eyebrow but says no more as we pull our jerseys on.

I'm not sure what to expect when I jog onto the floor for warmups, and my heart is in my throat as the familiar jumbotron and Outlaws logo at midfield come into view. The arena is lightly buzzing with activity and music as fans begin to find their seats. A roar rings out from the lower bowl, and I look up to find Genny, Chelsea, and Sienna standing to cheer for me.

A grin splits my face, and I hoist my stick in the air to acknowledge them. My girl looks stunning in a pair of jeans and my Outlaws jersey t-shirt. I blow her a kiss, and the flush in her cheeks is visible from here.

God, I love that this woman is mine. And that six months into our relationship I can still make her blush.

The Outlaws start to trickle out from the locker room, so I make my way in their direction.

The guys are happy to see me, and it feels good to get in some overdue hugs and stick taps. A few groups of nearby fans hold up "Welcome back, Lanes!" signs and cheer. *Maybe this won't be as bad as I've been envisioning.*

Jamie shoots on net, and I wave as he jogs by. His eyes catch mine, and what looks like resignation flashes in them before he slowly walks to where I'm standing at midfield.

"Are you avoiding me?" I ask with all the lightheartedness I can muster, when I've never been so serious about a question.

He looks past me and waves at Neil. "I'm trying to save you from my bad mood."

I tap my stick against his shin. "What's going on?"
He shakes his head.

I haven't seen Jamie act this low since his life took a hard left turn and he changed everything early in his NLL career. Before that, he would barely talk to me unless it was to snipe at me.

"Can we grab a drink after the game?" I ask. "I miss you."

His gaze snaps to mine. "I find that hard to believe."

I take an unconscious step back, thrown off by his unexpected tone. "What?"

"Forget I said anything," he grumbles before heading back towards the net.

Stunned, I watch him leave with an ache in my chest. I don't notice Wes at my shoulder until his voice startles me.

"He's in a funk," he explains with a half-hearted smile. "He's barely talked to any of us since you left."

"Is everything OK at home? With Connor?"

Wes leans forward onto the end of his stick. "As far as I know." He pauses. "I think he's having some big feelings about you accepting the trade to Miami."

I blink as I process what he's saying. "Why?"

He shrugs, but the look in his eyes tells me he has a good idea. "You'll have to ask him."

During the first TV timeout, the Outlaws play a Thank You video for me on the jumbotron. It's full of my most memorable moments and goals, including winning the Cup two years ago and the hidden ball trick I pulled off with Zeke last season. That might be my favorite trick shot ever.

I blink quickly as I watch the montage, praying my tears stay behind my eyes. This type of video is standard for longtime players returning to the Hideout after leaving for another team, so I knew it was coming, but I'm emotional nonetheless.

I wave to the crowd in gratitude at the conclusion, and the Outlaws bench bangs their stick handles against the boards as a sign of respect.

Home. This place is home. These teammates, these fans, this city is home. Nothing else comes close, no matter how nice it is.

"Nice video," Matt says, shaking his long hair back before pulling his goalie helmet on. "They must've really loved you here."

I squirt some more water in my mouth before reaching for my own helmet. "Well, the feeling is mutual."

The Storm are up by three with a minute left in the game, and barring disaster we'll go on to secure our spot in the semi-finals. Zeke just scored a gritty goal while the Outlaws were shorthanded, so we're lined up for the ensuing faceoff.

"Jammer." I acknowledge Jamie as he gets into position next to me near the face-off circle.

"Lanes." His voice is low and gruff.

Chauncey and the Outlaws' face-off guy are taking their time getting set, and each second feels like an hour standing next to a belligerent Jamie.

"You've gotta talk to me at some point, right?" I say without looking at him.

He nudges me with the end of his stick. "Do I?"

I glance over, hoping to find a teasing glint in his eyes, but find them expressionless. "Is everything OK? I can't read you."

He scoffs and jostles me with his hip as he adjusts.

The face-off specialists are jawing at each other, and this is taking for-freaking-ever.

"I hate losing," Jamie mutters, "and I especially hate losing to *you.*"

My eyes snap to his as the ref finally blows his whistle and the face-off circle springs to life.

"I don't like this anymore than you do," I say softly as we wait for someone to come up with the ball. "It's breaking my heart to be playing here tonight."

The ball squirts loose and I dart after it, but smack into a motionless Jamie instead.

"I don't think you actually care." He stares me down, and my feet forget how to move.

"What the hell, Jammer?" I try to dodge him, but he pushes me back.

"I. Don't. Think. You. Care." He shoves the side of my helmet and my chinstrap pops loose.

I shake him off but he's relentless, keeping pace with me as we head towards the Outlaws' end. "Are you trying to pick a fight with me?"

"Yes." He slashes my stick, and my feet get caught up in it. "You said you wanted to talk, so let's talk."

"Why are you acting like a grumpy teenager?" I stumble into him and we both crash into the boards.

Play continues around us as I struggle to push Jamie away, but he grabs my jersey and my balance tilts.

"Knock it *off*," I hiss, kicking at his sneakers.

He throws his gloves to the floor. "Hit me. You know you want to."

What in the ever-loving hell is going on here? "No, I don't." I turn to leave, but he clenches my collar and yanks.

We tumble to the ground in a mess of gear as the crowd cheers and a whistle blows. I shake my gloves off so I can better pry his fingers loose.

"Seriously, what the fuck, Jammer?" I heft my bodyweight so I can roll us and pin him, but he's not getting the message. "I don't want to fight you!"

He yanks on my facemask and sends my helmet to the turf before jettisoning his own. "You're pissed at me. Just hit me and get it out of your system."

"You're the one who's pissed, not me." We roll again, looking more like amateur wrestlers than prize fighters. I'm six inches taller, but he's got a slight weight advantage, and he's *strong*.

Gloved hands pull on Jamie's shoulders. "You don't want to do this, Jamie," Wes says. "Knock it off."

"Thirty-three, get out of there before you get hurt!" a ref snaps his way.

Arms hook around my torso as a braid flips into view. "Let him go, Jammer." Neil attempts to pull me away, but Jamie has a death grip on my jersey.

His fist connects with my face before I can register that it's even a possibility he would hit me.

I manage to cushion my fall before my head connects with the turf, but I'm reeling. Pain radiates from my cheekbone, and my vision whirls.

I'm vaguely aware of a flurry of activity above me before whistles frantically blow. The crowd is roaring a mix of boos and cheers. I try to count the blades of turf as I wait for my vision to stop spinning.

A gentle hand touches my shoulder. "Are you with me, Sawyer?"

The voice is familiar, but the figure in black is blurry. "I think so."

Paige crouches close to my face. "Your trainer is patching up a teammate in the locker room, so I'm helping out until she's back. What hurts?"

I sigh with relief at her presence. "Just my face and my pride. I'm dizzy, but it's getting better."

"Good. Can you sit up?" She holds out a hand and carefully pulls me into a seated position.

I blink at the ruckus across the floor. A yelling Jamie is heading towards the locker room, and a furious Neil stomps toward the penalty box.

"I can't believe he punched me."

Paige examines the back of my head for bumps. "Trust me, I'll be lighting into him about that in about two minutes. Follow my finger with your eyes, please."

Keegan appears at my side as she finishes. "Want a hand?"

He and Paige help me to my feet, and the remaining players hit their sticks against the benches in support.

"I can walk on my own, but thank you," I tell them.

Keegan cringes. "You somehow got a penalty for unsportsmanlike conduct, but Coach said to go to the locker room since there's less than a minute left in the game."

"Got it."

Paige follows me to the visitors' bench door with my gloves and helmet. "Tell your trainer to check for signs of a concussion. I think you're OK, but I'd feel better if she did a full check."

"Thanks, Dr. B." I hesitate. "Will you ask him if we can talk after the game?"

She gives me a half-smile. "I'll ask, but I wouldn't get your hopes up."

I sit in my locker stall, staring at the wall until my teammates come barreling in. They're in a celebratory mood, but all I can think about is how I managed to lose my best friend.

Chapter 45

Sienna

To say I feel stunned is an understatement.

My emotions were running high for Sawyer's first game back against the Outlaws, but I never could have predicted how things would turn out.

My hands fly to my face. "What is happening?!"

"Why is Jamie...oh!" Sawyer's mom, Marianne, gasps a few seats down from me when Jamie lets loose his punch.

"I can't believe this is happening," Chelsea says softly.

"He's OK. Look." Ellie grabs my forearm with a reassuring squeeze and gestures towards Sawyer sitting up on the floor with an Outlaws trainer.

Phew.

"Wes got knocked out last year, and it nearly killed me." Chelsea drapes an arm around my shoulders. "I'll text Paige and get an update."

"Is something going on with Jamie?" I ask again while watching Sawyer head toward the locker room.

She gnaws on her lip. "Yes, but I don't know what exactly. He's been a ghost since Sawyer's trade, and we've barely seen him. I can tell he's upset, but he won't talk about it."

Genny leans into view. "Has Sawyer said anything about it?"

I shake my head. "Just that Jamie's been hard to get a hold of. I didn't realize there was animosity."

Rich crosses his arms. "I might need to have a talk with Tom Montour."

"Richard." Marianne fixes him with a withering look laced with amusement. "Sawyer and Jamie are grown men. They'll work it out without getting their fathers involved."

Forty-five minutes later, I'm still waiting for Sawyer to exit the building, and my nerves are on edge. The rest of the Storm players and staff have come out to the team bus, and I convinced his family to head home across the border with promises to update them later.

Neil catches sight of me across the parking lot and jogs over. He pulls me in for a hug.

"Is he OK?" I ask.

He shakes his head. "Physically he's fine aside from the shiner he'll wake up with. Emotionally, he's a mess. He was right behind me, so he'll be out in a minute."

I nod. "He's staying at my place tonight, so I'll talk to him."

"Good." He squeezes my shoulder. "He needs you."

Neil disappears onto the team bus just as Sawyer comes out into the parking lot.

He looks like hell. Purplish bruising blooms across his cheek and under his eye, his white button-down is disheveled, and he looks like a guy whose world just turned upside down.

Probably because it did.

I hold out my arms to him, and he steps into them without a word. We hold each other silently for a while and let the sounds of the city pass us by. We have a hundred problems to solve, but we've got each other.

"Want to go home?" I ask.

"Yeah."

Sawyer's quiet on the drive back to Niagara Falls. He ices his face with one hand and holds mine with the other while I contemplate conversation starters.

The longer we go without talking, the more agitated I feel. It's hard to know where to start, because I need to dig through the web of unknowns he's woven.

"How are you feeling?" I finally ask.

He rubs his thumb over my knuckles. "Better now that you're here."

I side eye him. "I want to know how you *actually* are."

"Can't a guy be romantic?"

I turn into my apartment complex, put my car into park, and lean back against my seat. "What's going on, Sawyer?"

"I wish I knew."

I bite the inside of my cheek and fight to keep my breathing even. I want to feel calm and in control of my emotions but, as usual with Sawyer, I don't.

He slowly lowers the bag of ice from his eye. "You're upset with me."

"I admit I'm feeling frustrated."

"I don't know what's going on with Jamie," he says. "I've tried to talk to him ever since the trade, and he won't give me the time of day."

"I don't care about Jamie right now." I blow out a heavy breath. "I want to know why you haven't been honest with me about what's going on in Miami?"

He stills. "What do you mean?"

I grip my hands on the steering wheel and drop my head between them. "This is my own fault for not talking to you last weekend while I was there."

"Sen, I—"

My keychain jangles as I yank it from the ignition and throw myself out the door. I want to scream from overwhelm, and I don't trust myself not to say something I'll regret.

His steps sound behind me as he struggles to keep up. I hesitate for a moment, knowing I'm dragging around an injured man, before mounting the stairs to my apartment at a more normal pace.

"I'm so sorry, Sienna." He rests his shoulder against the wall as I fumble for my key. "I know I haven't given you all the information."

I stop before turning the knob. "But why? Why can't you trust me with everything in your life?" My eyes search his. "I was totally blindsided that you weren't happy in Buffalo, and now here we are again."

"I do trust you." He reaches for my cheek, but I bump the door open with my hip.

"Your actions suggest otherwise." I toss my keys onto the kitchen counter and rip open the freezer door.

"I know, I—" He looks down with surprise at the fresh ice pack I thrust into his hand. "Thank you."

I wrench a bottle of water out of the fridge and set it in front of him with a slosh. "You should hydrate."

"*Sienna*." He grabs my wrist before I can snatch it away. "Can we sit and talk?"

Tears sting my eyes. "We lost thirteen years together because we couldn't figure out how to communicate with each other. I'm so afraid we're falling into the same old patterns."

"Come here, love." He pulls me to him, and my resistance folds.

My shoulders curve over his as he lifts me and walks toward the couch. I bury my face in his neck and breathe deeply.

He gently sets me down and lays his head in my lap. "I love you so much, Sen. Please let me explain."

I wrap my torso around him and lose my fingers in his hair. "I'm listening."

His chest shudders on an exhale. "I'm assuming Neil told you about the team house?"

"Yes. He didn't realize I didn't know."

"Because a normal person would've told his girlfriend." He sighs. "At first I didn't say anything because I didn't want to worry you. But then I felt so tremendously stupid for pushing to make this trade happen when the Storm didn't even care enough to make sure I had a bed to sleep in."

"I wouldn't have felt that way." I lean back against the couch but continue playing with his curls. "It's not your fault."

"I've been so afraid you wouldn't want to keep a long-distance relationship going," he says softly, "especially when things were so clearly not working out with the team initially."

I tilt his head up with my hands. "Do you honestly think I would leave you after everything we've been through to be together?"

"You don't deserve to be saddled with someone like me," he rasps. "I'm a mess. Always have been."

"And I love your mess." I slide down to join him on the floor. "I always have. It's the perfect complement to *my* mess."

The tiniest smile tugs at his lips. "You're not a mess. You're beautiful, brilliant, and accomplished."

"I pulled a knife on you for offering to make strawberry shortcake with me."

He nips at the corner of my mouth. "Have I ever mentioned what a fucking turn on that was?"

"You're a psycho."

"Guilty as charged. I like you spicy."

He brushes his lips against mine, and I pull away with a groan. "Don't try to distract me. I'm still mad at you."

"I'm going to make sure you end the night *not* mad at me." He runs his palm down the side of my neck and I shiver. "I have a few ideas."

"Stop it." I bat his hand away. "I love your sensitive soul, but you have to quit thinking I'll leave if you show any vulnerability." I kiss the tips of his fingers. "I love you *because* of your vulnerability. Please don't take that away from me."

"I'm so sorry." He folds me into his arms. "It's hard for me to imagine anyone truly loving me with all my flaws."

"That sounds like your dad talking," I point out.

He blows out an exhale. "Ouch."

"Well, I don't appreciate lumping his opinions in with your real family and friends."

We hold each other for a minute. His heart beats strong and steady against my chest, and I melt into him.

"Are we OK?" Sawyer asks quietly.

"We're OK." I press a kiss against his jaw. "Unless you're keeping any other secrets from me."

"Not that I can think of. Oh, wait."

"Don't say that."

He flicks open the button at his wrist and rolls up his shirt sleeve. "I do have one last thing I haven't told you."

My eyes scan the familiar inky tapestry of his skin. "What's that?"

He taps on the small strawberry tucked amongst his forearm tattoos. "This is for you."

I still. "What?"

He pulls me onto his lap. "I got this when I was nineteen. Strawberries have always reminded me of you." He nuzzles my neck.

"But why?" I stare at the petite fruit. "We weren't even talking then."

I glance up when he doesn't respond.

"I was...pretty beaten up about our fight at the Tuscarora picnic that summer." He won't meet my eyes. "I was desperate to win back your friendship, but teasing you after you won the pageant went horribly awry, and I thought for sure you'd never talk to me again." He swallows. "I always hated calling you Princess, but I leaned into the villain role you cast me in. I regret it."

I stare at the tiny splash of ink and try to pull my emotions back from the edge. "You stopped using that nickname after our second time together in Jamaica."

He nods. "I couldn't keep up the act anymore once I was kissing you at every opportunity." I feel his gaze on me as I continue looking at the tattoo. "Seeing this strawberry used to make me think of the good years we had, and I'd look at it to keep myself steady when we'd bicker."

I'm pretty sure I can feel my heart physically cracking like the winter ice on Lake Erie. I grip his arm with a shaky hand and fight back tears. "Why didn't you tell me months ago?" I whisper.

"Because I knew you'd feel bad. And I figured this might be a step too far in the weird stalker direction."

It's hard to breathe through the heaviness sitting on my chest. "Can we be done with secrets and doubting each other now?"

"I'm done." He kisses me softly. "I promise. Let's start fresh."

"I'd like that." I cradle his face in my hands, doing my best to avoid his bruises. "Now, what are you going to do about Jamie?"

Chapter 46

Sawyer

I take a deep breath before raising my knuckles to rap against Jamie's front door. I'm balancing two cups of Tim Hortons coffee beneath my chin with the opposite hand.

My stomach rolls in waves as I wait on the stoop. Chances are high he won't talk to me, and I'm hoping I don't have to take my two cups of failed peace offering over to my mom and Rich instead.

I was scheduled to fly back to Miami early this morning, but Sienna convinced me to reschedule my flight to tomorrow. I get an extra day with her and my family, as well as a chance to patch things up with Jamie.

The Storm can deal with it for one day.

I'm about to knock a second time when the door opens on a shirtless and yawning Connor. He rubs his eyes. "Sawyer? You look like shit."

I chuckle weakly. "Hey Monty. Is your dad home?"

He yawns again. "Yeah, I think so. Come on in." He takes a few steps inside before realizing I'm not following.

I shift awkwardly on my feet. "I'll wait out here. I'm not sure if he wants to see me or not."

"Why wouldn't he—" His eyes widen. "Did he—"

"Yeah. We got into a fight last night."

"Damn. I'm sorry." He hesitates. "Let me see how he feels, OK?"

"Thanks, man."

I close my eyes and breathe through my anxiety while I wait. Jamie and I haven't raised our voices at each other since he turned his life around when I was in high school. He's been one of my best friends ever since, and the thought of losing him breaks me. Aside from my family and Sienna, he's the closest person in my life, and I need him now more than ever.

The door creaks open and Jamie peeks out. He's wearing rumpled sweats and sporting a fat lip with a flourishing bruise on his cheek.

"You look like shit."

My mouth quivers upward. "I've heard. You should see the other guy."

He barks out a sharp laugh. "Touché."

I raise the red cups in my hands. "I come bearing Tim's."

He looks at me for a few long seconds before speaking. "Do you want to come in?"

I hold out a coffee. "I'd like that. Thanks."

Jamie pulls on a threadbare Six Nations Minor Lacrosse t-shirt from a laundry basket while I sip my coffee at the kitchen table.

"As much as I'd like to take credit for that face you're sporting, I know I didn't hit you," I say.

He slides into a chair across from me. "You can thank Neil. He kicked my ass after I punched you."

A slow grin spreads across my face. "Did he really? He never fights."

"Well, I guess I deserved it."

I take a long sip of coffee. "You said it, not me."

"Asshole."

We drink in silence for a minute, and I turn over every possible way to bring up the elephant in the room before Jamie finally does it.

"I'm sorry about last night," he says quietly. "I completely lost my shit, and you didn't deserve that."

"What's going on, Jammer?" I ask. "Tell me how I can fix things."

He shakes his head. "It's not you. I mean, it is, but not really."

I give him time to collect his thoughts without filling the space with more questions.

He sighs. "You were one of the first people to give me another chance after I nearly threw my life away when Connor was little. It gave me hope that, with time, I could earn back the trust of my family and friends." He pauses for a sip. "I advocated for the Outlaws to draft you because I knew you had what it takes to succeed in the league. You're resilient and a true team player."

I nod.

He fidgets with the lid of his coffee cup. "Selfishly, I always wanted you to play with me. Because I trust you and I care about you."

I smirk. "I love you too, man."

Jamie rolls his eyes. "My life is changing. Connor only has a year left before he's off to college. I'm not sure how many years I have left to play professionally."

I open my mouth to disagree, but he cuts me off with a look.

"You know it's true. It's getting harder to recover in my late thirties, and I don't know how much longer I can keep up this pace," he continues. "Now you're playing in Miami, and I'm sitting at home bored after an early playoff exit. Everyone's paired off with great women, and I'm just...alone."

I tap my cup against his. "I would tease you about going through a midlife crisis, but..."

"Not the time, Lanes."

I chuckle. "So, I left you alone to fend off the legions of aunties that swoon over you on a daily basis?"

He kicks me under the table. "There are no legions of aunties."

"I think you choose to ignore their existence. I see you getting checked out whenever we go anywhere."

"Whatever," he mutters. "*Anyway*, all this to say I probably am going through a midlife crisis. But also, I'm worried about you."

I frown. "Why?"

"You're chasing a level of fame and success that would come naturally if you just trusted yourself and let the medicine of the game work through you."

An uncomfortable sensation grips my chest. "What do you mean?"

He leans back in his seat. "Whose idea was it to go to Miami?"

"The team got a trade offer, and I agreed to it, so…mine."

"I really wish you'd talked to me before you accepted," he says quietly. "You don't actually care about social media posts and flashy uniforms. I'm willing to bet your shitass of a father is feeding you crap, as usual. You're bougie, but you need community more than anything."

I stare into my empty red cup. "It wasn't about that. I've been feeling stalled out in my career for a year or two. You're the uncontested leader of the Outlaws. Our captain. Zeke's our best all-around player. Wes is on the cusp of superstardom and still on his rookie contract. Where do I fit in?"

"How do you not realize you're the heart of the team?"

I lift an eyebrow. "Have you started drinking again?"

"Come the fuck on, Sawyer." He leans forward on his elbows. "The Outlaws are who we are because of *you*. We're always contenders because of the X factor your play gives us. The fans have a blast coming to games because you play loose and score on those ridiculous shots. The number of marriage proposals I've seen on your socials is unreal."

Laughter bubbles out of my chest. "One of those things is not like the others."

"You're a fan favorite, and you give the team its character. You bring out the best in everyone. I probably only have a couple of seasons left in me, and I could absolutely see you or even Wes taking over for me as captain."

I sit back in stunned silence. "You're not just saying that because you're my friend?"

"When have I ever been a bullshitter?"

My head falls forward into my palms. "I don't know what the hell I'm doing, Jammer. I've made a mess of everything."

His chair scrapes the tile floor as he pulls it closer to mine. "You haven't. I think you needed to try something new to figure out what you actually want. Sometimes I forget how much younger you are than I am."

"Trust me, I never forget."

He puts me in a headlock and pulls me in for an aggressive hug.

"Are we good now?" I ask as I clap him on the back.

"We're good. I'm sorry about the black eye. And for avoiding your calls."

"Please don't ever be a jerk to me again. My sensitive heart can't take it."

Jamie smiles. "We really miss you in Buffalo."

"I miss you, too," I say quietly. "I miss home."

He squeezes my shoulder. "Well, go win a Cup and then think about coming back."

I swallow over the knot in my throat. "I want to, but I'm also making some good connections on the Storm. It's been really fulfilling to make a difference on a young team."

His grin wavers. "They're lucky to have you, and you need to do what's best for you. My opinion may differ from yours, but I'm trying to be OK with that."

"Thanks, Jammer," I whisper. "Can I call you this week to talk about it more?"

"You fucking better, or I might give you a matching shiner."

Chapter 47

Yunęhrúha'r

Lacrosse

Sawyer

The Storm's Cinderella run continues with a semifinals sweep over the Las Vegas Rattlesnakes. Coach put me, Neil, and Keegan on a permanent line together, and we're lighting up the scoreboard on a regular basis. I bought an air mattress for the living room, my roommates are hitting the gym with me, and the medicine is starting to return to my game.

It feels...good. And that scares me.

We lost the first game against our finals opponent, the Georgia Hive. We play them again tonight, and if we win, we continue the best-of-three series next weekend. If we lose, then our season is over.

I'm breathing through the pain of a recovery ice bath when my phone rings.

Aidan glances at the screen as he dries off across the room. "Dom's calling. Do you want me to answer it?"

My blood freezes, and it's not from the water. "Uh, I'll call him back once I'm out. I'm trying to stay alive at the moment."

The last time the General Manager of the Storm called me, he was offering a lucrative contract in free agency. What could he need from me on what may be our last day of the season?

An hour later I'm warm, spiffed up, and about to walk into Dominic Ocean's office four hours before game time. I fix my hair and smooth my cream polo in the reflection of a framed photo next to his door.

"Sawyer!" Dom booms. "Good to see you. Come sit."

I awkwardly arrange my long frame in the spacious leather chair facing his desk. It was only two months ago I was doing the same in Coach Travis' rickety office chairs, but it feels like another lifetime.

"You look good," he says with a grin. "The Florida sunshine agrees with you."

I chuckle and brush an imaginary piece of lint off my tanned forearm so I can take in a dopamine hit from my strawberry tattoo. "The quality of life is pretty great down here. Sun, sand, delicious Cuban food."

"I knew you'd fit right in." He folds his hands in front of his chin. "Any chance I could convince you to stay longer? Let's say...a three-year deal?"

"Is this an offer to extend my current contract?" I draw in a steadying breath.

"It is." He pushes a stapled document towards me. "Take a look and tell me what you think."

I flip through and scan the major details. A small bump in pay over what they offered last August. Money for relocation and ongoing training costs. On paper, it looks great, and it's a validation of the value I've brought to the team in our short time together.

I should be happy. I should grab a pen and sign it on the spot. But every muscle in my body screams, *wait.*

My jaw twitches. "I can't sleep on a couch for another three years, Dom. The team wanted me down here full-time, but then you didn't provide me with an actual place to live."

He shrugs. "I know it wasn't ideal, but it saved us a lot of money. With this new deal, things will be different. You can rent a place of your own, if you'd like." He pauses. "Or with a roommate."

"I'd like to have some time to discuss this with my family."

Dom frowns. "If we're going to extend you, it has to happen before the end of the current season. Which may be tonight, if we lose."

A flicker of annoyance hits my veins. *I'm getting tired of being rushed into decisions I'm not one hundred percent comfortable with.* "So I have four hours to sign, or…?"

He sits back in his chair. "I can't promise what an offer would look like in free agency. The owner is re-evaluating our finances this summer."

"So, you want me to sign now, without talking to anyone else, so the team gets me at a discount?" My eyebrow ticks upwards.

He stares at me for a few silent seconds.

I glance down at my strawberry ink before pushing the paper across his desk. "Call me in August if the Storm has an offer. I've got a game to get ready for."

We battle hard and keep it close, but Georgia is a wagon this year and we can't pull off the upset.

"Hell of a season, boys. You should be proud of yourselves." I stand at the entrance to the locker room and give every single teammate a hug or a helmet tap. "This team is going to be a real problem for the league next season."

"Hey, that's my job." Coach claps me on the back. "You were a great deadline acquisition, Lanes. Maybe I'll see you back here in the fall?"

I smile warmly. "I enjoyed working with you, too, Coach. We'll see what the future brings."

"Tough way to end the season," Neil says as we pack up our gear. "It's hard to come so close to a championship."

"It is." I fire off a text to Sienna before she falls asleep. "But this team will be back."

> **Me:** I'll be home in the next couple of days. Makes it easier to stomach a loss.

My Girl: I'm sorry you didn't win, but…

Me: Yeah, I'm feeling the same way. When is Noah's big game? Maybe I can get back in time

Neil brushes out his long, wet hair. "Think you'll be back here next year?"

I glance quickly around us before leaning closer. "I'm not closing off the idea entirely, but…I just turned down a three-year extension."

His eyes widen as he begins braiding. "No shit? Like, today?"

I nod. "Dom called me into his office a few hours before the game and wanted me to sign on the spot."

He rolls his eyes. "Why am I not surprised?"

My phone buzzes.

My Girl: Tomorrow at 10am in Rochester. Don't worry about it. I'll let him know you would've been here if you could

I mutter under my breath. "Do you think I could get to Rochester by ten tomorrow? The high school near the Tuscarora rez is playing for the state lacrosse championship."

Neil whistles. "Not sure you can pull that off. Have you looked for flights?"

"Not yet. I still need to pack up my stuff at the team house, and…" I blow out a heavy breath. "This probably won't work."

"Never say never. I'll help you pack while you book something, how's that sound?"

I grin. "It sounds like I've got a damn good friend."

Hot diggity. Thirty minutes later I've got an early morning reservation into Rochester and a whole lot of excited energy.

Saying goodbye to my roommates is hard. They're not entirely likeable characters, but I enjoyed living and playing with them. Keegan's the most broken up to see me go, and if I come back to Miami, he would be a big reason why.

I greet Wes with a collection of bags outside the airport. The sun is bright on a late May morning, and I'm feeling fantastic.

"My car is not big enough for all your crap, man." Wes throws his body against my oversized bag of lacrosse gear so he can squish it into the trunk of his sedan.

I chuckle. "Thanks again for the pickup. I know you hadn't planned on driving out to Rochester this morning."

"My pleasure."

We have to park far from the field due to our lateness, but we'll make it before the second half. I zip a fleece jacket over my Falls Creek High School t-shirt and we book it towards the stadium.

"So, are you back for good?" Wes asks.

"Maybe. Probably. Damn, it's chilly here."

He laughs. "It's fifty-seven degrees. You've turned into a Floridian."

"Maybe I should think about re-signing down there after all." I dodge his elbow with a smile. "I'm so freaking happy to be home."

He grins back. "Trust me, the feeling is mutual."

Chapter 48

Sienna

F alls Creek is down by three at the half, and I've bitten all of my fingernails to the quick. Sawyer texted when he landed, but otherwise I've been too nervous to check my phone.

A handful of Tuscarora kids are on the team, and my Uncle Randy is the head coach, so there's a strong contingent of Native families in the stands with us. Noah's mom, Amber, sits on one side of me, with Jamie and Connor on the other. My parents and Hazel are sitting nearby. Purple Haudenosaunee flags and shirts pepper the audience.

"I'm so relieved everything's good with you and Sawyer," I say quietly to Jamie as the whistle blows for halftime.

He smiles warmly beneath the fading bruises on his cheek. "Yeah, we're good. I'm lucky he's so forgiving. I'll be making it up to him for a while."

Amber gets to her feet. "I'm going to take a quick walk. I'm too nervous to sit here waiting for the second half to start."

"I'll join you if you don't mind. I've got some nervous energy, too."

The two of us weave our way down the bleachers and exit the stadium tunnel through crowds of people. We walk in companionable silence around the grounds of the local college hosting the game.

I don't know what the future holds for Sawyer's career, but I feel secure in the knowledge that we'll navigate it together. He's home for the foreseeable future, and I plan on savoring every day we have together. He'll be living with me until free agency in August, at least, and I'm looking forward to easing up on my work hours so we can enjoy each other.

I never thought I'd happily close my laptop at 5pm each day, but knowing he'll be waiting for me at home makes it an easy choice.

We're heading back up the bleacher stairs to our seats when I hear my name called by a familiar, deep voice.

I spin around with a wide grin splitting my face and immediately run back down. I fling myself down the remaining steps and into Sawyer's arms.

He catches me easily and holds me close as my feet dangle several inches off the ground.

I bury my face in his neck. He smells like shampoo and sunshine. "You made it."

"There's nowhere else I'd rather be." He nudges my cheek until he can bring his lips to mine. "Sorry I'm late."

My body noticeably relaxes in his presence. "Welcome home."

"It's damn good to be back." He kisses me again while gently lowering me.

Noah scores with a minute remaining, and the Falls Creek contingent goes wild. If the team can hold on, they'll win the first state championship in school history.

We stand up to watch the scoreboard clock tick down. *Thirty, twenty-nine...*

Amber grips my upper arm as our opponent mounts a frantic comeback attempt, throwing all their best shooters into the offensive zone and shooting rockets on net.

Wes leans over from the other side. "Their defenders are doing a great job. Just need to keep their nerves calm and outlast the onslaught."

Eleven, ten...

Amber throws her hands over her eyes. "I can't watch."

Falls Creek intercepts a particularly dangerous pass and slings it downfield with eight seconds to go.

I scream with excitement, and she looks up in panic. "What happened? Oh my God."

"They did it!" I throw my arms around her and jump up and down. "They're state champs!"

Sawyer scoops the three of us into his wingspan and crushes us together for a group hug. "What a game! Those kids played their hearts out. You should be so proud of Noah."

"I am." Amber blinks back tears. "And I'm so appreciative of everything you've done for him this year. He's thriving."

He squeezes us. "He's easy to coach."

The field is pure chaos as families spill onto the grass to celebrate. We slowly make our way down in search of Noah and my uncle.

Noah is sweaty and overjoyed. "I can't believe you're here!" he says to Sawyer. "You played in Miami last night. Sorry about the loss."

Sawyer smiles. "I got lucky with flights. I didn't want to miss this."

Noah jostles me with his elbow. "Did you want to...?"

"Now?" I ask, and he nods. "We can do that."

"What's that?" Sawyer inquires.

"Uncle Randy, could you grab the..." I nudge my head towards Sawyer.

My uncle grins. "Sure. I'll be right back."

Sawyer's eyebrow elevates. "What's this about?"

"We got you a gift." I thread my arm around his waist. "Noah, Randy, and I."

His smile grows. "What's the occasion?"

"No occasion. Just because we love you." I squeeze his hip bone. "I guess you could consider it a Welcome Home gift."

"You didn't have to do that." He tucks me under his arm.

Uncle Randy jogs back from the sideline pile of team gear with a duffel bag slung across his shoulder. "Here you go, kid. You should've had one of these a long time ago."

Sawyer cocks his head before taking the bag and setting it on the ground. He drags the zipper open and pauses.

I crouch next to him. "It's from a stick maker down the road from my shop."

He blinks. "I can't—"

"Yes, you can." Randy comes down to our level. "You may not have been born Tuscarora, Sawyer, but you're one of us. You know our traditions, you're learning the language, and you give back to our youth. We love, accept, and trust you. Nothing would make me happier than seeing you play with a wooden stick at our next community game."

"You've always been worthy enough to carry one of these." I wrap my hand around his wrist and brush my thumb against his strawberry tattoo. "You just needed to believe it."

Sawyer runs a palm over his face. "I don't know what to say."

"Say you'll shoot around with me," Noah says with a grin. "You've got to break it in."

Sawyer chuckles and carefully pulls the lacrosse stick out of the bag. "*Nya:we* to all of you. This is an incredibly generous gift. I can't thank you enough."

"*Nya:we,* Sawyer." Noah holds out his hand for a fist bump, but Sawyer pulls him in for a hug. "You inspire me so much, and I wouldn't be the player I am without your help this year."

Sawyer's eyes are watery as he claps him on the back. "You've got a bright future ahead of you, Prints. I'm honored to have played a small part in your journey."

Noah and Uncle Randy are accosted by more well-wishers, and Sawyer takes the opportunity to fold me into his arms.

"I love you so damn much, Sen," he whispers before kissing me deeply. "Thank you for doing this."

I giggle and push him back slightly. "There are people watching."

"Good." His mouth finds mine again, and I let him have it.

Epilogue
Kanęhsé·økye / Longhouse

Sawyer

"Is it all right to feel nervous?" I ask, looking around at the grounds blooming with people decked out in their finest regalia.

"Why are you nervous?" Sienna smoothes the front of the ribbon shirt her mother made for me. "You look hot as hell in this, by the way."

I smirk and pull her closer. "Oh yeah? You like pretending you're dating a Native guy?"

"Trust me, I like you just the way you are." She brushes a kiss against my cheek. "Why are you nervous?"

"This is my first time at a longhouse. Rich would invite me and Alex, but I never felt it was my place to attend." I drape an arm around her shoulders, careful not to disturb her hand-beaded collar.

She nods. "You would've been accepted, but I imagine it felt intimidating."

"Well, I'm glad you're here to coach me through my first one." I wave at Zeke as he walks by with some of his brothers.

He grins and splits off in our direction. "So glad you guys are here." We exchange hugs.

"Wouldn't miss it. Especially after I hit on Genny the first time you brought her around," I tease.

Sienna raises an eyebrow as Zeke guffaws.

"I'll tell you about it later." I drop a kiss on top of her head.

"There's the groom." Wes slides in beside me, his green and white ribbon shirt coordinating nicely with Chelsea's blue and green ribbon dress. "Congratulations, man."

Sienna and Chelsea chatter while admiring each other's traditional clothing.

Zeke glances behind him. "I'm being summoned by my mom. I'll see you all in there?"

"Definitely. Good luck." I clap him on the shoulder.

"No luck necessary." His smile outshines the sun. "I'm marrying my best friend."

Sienna slips her hand into mine. "They're so sweet together."

A huffing and puffing Jamie appears in our circle. "Sorry I'm late. Bridge traffic is killer today. Are we ready to head inside?"

"Let's do it." I tug on Sienna's palm, but she stays rooted to the spot. "What's wrong?"

She chuckles. "I'm going with Chelsea. You need to go with the guys through the men's entrance."

"Oh."

"Come on, Lanes. I'll show you what to do." Wes crooks his head in the opposite direction.

"I don't get to be with you?" I ask her quietly.

She smiles. "I'll sit with the other Beaver clan members. You'll be with Wes and the Bear clan."

I frown and she pecks me on the lips. "Wes will take care of you. I'll see you afterwards."

"People sit according to clan at ceremonies," Wes explains as we enter the longhouse. "Jamie and Chelsea will be with the other Turtles, and you're with me since anyone can sit with the Bears."

"So your clan takes in all the riffraff?"

"Basically. We're nice like that."

The ceremony is beautiful, with a focus on the union of two families rather than two individuals. Both mothers are heavily involved and need to formally agree to the marriage. There are several speeches, a dance, and the bride and groom exchange traditional baskets as well as rings. Genny is resplendent in white regalia that must've taken months to bead.

"How long until this is you and Chelsea?" I whisper to Wes.

He smiles. "Not for a little while, but hopefully at some point."

Sienna catches my eye from the other side of the ceremonial fire, and I give her a wink.

The wedding reception takes place a few hours later at an event space along the shores of Lake Erie. We eat, drink sodas, and dance until we're sweaty and exhausted.

I tug Sienna outside to take a break with me on a stone wall overlooking the lake. Her jade green dress is gorgeous against her caramel skin. Her long hair is pinned up, showing off her back and the halter tie cascading along her spine.

"Can I ask you a question?"

She turns her gaze from the softly lapping waters to look at me. She's gorgeous with the colors of a summer sunset casting their soft glow on her hair and skin. "Of course."

My stomach clenches with my sudden loss of nerve. I pull her to my side with one arm, and she rests her head on my shoulder with a contented sigh. We sit silently for several more seconds before she asks, "What's your question?"

I clear my throat and toss up a prayer for bravery. "Do you want to get married?"

She stills, and I force myself to keep an even breathing pattern. *In and out. In and out.*

"Are you—?" She tilts her head up towards mine.

"This isn't a proposal, so you can relax." I squeeze her shoulder. "I'm wondering how you feel about marriage in general. If you want something like what Genny and Zeke have today."

Her dark eyes reflect the golden streaks in the sky. "I've always pictured myself getting married and raising a family. I just didn't know if it would happen."

"Same here." I cup her jaw with my palm and dust a soft kiss across her lips. "How would you feel about marrying *me*?"

"I thought you said this wasn't a proposal."

"It's not." Another kiss. "I'm just testing the waters."

Her hand drifts upward to tangle in the hair at the nape of my neck. "Do you think about marrying me?"

"Every minute of every day."

Her tiny intake of breath is so quiet I might have missed it if she weren't so close.

"You're the love of my life, Sen." I run my thumb over her cheek. "I don't want anyone else but you, and I never will. We were made for each other, and I was lucky enough to meet you when I was young and dumb. But I still knew how special you were."

"Sawyer," she breathes.

"So, tell me if you feel the same way. If you don't, and if you want something different for your life, I'll be devastated but I'll understand." I scan her eyes for an answer. "I don't want you to feel trapped because you're afraid of hurting me."

Her eyes flutter shut. "You would break up with me?"

Panic rises in my throat. "No, I—I mean, only if you didn't want to be—"

She pulls my mouth to hers, and I exhale into the kiss. My fingers follow the long sash tied at her neck as it cascades down her bare back.

"Shut up for a second," she mumbles against my lips.

"Good idea."

When we finally come up for air, she fists my shirt collar and holds me close. "I want to raise my kids in the Tuscarora culture, so it's really important for me to live on or near the reservation. Is that something you're open to?"

My heart's about to beat out of my chest. "Absolutely. I want that, too."

"And I want to keep working. It would be challenging while you're still traveling for lacrosse, but I want to grow my business for a long time."

I nod. "I never considered asking you to stop. I'll support however you want to parent."

"Good." I track the bob in her throat as she swallows. "One more thing: is cookie dough still your favorite flavor of ice cream?"

A laugh bubbles out of me. "What?"

"I need to know. This is important."

I tuck a strand of hair behind her ear. "Yes, cookie dough. Is black raspberry still *your* favorite?"

A smile creeps across her face. "You remember."

"Of course I remember. I've thought about you every day since I was twelve." I graze her lower lip with my teeth. "I get to learn so many new things now, but I still remember the essentials."

"OK," she whispers with a grin.

"OK, what?"

"OK, we can continue this discussion in the future." She traces my cheekbone with her fingers.

"Fantastic. One last question." I thread my fingers between hers and kiss her knuckles. "White gold or yellow gold?"

She cocks her head before realization dawns in her eyes. "Oh. For a ring?"

"Mmm hmm." I slowly dust kisses up the inside of her forearm. "I want to make sure you get something you love."

Pink blooms beneath her skin. "Yellow gold, I think. Something simple that won't get in the way while I'm working."

"Of course." I spend some time in the inner crook of her arm.

"Sawyer?"

"Hmm?"

"Thank you."

"For what?" My lips caress her shoulder, and I need to be careful, or this dress is going to be around her waist in another minute.

"For loving me." She tugs at my hair to bring my mouth back to hers.

"I think you put it perfectly earlier this year. Loving you is the easiest thing in the world." I tip her head back to kiss her more deeply. "It's as natural as breathing."

Acknowledgements

Niawen'kó:wa to the Haudenosaunee community across Turtle Island for the welcome I have always received as a *Kanien'kehá:ka* woman who grew up off-reserve. There's always more to learn, and it is a joy to do so.

Thank you to my friends and editors Reannen and Carole. My books grow so much under your thoughtful feedback and encouragement.

I am deeply grateful for my husband, Brad, who steers our family's ship while I spend every free moment writing. He's cooked a lot of dinners, washed a lot of dishes, and helped solve countless math problems. Thank you, my love.

Growing up as an urban Native of mixed ancestry, the opportunity was there for my parents to disregard our Mohawk traditions. Instead, they fought for them. *Konnorónhkwa*.

I consulted a number of authentic voices in my research for this book:

The Tuscarora Band of Six Nations Indians (https://tuscarorabandindians-govtribe.co/home)

Tuscarora Language Resources: Six Nations Public Library

Connect With Me

The Medicine Game Series

- **Over and Back:** A childhood friends-to-lovers, second chance romance on the Seneca Nation

- **Hidden Ball Trick:** A friends with benefits, secret dating romance featuring the Oneida Nation

- **Trick Shot**: A frenemies-to-lovers, second chance romance involving the Tuscarora Nation

- **A Fresh 30**: An age gap, workplace romance spotlighting the Mohawk Nation

About the author

S.E. Martin is an enrolled member of the Mohawk Nation at Six Nations of the Grand River reserve in Ohsweken, Ontario. She grew up in Niagara Falls, NY and currently resides in New England with her husband and children. She's been writing personally and professionally since her teenage years. She has always been captivated by the power of a good story. She's writing The Medicine Game series in order to share the beauty of Haudenosaunee culture and the game of lacrosse with a wider audience. When she's not reading or writing, you can find her losing years off her lifespan by cheering for Buffalo sports teams.